"I am honored to be your husband, if only for a short time."

Bliss sighed and rested her hand on his arm. He placed his hand over hers, his warmth not only running through her, but also his strength. He was a man of great courage and conviction, and a man who loved deeply.

"You tremble."

She stared at him a moment. She did tremble, but inwardly, and he had felt it.

"I must explain."

"No need. I understand how difficult this incident must have been for you. I will see you safely home." He reached for her hand and closed his fingers firmly around hers. Bliss could not help but think how his innocent gesture sealed what Fate had decreed.

She tugged at his hand, forcing him to stay put. With a more adamant tone she said, "We are husband and wife."

He nodded, clearly not understanding. "Aye, we should continue to appear so in case other soldiers approach."

She shook her head a bit too frantically, worried that he would fail to understand the truth, and poked his chest to make him pay closer attention. "You," she tapped her chest, "and I, are wed. We are truly husband and wife."

By Donna Fletcher

DONNA FLETCHER

WED TO A HIGHLAND WARRIOR

AVON

An Imprint of HarperCollinsPublishers

This is a work of fiction. Names, characters, places, and incidents are products of the author's imagination or are used fictitiously and are not to be construed as real. Any resemblance to actual events, locales, organizations, or persons, living or dead, is entirely coincidental.

AVON BOOKS
An Imprint of HarperCollins*Publishers*
10 East 53rd Street
New York, New York 10022-5299

Copyright © 2012 by Donna Fletcher
ISBN 978-0-06-203487-8
www.avonromance.com

First Avon Books mass market printing: November 2012

Avon Trademark Reg. U.S. Pat. Off. and in Other Countries, Marca Registrada, Hecho en U.S.A.
HarperCollins® is a registered trademark of HarperCollins Publishers.

Printed in the U.S.A.

10 9 8 7 6 5 4 3 2 1

WED TO A
HIGHLAND
WARRIOR

Chapter 1

Bliss waited, not sure of her fate.

She often wondered why she could see the providence of others and yet when it came to her destiny, she was blind. At times it made sense to her. After all, it was a burdensome lot to unwillingly peer into the future and see not just happiness but pain and sorrow. Certainly, if she saw that for herself, life could possibly become unbearable. Even knowing the destiny of others brought a burden that, at times, Bliss would much rather not carry though she had no choice.

This gift, as her people, the Picts called it, or curse as others often referred to it in whispers, had been part of her as long as she could remember. There had never been a time she had been without her knowing, and while she could see small, incidental moments in her future, she could not see the whole of it, the important moments in life that had others seeking her knowledge.

If her knowing wasn't enough, there was also her ability to help heal. Her touch held power, not that she understood it, but nor did she question it. Like her knowing, it had always been a part of her, and she had always willingly shared it with those in need.

At the moment, though, her instincts warned her that this was where she must stop and wait. Why, she did not know. She truly had no time to dally. There was an ill woman in need of healing, and she was still a day's journey away. But to ignore fate's warning could prove unwise.

Bliss hugged her dark blue wool cloak more closely around her. Winter's bite was sharp in the air, leaving no doubt it would be a bitter one. She wished, however, this year she need not spend the cold days and shivering dark nights alone. Being one-and-twenty years, she had thought for certain, though had never foreseen it, that she would have a husband and children by now. She didn't, and she worried that she never would.

Respected for her abilities by her people, she also found it a deterrent to finding a mate. Most men feared her knowing, one fellow being adamant about it, saying, "There would be nothing I could keep from you—nothing."

Bliss realized then that she wanted no husband who would hide things from her. She wanted honesty and trust from the man who would be her husband, or she would remain alone.

The crunch of leaves alerted her to heavy footfalls, and it was easy to tell that more than one person approached. In an instant, she knew that soldiers headed her way. Normally she would detect their presence much sooner giving her time to flee to safety.

Why had she been cautioned to wait for those who could very well do her harm? Could they possibly be in need of healing? Or had she been mistaken? She dismissed the foolish thought as soon as it entered her head, reminding herself that fate knew well life's course and she need not fear.

Three king's soldiers broke past the trees and into the clearing where she stood. Apprehension fluttered her stomach, but she remained confident that all would be well.

"We've found ourselves an angel," one young soldier said with a grin.

"She is a beauty," remarked another with a sneer that warned that his thoughts bordered on carnal.

All too often, men remarked on her beauty so much so that the words no longer meant anything to her and certainly not from this lot. Someday, she hoped to find a man who would look past her features and see her true worth. But at the moment she needed to wait, for she sensed these soldiers were not why fate had her linger.

A sudden ill wind blew around them scooping up leaves and twigs and swirling them in the air before carrying them off on a rush of wind. A fast-moving mist followed, sweeping in along the ground. It would not be easy to take a step or find one's way if it grew any thicker.

Gray clouds rushed in overhead, warning of an impending storm, or was it a portent of someone's arrival?

Bliss shivered, sensing someone's approach, someone of great power and strength, someone who would stand before these soldiers with courage and someone she was destined to meet.

"What is a beautiful lassie doing out in the woods all alone?" the youngest soldier asked, inching closer.

"I wait." Bliss let her cloak casually fall away from her arms to reveal the drawings on her wrists.

Another soldier gasped. "She's a Pict."

"We don't mix with pagans," the older soldier, who had remained a distance from the other two, said.

"Why?" the young soldier asked boldly.

The older soldier slowly shook his head. "They are strange ones."

Bliss sensed that the younger soldier would not pay heed to the wisdom of the older one. He was brash in his bravado and intent on proving his courage. Warnings from the older soldier, to him, were nothing more than fear and old superstitious nonsense.

"Because they paint symbols on themselves?" the young soldier asked with a shake of his head and a laugh. "There will be no more Picts soon enough."

Bliss's fair cheeks flared red, and her pale blue eyes darkened ever so slightly. "Mark your words wisely, young lad, for Picts have walked these lands far longer than you know and will continue to claim these lands long after you're gone."

"Is that a threat?" the young soldier demanded, his chest expanding as he drew his shoulders back and approached her with swift steps.

He didn't in the least intimidate Bliss. She stood firm, her head up, her pride and courage evident. "It is the truth."

"And I say with as much truth that the likes of you and your kind will be no more," the soldier challenged, his comrades encouraging him with cheers.

"You can say or claim all you wish, but the truth is written and cannot be erased," she said confidently.

"She's a seer," the older soldier said with a shiver. "Stay clear of her, or she will steal your soul."

The young soldier scurried away, tripping over his feet as he went, his pretentious bravado failing him.

"What do we do with her?" the other soldier asked taking several cautious steps away.

"She might prove helpful to King Kenneth," the young one suggested.

"Fool," the older one spat. "The king has his own seer, and he keeps his distance from the Picts; being pagans, they cannot be trusted."

Bliss felt a sudden catch in her stomach though she moved not a muscle. It intensified as the unknown man continued his approach. From how palpable his strength, he was no doubt a warrior. They were an easy lot to sense, their potency far-reaching. Though there was a force about this particular one that caused her to shudder. Passion tickled at her flesh, and a heady scent soon followed, wrapping around her like a lover's strong embrace.

This was the man she was meant to meet, and

why fate had her wait. A tingle of anticipation ran through her, and without warning, as was the way of it, a sense of knowing struck her like a mighty blow. Only this time it was about her.

She could foolishly doubt it, but it would do no good. The sense of what was about to transpire was much too strong, too rooted in her knowing. Still, it was difficult to believe, and yet she knew without a doubt that fate had her wait here—she took a deep breath, not sure if she was ready—to meet her future husband.

"What do we do with her then?" the young one asked anxiously.

Her answer spilled from her lips, shocking her. "My husband has come to get me."

He walked out of the mist then, as if summoned, emerging slowly, the fog dissipating around him with each confident step he took. He was a formidable figure: tall, his shoulders broad, his body lean, his eyes intense, his long auburn hair blown wild by the irate wind, and his long, slim fingers resting heavily on the hilt of his sword. A Highland plaid, the colors a near match to his dark hair draped proudly around him and a black wool, fur-lined cloak hugged his wide shoulders.

The three soldiers shuddered, and a shiver ran through her.

Trey MacAlpin.

Bliss knew this man, had helped heal him and kept the secret that he and his three brothers shared—one of them was the true king of Scotland and would soon take the throne.

"Husband of mine, finally you arrive," she said,

walking over to him though her legs trembled. She stretched her hand out, knowing he would not refuse her.

His hand reached out, taking hold of hers tightly and drawing her intimately up against him as only a husband would. The vision came swiftly and left with the same haste. There was no time to consider it. She had to pay heed to the present, and so she tucked it away to examine later.

The young soldier wanted more confirmation, and asked, "This Pict is your woman, your wife?"

Trey didn't hesitate. "Bliss is my wife."

Bliss spoke the words that would seal their fate. "Trey is my husband."

"You are on MacAlpin land," Trey warned.

"King Kenneth owns all land," the young soldier challenged. "And all on the land serve him."

"I serve the true king," Trey boldly announced.

The young soldier stepped forward, his bravado regained and his hand going to the hilt of his sword. "There is only one true king, and perhaps it is time you served him."

"Take another step, lad, and it will be your Maker you'll meet and be serving," Trey warned with a cold, hard stare that froze the fellow in his steps. "Go back to your king and tell him that the time draws near, and soon he will be king no more."

Anger had the young soldier taking a hasty step forward as he shouted, "There is only one of you and three of us."

"Unfair odds for sure, but I have no time to wait for you to fetch more soldiers," Trey said without a trace of a smile.

Bliss marveled at his confidence and courage. But, then, his bravery wasn't foreign to her; she had felt the heart of it pulsing through her when she had helped heal him. She knew then the strength of this man and what he was capable of; but there had also been a moment when a shiver of fear had run through her. He was also a man heavily burdened, and it had troubled her heart to feel his sadness.

Now it troubled her that she had not sensed the connection between them sooner, but then Bliss had learned at an early age that fate often worked in mysterious ways, and it wasn't for her to question.

The young soldier looked quickly to the other two soldiers, his hand already beginning to draw his sword from its sheath.

"MacAlpin warriors are superior swordsmen," warned the older soldier.

"I heard tell that one took ten soldiers down on his own, without an ounce of help," the other said.

"That would be my brother Reeve," Trey said proudly.

"And another brother survived wounds that would have killed most men," the older soldier said. "Some say he cannot die."

Trey nodded. "That would be me."

The two soldiers took a step back and the young one spat at them. "Cowards you are. Death claims everyone, and it will claim him today."

Bliss raised her voice before the soldier took a step. "Death will claim someone this day, but it will not be my husband."

Her prediction caused all color to drain from the young soldier's face and his sword slipped down into its sheath as his hand drifted off the hilt.

"Now be gone, and take my message to your king," Trey commanded.

They obeyed, disappearing into the woods without a backward glance.

Bliss smiled when Trey turned his attention on her. "It is good to see you have healed well."

"With your help, *wife*," he said smiling.

Her heart gave a catch, as if his smile had stolen a beat. Certainly, fate had had a hand in his defined features, making him the handsomest of men. But it was his eyes she found the most compelling, for she could not be sure if they were blue or green. They seemed to change from one color to the other right before her eyes.

She shook her head. With more important matters at hand, she had no time to be musing over her husband's good looks.

Husband.

How did she explain this to him?

First she had to take a step away from him. His arm around her waist felt too intimate. It made her want to step closer to him, rest her body to his, run her hand across his chest, feel his heart beating as rapidly as hers, and wonder if love could truly come from their strange joining.

Bliss slowly slipped out of his embrace, and she thought she detected his reluctance to let her go. "I should explain—"

"Not necessary. You followed your instincts, and it worked well."

"Yes, though—"

"I am honored to be your husband, if only for a short time."

"And I am honored to be your wife."

"We still pretend then?" Trey asked, stepping closer.

Her thoughts turned foggy. She had spent time healing him and had not felt a tug, a pull, a tingle of interest in him. But then she had no visions of him as her future husband. She couldn't help but wonder why now it was different? Why had fate chosen this moment and this way to bring them together?

She sighed and rested her hand on his arm.

He placed his hand over hers, his warmth not only running through her but his strength. He was a man of great courage and conviction and a man who loved deeply—and a man who was still recovering from the loss of a love.

Whatever was fate thinking sending her a man who still loved another woman?

"You are upset," Trey said. "You tremble."

She stared at him a moment, for she did tremble, but inwardly, and he had felt it. "I must explain."

"No need. I understand how difficult this incident must have been for you. I will see you safely home."

She shook her head.

"I insist."

Bliss continued shaking her head, though not because he insisted on escorting her home. "I must tell you something."

"I'll listen as we walk."

He reached for her hand and closed his fingers firmly around hers. Bliss could not help but think how his innocent gesture sealed what fate had decreed.

She tugged at his hand when he went to walk, forcing him to stay put. With a more adamant tone, she said, "We are husband and wife."

He nodded, appearing not at all upset by her resolute words, and clearly not understanding what she was trying to convey to him.

"Aye, we should continue to appear so in case other soldiers approach us."

She shook her head a bit too frantically, worried that he would fail to understand the truth. She poked his chest repeatedly, hoping to make him pay closer attention. "You"—she tapped her chest—"and I, are wed. We are truly husband and wife."

Chapter 2

Trey almost laughed aloud, the jabs to his chest having amused him since he barely felt them, but when he saw that Bliss was quite serious, he curtailed his humorous response. Her lovely pale blue eyes, which only moments before had sparkled, appeared shadowed with concern. And though her words made no sense, no vows having been exchanged, he sensed that there was more to her claim than he realized.

He did not know this woman well though he knew well the comfort and skill of her healing touch. She had stroked his brow, had touched his wounds, and had used whatever power had been granted her to heal him. He had been drowning in a sea of frightful visions and consumed by such suffocating heat that he had thought he had died and gone to hell.

Then, suddenly, a gentle, cooling hand had pulled him free. And he had caught a brief glimpse of an angel's exquisite face. That angel now claimed that he was her husband.

"What exactly do you mean that we are truly wed?" he asked.

"Picts wed by laying claim to each other."

It took a moment for him to realize what she meant. "When I said you were my wife, I took you as my wife?"

"Aye, and I sealed our spoken vows when I claimed you as my husband," she said. "Both must proclaim the other as husband and wife for the vow to be final. In the eyes of my people, we are husband and wife."

"A few words, and we are sealed as one? No documents to sign? No arrangements made? Simply an exchange of words?" He found it difficult to believe, but, surprisingly, he was not troubled over the situation. No doubt it could be rectified.

"A few words can hold so much more power than people know. Just think of the tremendous power of the three words—I love you."

His heart jolted with the memory of once not only hearing those words but speaking them. "You're right. Three small words can bring tremendous happiness—or great pain."

Bliss smiled. "To say I love you means you will surely taste of happiness and pain. That is why it is so important to choose carefully the words you speak, for often they cannot be rescinded."

"What of Pict wedding vows?"

"A few clearly stated words, and our wedding vows can be rescinded as easily as they were made."

One did not take wedding vows lightly, even if spoken in haste. And he needed time to consider this. "I don't believe it would be wise of us to rush and do that. It may be better to remain husband and wife until I deliver you safely home." It was a sensible decision not to separate from her just yet. She needed protection, a woman on her own, and if being wed to him brought her that, then married they would remain until he was certain she was safe from harm. And he could sort this strange situation out for himself.

Perhaps this tug he felt to protect her was nothing more than indebtedness for what she had done for him though she did intrigue him. She was a pagan, her beliefs far different from his, and she was beautiful. Tall and slim, with long hair that shimmered as if spun with gold. A pale, smooth complexion, a round face with lips the color of a pink rose at first bloom. She startled his eyes, tightened his groin, and tempted him to abandon all sound reason—and kiss her.

The thought jolted him, and he realized she had yet to respond though he couldn't recall what he was waiting for her to respond to. When he remembered it concerned not rescinding their vows just yet, he wondered what caused her delayed reply.

Was she regretting her actions and anxious to correct them? Or was she weighing what was best for her? Then he recalled that she was a seer and wondered what she knew that he didn't.

"Is there something you're not telling me?" he asked with distinct firmness to his tone.

"I share the truth with you."

"What of your visions?"

She nodded understanding what he asked. "I knew that a powerful warrior would emerge from the woods to help me." She did not share the part about his being her future husband.

"So you would have claimed any warrior as your mate?" he asked with a shred of annoyance.

"You are not any warrior. You are one of four brothers, though not blood related, one of which is the rightful king of Scotland."

He grew annoyed at himself for not having realized the implication of her skill and grabbed her arm. "We have to get moving. That young soldier will realize soon enough that you can foresee the true king's identity, and no doubt he will gather more soldiers to come find you."

"The king has a seer of his own, so claimed one of the soldiers. She could provide the answer he seeks."

"Evidently, she's not as skillful as you or else the true king's identity would be known by now."

He hurried her along, keeping tight hold of her arm as thunder rumbled in the distance, gray clouds gathered in force overhead, and chilled air nipped at their skin.

"We need to find shelter before the storm hits," he said. "Old Jacob's cottage is not far."

"It blusters, but little rain will fall. And I must make use of what daylight is left. An ill woman, a friend, needs tending," she said, and eased them to a stop. "I do appreciate your help, but it's a good day's journey I must make, and you should not delay your task any longer. Tell me that you no longer wish me as your wife, and I will acknowledge the same of you, and you can be on your way."

Trey couldn't say why he hesitated. He was concerned that the soldiers would come after her, and they would not be so easily discouraged this time.

She had something the king wanted, and no doubt the king would order a decree—bring her to him or die trying.

But that was no reason to remain wed to her. Even if the soldiers did find them, they would assume they were still wed. So why not speak the words and be done with it?

Instead, he asked, "You journey home to tend this woman? I could see you safely there."

Her people were fine warriors and could well defend her. Though he worried that such important information could have the king break his habit of keeping his distance from Pict territory and attack them. She would be safer with him and his brothers, and so would the true king's identity. But could he convince her of that?

"She lives beyond the Pict border."

"Then I go with you," Trey said. That would give him time to convince her to return home with him until—that was the question. Until the true king's identity was known, she would not be safe.

"That isn't necessary," Bliss said. "I do not know how long the healing will take and—"

"It matters not. I will stay with you as long as needed."

"Your family will wonder where you are and worry. And are you not needed there?" she asked, resting a gentle hand on his arm.

"They can make do without me for a while, and if I leave you unprotected, I leave the true king vulnerable. That I cannot do. I go with you whether you want me to or not," he said. "We will stop at Old Jacob's place, where Willow and Stone wait, and I will let them know I will not be returning with them. This will settle any worries my family would have over my absence."

Bliss had met Stone, a fine seer in his own right, while healing Trey. He was a good friend of Tara's, Reeve's wife, and had helped her solve a difficult problem.

"What of Stone? He would know the true king's identity. Is he not vulnerable?" The answer came to her before he could respond. "He cannot see which one of you is the king."

Trey nodded. "Stone spoke with my da and brothers and explained that he sees what he is meant to see and no more. And it appears he was not meant to know the true king's identity. You apparently are, and therefore, I will see you safe, not only for your protection but for the king's."

"I sense there is no point in arguing with you. Your reasoning makes sense, and you will have your way."

"That I will," he said, and, taking her hand once again, they continued walking.

She followed alongside in silence, recalling the image that had assaulted her when he had first taken her hand. A blond woman crying and running into his arms, and he hugged her tightly. It had upset Bliss. Why? She didn't know. She tucked the vision away once more, knowing one day it would surface, and so would her upset.

"We must not delay," she said, "though it will be good to see Willow again."

"A brief stop; though with its being months since you last saw Willow, you two may not stop talking."

She laughed. "That is true. I do favor your family, and I made good friends with Mercy and Tara, Duncan and Reeve's wives. Your mother was very nice as well."

"You're the only woman I know that my mum did not dictate to."

"Your mum wanted my help. Her only concern was for you to survive and be well."

Trey stopped, bringing them to an abrupt halt and shook his head. "That may be so, but my mum has a way about her, abrupt more times than not."

"Though not out of malice, more out of concern for her flock."

"But not once was she that way with you," he said, shaking his head again. "I heard Mercy, Tara, and Willow speaking about it when they thought I slept. All three were amazed at how kindly my mum spoke to you, not a bite or sting to her tongue."

"She would not talk such to the person who she hoped would help heal her son."

"That proves you don't know my mum."

Bliss smiled. "I know your mum better than you think."

This time he nodded and kept nodding as he spoke. "You know something about her. Something she fears you will reveal, and so she speaks more respectfully to you than to others."

"I know she is a good woman with a good heart—and a heavy burden."

"How can I help ease her burden?"

"You cannot. It is for her to carry and release when the time comes," Bliss said, impressed he had not demanded she reveal what she knew but instead asked how he could help his mum. And he didn't argue, protest, or debate her response, and that pleased her. He accepted her explanation and let it be.

They started walking again, this time keeping a steady pace.

Bliss was surprised that their hands remained joined, firmly locked together as if neither of them wished to let go. It seemed an instinctive action, natural, something they did often and yet, they hadn't.

She thought back to the moment when she first sensed that it was her future husband who approached. She wished she had sensed more in regard to him. Though it had been clear he would be her husband, there had been no indication of anything else. Did that mean they were destined to remain husband and wife? Was she meant to love this man and was he meant to love her? Were they truly meant to be together?

She wished for answers, but none came. In time, things would be revealed to her. She'd be patient—at least she hoped she would.

They came upon the cottage, and Willow ran to them, her red hair blowing wildly around her face.

"Soldiers are near," she said after giving Bliss a hug. "Stone spotted them while he searched the area. He told me to pack fast and warn you"— she nodded at Trey—"when you returned. Stone is keeping watch now. We're to meet him at the north end of the croft."

Willow smiled at Bliss. "There'll be time for us to talk when we reach the keep. Mercy and Tara will be so pleased to see you."

"I can't come with you," Bliss said, and tried to slip her hand free of Trey's, but his grip was strong, and he refused to let go.

"As much as I'd prefer to take Bliss home and see her safe, there is an ill woman in need of her skill," Trey said, and Willow nodded. "Go join Stone and explain to him what has happened and make sure to let my family know so they do not worry."

Willow hugged Bliss again, and whispered, "Tell me I'll see you both again, so that I may leave without concern."

"You will," she whispered in return, and Willow smiled.

"Go," Trey urged.

"I filled two sacks with food. I will take one; you take the other. It's by the door," she said, pointing. "And take blankets from the house—the day is growing colder."

With a hug to Trey and a wave to them both, she was gone.

"We have no time to spare," Trey said. "No doubt the soldiers will show up here to see if anyone has returned."

"They are not far," Bliss warned.

"Then we hurry."

Bliss collected blankets while Trey grabbed the sack and kept watch. As soon as she was out of the cottage, Trey once again took hold of her hand.

"Can you keep a fast pace?" he asked, as they hurried off, the cottage disappearing from view behind them.

She smiled. "One you no doubt will have difficulty matching."

He laughed. "I doubt that."

They were a good match, their steps perfectly aligned and in rhythm. They spared no time for talking, their focus strictly on keeping a good gait. Only when dusk drew near did Trey slow them to a stop.

"We need to find shelter for the night," he said.

"There is a grove of trees not far that would provide sufficient shelter."

Trey nodded, and it wasn't long after that they arrived at the secluded grove.

The circle of oak trees stood like alert sentinels, followed by another and another and another circle of oaks that eventually brought them to a small clearing.

"We may build a fire, but use only the broken branches and sticks on the ground. You must not break any branches off the oaks," Bliss warned. "This is a scared grove and must be respected."

"A sacred grove?" Trey asked.

"Aye, this land was once solely Pict territory, and many would come here to exchange vows or ask for help or simply seek a peaceful moment."

"So this is like a church of sorts," Trey said.

"To those who believe in our ways, aye it is."

He released her hand and walked around the confined area. "The soaring height of the trees and the magnificent branches naked in preparation of winter's rest make for an incredible roof and the thick trunks make for solid walls, and"—he nodded slowly—"it is peaceful here."

"And safe," she said. "The grove only welcomes those who know the way in."

They went to work gathering wood and setting a campfire. Bliss spread out wool blankets on either side of the roaring flames, their cloaks serving as blankets.

After eating a light fare, they each stretched out on the blankets. Bliss wrapped her cloak snug around her and lay on her side, facing the fire.

Trey lay on his back, looking at the canopy of thick branches. "There is a soothing quietness about this place that calms the soul."

"Why my people still seek its comfort."

He turned on his side to face her. "People come here to exchange wedding vows?"

"Those who wish for a long, fulfilling life together, for vows exchanged in such a scared place are never broken."

"The vows would be spoken as we exchanged ours?"

"Nay, it would be different."

"How? Tell me what you would say if you exchanged vows here with me," he said.

She felt a sudden desire to show him how it would be done, and so she spoke with love from the heart. "I take Trey MacAlpin as my husband. I give my heart to him and only him. And I will love him for all the days of my life and beyond."

She heard him mumble but could not understand him. "What did you say?"

"The vows would then be sealed?"

"After the husband-to-be vowed his love, they would be sealed, and the vows honored, for I would not speak them here if I did not mean them."

"I thought as much. And you would love the man who stood here beside you."

"I would not bring him here if I didn't," she said.

"And you would never stop loving him?"

"I will love only once in this life, and it will be a strong, devoted love. And as I said, I will love him for all the days of my life and beyond, for death will not stop me from loving him."

"Your husband is a lucky man."

"That he is," she said with a grin.

Sleep soon claimed Trey, but Bliss lay awake, her eyes wide and her thoughts churning. Trey had said, "Your husband *is* a lucky man." And she had agreed with her own words. "That he *is*." Neither he nor she had said her husband *would be* a lucky man.

It was as if they both acknowledged Trey as her husband—now and forever.

Chapter 3

Trey woke, along with the first light of day. It barely filtered through the treetops, though a spark of light poked through here and there. The fire had died out, but it didn't matter, they would not linger long this morning. He wanted them on their way, get Bliss where she needed to be, then take her home and see her kept safe. She might object, but perhaps her visions would show her that it was for the best.

Besides, he needed time to make sense of this sudden marriage.

He stretched himself up to a sitting position and gave a glance her way. She still slept, looking so very peaceful in slumber. Her beauty couldn't be denied though Trey found her kindness and unselfishness more attractive. She thought of others before she gave thought to herself. And she would not betray trust, a quality he much admired.

His da had told him how she had spoken with him and his brothers, giving warning of things that had been and were yet to be, and though she never acknowledged that she knew the identity of the true king, she had pledged her silence.

Once others realized what knowledge she possessed, there was no place she would be safe, except with him. She was, after all, his wife, and he had a responsibility to protect her.

He stood with another stretch and glanced around at the circle of trees. He could well understand why the place was sacred. It brought peace to the soul, and he could use that right now.

He stretched again, his muscles sore but the ache of losing Leora, the woman he loved, was suddenly less painful. Had this sacred grove brought him some peace, or had it been Bliss who helped ease his pain?

That he was attracted to her he could not deny. That he felt somehow connected with her he also could not deny. That he favored her company—he shook his head. He was trying to make sense of why he did not at all, in the least . . . feel troubled being wed to her.

Was he feeling alone, with his brothers having found women they loved, and good ones at that? Or could he finally, possibly, be on the verge of allowing himself to love again?

When he had lost Leora, it had felt as if his heart had been ripped out of his body, the pain was so great. At times he hadn't thought he could bear it another moment. And then he had turned numb, devoid of all feeling, swearing he would never allow himself to love again.

Then Bliss happened along. And he wondered if she had healed more than just the wounds on his body. He wondered if she had healed his broken heart.

"Have you been awake long?"

Trey turned to Bliss just as a ray of sunlight kissed her face, and her beauty startled him. He had thought he would never think another woman more beautiful than Leora, but Bliss far surpassed Leora, and the thought surprised him.

"Not that long," he said. "I intended to wake you soon, so that we could eat and be on our way."

Bliss sat up, running her fingers through her silky blond hair. "I'm rarely hungry in the morning, so please do not wait on me."

"A hunk of cheese and bread will suffice as we walk," he said. "I much prefer to be on our way."

"I am just as eager," she said, bouncing up to gather and fold the blankets. "I feel the need to get to my friend as fast as possible."

While he wished the same, to have this done with and see her safely to his home, he rather favored having time alone with her. It was odd to feel the stirrings of more than just attraction. And he wanted the chance to see if it was real or only gratitude for her having healed him.

They were on their way shortly, their hands joining as soon as they left the grove. They both reached out for the other at the same time, their hands clasping, their fingers lacing, and their grip strong.

"Where do we go?" he asked, having let her set the course.

"Not that far from my home, though not on Pict land," Bliss explained. "It will take most of the day to get there."

"You travel alone much?" he asked once again, her safety concerning him.

"More times than not."

"It is not safe."

"Fate watches over me."

"Fate can be a cruel mistress," he said with more anger than he intended.

"I have found through the years that fate is often wiser than we are."

Trey shook his head. "I cannot agree with that. I believe man determines his own fate."

Bliss smiled. "With help."

"I believe you are tenacious in your opinion," he teased.

She leaned close. "Beware. I am tenacious in more than just my opinion."

Trey laughed. "At least you are honest about it."

"To a fault at times, or so I've been told."

"How could honesty ever be a fault?" he asked.

"When it hurts?"

"If someone doesn't want to hear the truth, he should not ask the question."

"Sometimes a person cannot help but ask," she said.

They continued talking as they walked, Trey finding her a delight to converse with and finding their thoughts and ideas much alike.

They both sniffed the air at the same time, but it was Trey who first said, "Fire."

"It is a distance away yet," she said.

He sniffed the air again while bringing them to a halt. "It smells as if it smolders." He shook his head, his features turning angry. "It could be the king's soldiers. They have grown bold, attacking defenseless crofts on the outskirts of MacAlpin land."

"We need to see if there are those in need of help," she said, urging him with a tug to hurry.

"It will delay us," he informed.

"It cannot be helped," she said.

He nodded, and as they hurried off, he could not help but admire her courage. She gave no thought to her own safety, only to those of others in need. And what made him admire her all the more was that he knew if he were not with her, she would still tempt fate and see if there were those she could help. Or perhaps fate took her where she was meant to go.

He almost smiled, for he realized he was beginning to understand *his wife.*

Almost an hour later, Trey urged Bliss behind him with a gentle hand, and she went willingly as they approached the edge of the woods. Beyond, through the sparse trees, they could spy the smoldering croft. The cottage was all but gone, with only embers left glowing.

Trey came to a halt, and she stepped around him, his hand shot out to stop her from going any farther.

She gently pushed it aside. "There are no soldiers here, but there is a child in need of care." She was relieved that he didn't doubt her and hurried forward with her.

A mother with a young lad no more than five cradled in her arms staggered to her feet in what was once a garden beside the cottage. Bliss rushed to her, but Trey was faster and had her and the child up in his arms by the time she reached them.

"On the ground by the tree," Bliss said, directing Trey where to put the pair.

Bliss immediately went to work on the two while Trey went in search of water. Working together, it didn't take long to ascertain that the pair suffered no serious wounds though both suffered the loss of a husband and father.

"The soldiers took my Kevin," she cried, hugging her son to her.

"How many soldiers?" Trey asked.

"Four," she said through tears. "I do not understand. I thought we were safe on MacAlpin land."

Bliss almost gasped, sensing the raging anger that ran through Trey. She wanted to reach out and calm him, but he stepped away from her so fast she had no chance.

Trey slipped off the rolled blankets and sack he carried on his back and dropped them to the ground. "Did you see which way they took Kevin?"

The woman pointed. "Away from MacAlpin land."

Trey nodded. "I'll find him. Get yourself and your son ready to leave as soon as I return. You'll head to the MacAlpin keep, where you'll be safe.

You can return home once the true king takes the throne."

The woman nodded while tears trickled down her face.

Bliss stood and placed a hand on his arm. Try as she might, she could not see the results of his sudden decision, and it frightened her. She wanted to warn him not to go, warn him to be careful, warn him that she could not see his fate, but she didn't. His heart beat strong and steady with the strength and confidence of a Highlander warrior. There would be no stopping him; he would fight this day.

She did something unexpected, but that seemed natural. She kissed his cheek, and whispered, "Stay safe, husband of mine."

He smiled and returned the kiss, only his kiss was on her lips. It was a light kiss, as if left unfinished. It sent a tingling shiver to the tips of her toes and left her waiting impatiently for more.

Bliss watched until he was gone from sight, then turned her attention to mother and child. Her name was Sara and the lad was Patrick. It was remarkable how different the pair was after Trey left. Tears subsided, and Sara hurried her son to be ready for his da's return. She trusted Trey, believed his word, and had no doubt he would bring her husband home.

The lad wiped his tears from his smudge-ridden face and hurried to obey his mum. Bliss helped them scavenge what food they could find and shared some of what Trey and she had.

Sara informed her that they never had a chance

to defend themselves. The soldiers swept down on them, one grabbing Patrick and threatening to take him if Kevin didn't cooperate. They ransacked the cottage, winter garden, and field, then told Kevin he would now serve King Kenneth. He didn't dare protest, for fear that his family would be hurt. They set the cottage on fire just before leaving.

Bliss wrapped a comforting arm around Sara. And though she didn't see or sense anything, she encouraged with hope. "If anyone can free Kevin from the soldiers and return him home, it's Trey."

Sara nodded and wiped away threatening tears. She turned to her son, who had busied himself with a stick and a stone, and smiled. So did Bliss, for leave it to a child to find a sense of peace in simple play during troubling woes.

Time passed slowly, and the more it did, the more worry wore on Sara's face and began to creep over Bliss. She reminded herself how confident Trey had been when he had informed the young soldier that he had no time to wait while the three gathered more help to fight him. He hadn't boasted. He had been quite serious and quite confident.

Still, she worried for his safety, this Highlander warrior—this stranger—who was her husband for not a full day yet.

Hours passed, and Patrick complained about being hungry, and while he enjoyed his food, Sara and Bliss ate sparingly. Silence followed the meal, the lad returning to play and the two women lost in their worrisome thoughts.

It annoyed Bliss that she could not sense if Trey was safe or in harm's way. And so she sat in silent vigil, hoping somehow something would come to her and relieve her concern. It wasn't long before a smile lit her face, and she scrambled to her feet, urging Sara along with her.

Before she could explain to Sara, Patrick yelled, "Da!" And he went running into his da's arms and was scooped up. Sara followed, her husband reaching out and grabbing her tight against him, their son's skinny little arms winding around their necks and hugging, as if he would never let them go.

Joyful tears flowed freely, Bliss's included, and she hurried to Trey. He spread his arms wide, and she ran into them. He hugged her tight, and she returned the embrace with just as much enthusiasm. His strength rippled through her, followed by comforting warmth. She closed her eyes, lingering in contentment and wishing for it never to end.

But it did. Kevin spoke up, saying, "Your husband is a brave warrior, and you are a brave woman. We are forever grateful for your help and protection."

"Take your family and do as we discussed," Trey said. "You will be safe there, and when all is settled, you will be able to return home."

There were hugs and more words of gratitude before the family left, and Bliss and Trey were on their way.

His hand slipped around hers after they had taken only a few steps, and the vision hit her then. With a heavy breath, she said, "We don't need to worry about meeting up with those soldiers, do we?"

He kept walking, and said, "No, they will not bother us—ever."

Bliss made no comment; she continued walking alongside him in silence.

They walked for a few miles before Trey finally spoke again. "I'm afraid we won't make it to your friend's place today."

"It can't be helped. If we keep our pace steady until near dusk and leave with the rising sun, we should be there by noonday tomorrow."

His lack of response drew concern, and she quickly sensed he kept something from her. "What aren't you telling me?"

"I saw more tracks that indicate more soldiers in the area," he said, shaking his head. "Something is wrong. Small groups of men are usually sent to scout and discover. King Kenneth is up to something."

If he expected an answer, she didn't have one. And there was no point in her trying to envision one. She knew she would get nothing. For some reason, she was not to have an answer—at least not yet.

He turned to her, a worried look scrunching his brow. "We need to get you home as soon as you see to your friend."

"It shouldn't take long," she assured him. "And with Pict territory being so close to my friend's home, once we arrive, you can leave me there and be on your way."

He brought them to an abrupt stop and shook his head. "We discussed this. Once you're done with your friend, you'll be coming home with me to MacAlpin land."

"That's truly not necessary."

"Aye, it is. I protect what is mine, and you're *my wife*. You'll be coming home with me."

Chapter 4

Trey didn't give Bliss a chance to object to his plan. "Coming home with me is what is best for you, and that is what we will do."

He continued talking as they walked. Bliss kept a tight lip, and he wondered what she was thinking. She didn't look happy with his suggestion though it was more a command. And he could understand her objecting though eventually she would see the wisdom in his decision and agree—or so he hoped.

When words finally failed him, he said, "Your thoughts?"

"I'm allowed them?" she asked with a tinkle of laughter.

He was relieved that she responded with humor rather than anger. Not that it would change his decision; that would stand no matter how she felt. It was, after all, for her protection. It was just that he didn't wish to anger her. He liked the way she wore a smile, never forced, always so natural and lovely. And he much preferred seeing her that way rather than with a frown he had caused.

"I want you safe," he said.

"I have looked after myself many years, and my people protect me. You need not be alarmed."

"But you have a husband now"—he shook his head when she went to speak—"No, I know what you will say, but we will not end this marriage of ours until I am sure you are safe."

"It is honorable of you to feel this way, but fate guides and guards me well and has for some time."

"What of your parents? Siblings?" he asked, curious about this woman who had suddenly become his wife.

"My da died in battle when I was five years old. My mum died of fever two years later though I think her heart had broken when my da died, and she just did not want to go on without him. My grandmum raised me."

Bliss smiled, and Trey smiled along with her, glad that she had loving memories to recall.

"Grandmum's skills were so much stronger than mine, but she encouraged me, insisting that one day my skills would far surpass hers. She was ever so patient with me and my hundreds of questions."

"She answered them for you?"

"Some, but she had insisted, it was the question that mattered more and not to worry if an answer wasn't found."

"She sounded like a wise woman," Trey said. "I wish I could have met her."

"She is near and watches over me and will be on her way when she feels it is time." Bliss glanced at him, her smile fading.

"What's wrong?" he asked, giving her hand a comforting squeeze and wanting her to know there was nothing to fear.

"I have not felt safe sharing that information with anyone, for fear of the consequences such unacceptable knowledge could bring."

"I am glad you trusted me," he said with a wide smile, and briefly raised their joined hands. "Besides, we are one—husband and wife—and we can share anything without fear of repercussions."

Her smile bloomed once again.

God, but he loved when she smiled. It was as if light were cast on darkness, and joy drove away despair. He almost shook his head. Whatever was the matter with him? He was sounding like a fool in the throes of love. He and Bliss barely knew each other, or did they?

She had healed him with tenderness and caring, and such a deep, abiding love that he longed to feel again. He had felt a distinct emptiness when she had left, that he had wondered over it. Had that been the way of it, or had something happened between them that neither had realized?

"Tell me more of your grandmum," he said eagerly.

And she did, regaling him with stories that allowed him a peek into her past and a peek more deeply inside her.

After a time, Bliss said, "I have talked enough about myself. What of you?"

He grinned. "Your tales are entertaining, mine would not be so."

"I would rather determine that," she encouraged. "Besides, I did hear some stories while at the keep."

Trey winced as if wounded. "You must not believe all you hear, especially if it comes from my brothers."

Bliss laughed. "I often wished for siblings. You are lucky to have them."

"You will think differently when I tell the tales," he said, and soon had her laughing with stories of his childhood.

"So no matter how many times you hid in the trees to escape your brothers, they did not find you?"

"I climbed higher and higher each time, so they could not see me amongst the leaves and branches." He grinned proudly. "And from my perch, I delivered deadly dirt bombs I had skillfully armed myself with, and won many battles."

When he finished detailing various victories and her laughter subsided, she said, "I hope to have many children so that they will have the chance to tell funny and endearing tales like yours."

"Aye, I wish the same," Trey said. "Seeing my brothers and their growing brood, I long for a family of my own."

Silence settled over them after that, he lost in his thoughts and she in hers, both thinking of the future and what it might bring.

With dusk not far off, they needed to find shelter. There was a glen not far ahead, and it they decided that it would be best to climb the rise and settle in the valley below for the night. Bliss was sure that a stream with cool, clear water waited there.

It was an easy climb, especially with each having the other to rely upon, and they stopped for a brief rest once they reached the top. Trey didn't wish to rush her. They had walked a good distance and kept a good pace today, and she had not complained once. But dusk was fast fading to night, and he wanted to get a fire started to chase away the chill, which grew ever colder with the fading light.

"We should go," he said, and she agreed with a nod.

The arrow came out of nowhere, slicing past Bliss's arm and causing her to stumble and lose her footing, sending her tumbling down the hill so suddenly that her hand was ripped out of his. Trey knew it would be a waste of time to look back and try to spy the culprit. He was more concerned with trying to reach Bliss. He charged after her, but her tumbling body gained momentum as she continued to roll rapidly down the hill. Try as he might, he could not catch her and stop her plummet.

His heart hammered in his chest as he raced down the hillside. Fear prickled along his skin, and worry gripped him like never before. She lay in a heap when the tumble finally was over, and he fell to his knees beside her when he reached the bottom.

He wasn't sure what to do. She was the healer, but instinct took over, and he gently eased her on her back. He pushed the strands of blond hair out of her face, which looked to have suffered no more than some dirt and scratches. A quick glance over her found no signs of blood, but there were broken bones to consider.

There was also the worry about those on their trail. He grew angry with himself. He had been so engrossed in conversation with her that he hadn't paid heed to his surroundings. He knew better than that. He had allowed his interest in her to interfere with common sense. And now she had suffered the consequences.

He had to get her somewhere she would be safe. Night being near upon them would help. Those who followed would not be able to track in the dark and would likely wait until dawn. It would be wise to put as much distance between them before that if possible.

Traveling in the thick of night was not new to him. He and his brothers had been trained well, and night travel had been part of that. However, carrying Bliss would slow him some, but it couldn't be helped. At least he could gain some distance before morning.

Bliss moaned, her eyes fluttering open. She moved to sit up.

"Slowly," he said, slipping his arm around her to help her. He felt the sticky wetness through her cloak and fear twisted his gut. He moved his hand as soon as he was certain she could sit up on her own. He was surprised and upset to see that blood covered his hand. "You're bleeding."

"A minor wound," she said, trying to stand.

"That much blood is not a minor wound," he said, his arm going around her waist and lifting her to her feet though he didn't release her.

"Trust me when I tell you it is minor. Right now we need to leave. They follow."

She saw and knew, so he asked, "How many?"

"Two," she said. "They were sent—"

"To find and return you and kill me," he finished. "That young soldier realized his mistake fast enough and, no doubt, is one of the two who follow. He wants to impress the king by capturing you."

"Aye, he does," she said, nudging him away to allow her stand on her own. "But we must hurry."

"You're injured; I'll carry you, and we'll put distance between us and them." He reached out to scoop her up, but she brushed his effort aside.

"No," she insisted. "I am fine for now. It is the two soldiers we must worry about. They follow. We cannot outrun them. We must—"

"End this now," he said, knowing it was the wisest choice. Otherwise, they would continue to be chased by the pair. "You are certain there are only two? There isn't one who has been sent back to report our location?"

"The young soldier isn't the only one who wishes to impress the king. The one who joined him wants the same, and neither is considering anything but his own glory."

Trey gave a quick perusal of the area, and Bliss did the same though she was faster to decide and hurried forward. He went along with her, not liking the way she held her arm close to her body. She was in pain and trying to hide it.

She stopped suddenly and pointed at a towering pine. "The tree. You can get me up there to hide the way you did as a child."

"What?"

"We have no time to discuss this. It will provide cover for me and ease your concern for my safety."

If she could sense his concern for her, what else could she sense? He had no time to consider it. She was right. If he could stow her away—

"Hurry," she urged. "They are not far off."

"Get behind me, lock your arms around my neck and your legs around my waist, and hold tight."

She nodded as she did so, and when he was certain she had a firm hold on him, he reached up for the lowest branch. It took him no time to climb into the densest part of the tree branches even though the pine needles jabbed at him as if annoyed at the intrusion. He found a spot where two branches formed a nook and settled her safely there with the extra blankets and food sack.

He then slipped a dirk from his boot and handed it to her.

She shook her head. "It won't be necessary."

He slipped it back in his boot and leaned in close. "I will be back for you; then I'll see to that wound of yours." He kissed her lightly on the lips, as though it were the most natural thing for him to do. "Rest and stay as still as you can."

He disappeared through the tree branches and was soon out of sight.

Bliss rested her head back against the tree trunk. His gentle kiss had comforted and left her with a sense of calm that all would be well and she need not worry. She liked that he took a moment to kiss her, and though it was a mere tender, friendly kiss, it had tickled her senses and sent a rush of goose-flesh over her.

Here she was perched high in a tree, her arm paining her considerably, and where were her thoughts?

Kisses.

She settled for a smile though she would have preferred to laugh aloud. It felt so wonderful to be kissed, even a light, friendly kiss. And to know that he cared and worried over her safety and well-being and—that he had held her hand.

The simple act of holding hands stirred something in the soul, and it had been stirring hers since Trey had walked out of the mist and into her life.

She winced, a pain suddenly shooting through her arm. The wound needed cleansing and bandaging and a touch of healing, though healing herself was not always easy. For some reason, her touch worked better on others than on herself.

Voices interrupted her thoughts, and she listened as they drew closer. The quiet woods carried the voices along on the cold night air, making them sound closer than they actually were.

"They couldn't have gotten far," said one, who no doubt thought he whispered.

"They would never expect us to follow in the dark," said the other.

Bliss recognized his voice. It was the young soldier, and she grew sad that he had not paid heed to her warning that it would not be her husband who died this day. Perhaps Trey was right about man deciding his own fate. The soldier had been warned and chose to ignore it, thus choosing his fate.

Their voices drifted away as they went to meet their destiny.

Bliss closed her eyes and rested her hand beneath the arm that pained her. She would need to tend it as soon as Trey returned. And then she would sleep. It had been a long and tiring day, and she longed to curl up on a blanket before a nice warm fire and drift into a pleasant sleep.

It had been a brief scuffle, Trey having surprised the two soldiers and neither having been as experienced with swords as he should have been. He left their bodies for Mother Nature to dispose of as She saw fit. He was eager to return to Bliss, see to her wound, and settle them for the night.

He worried when she didn't stir upon his arrival. When he reached out to gently rouse her, she winced, and he hadn't even touched her arm.

Her eyes fluttered open, and she gave him a weak smile. "I'm so glad you're back."

"Your arm?" he asked anxiously.

"Too much pain, something is wrong."

The pain had increased, and she had weakened since he had left her. She would not be strong enough to hold on to him as she did when he had climbed the tree. He didn't waste time. He needed to get her settled and see to her wound.

He tossed the rolled blankets and food sack to the ground and moved to the side opposite her wound.

"I'm going to help you stand," he said. "Slow and easy we'll go." He wrapped her arm around his neck, and, with his arm strong around her waist, he eased her up.

She gasped, and he stopped. "What's wrong?"

"The pain. There has to be a reason for so much pain."

"Can you keep one arm around my neck and curl your one leg around mine?"

"I believe so."

"I can get us down if you feel strong enough to do that," he said.

She nodded.

Once she did as he asked, he started their descent though it didn't go as easily as he had hoped, and the darkness didn't help. Pine needles poked and jabbed her injured arm, and by the time they reached the bottom branch, he could feel that her strength had waned.

He held her tight and, with one hand, took hold of the last branch to lower them to the ground. Her body went limp in his arms, and he knew she had fainted. He didn't hesitate. He eased her over his shoulder and got them quickly to the ground.

Chapter 5

The pain woke Bliss, her eyes springing open. She lay next to a crackling campfire, a blanket beneath her and another one covering her. Her cloak was gone and the sleeve on her right arm was ripped wide, exposing her wound.

"You're awake," Trey said, bending down beside her.

"I fainted?" She reached out anxiously for his hand. "I have never fainted."

As soon as his hand took hold of hers, she calmed, and her apprehension began to dissipate.

"You had good reason; a small part of the arrow splintered and broke off in your arm."

"That explains the pain," she said. "You'll need to remove it."

"Already done," he said with a smile. "I thought it best to get it done before you came to though it wasn't difficult. I got a good grip on the small piece, gave a tug, and it was out."

She looked quickly at her arm. "Bleeding?"

"Not as much as I expected. I was just about to clean and bandage it for you."

She smiled. "I see that I am in capable hands."

"Aye, you are," he confirmed with a smile.

His confidence eased her concern, and she allowed herself to rest as she watched him work. He bent over her, his focus intense, his touch gentle. She had studied his face often when she had helped heal him. You could tell much by watching a face. And even though he had been unconscious through most of the healing process, his face had shown discomfort, pain, worry, sorrow. But now—now she saw concern there, and it was for her.

He genuinely cared, and he was upset over her suffering, as if he suffered along with her. This caring part of him seemed in such contrast to his warrior side. He had taken two lives a short time ago, and now those same hands were gentle and healing.

He was a good man, this husband of hers, and the more time she spent with him, the more she learned about him, the more she liked him. She still wished she could see beyond these moments, but visions of him came sparingly.

"I'm afraid I have to tear a piece of cloth from your other sleeve to use as a bandage," he said. "But worry not; I'll see that another blouse is stitched for you."

She did not object to his kind offer and she was resting her hand on his arm to thank him when a vision struck. It was of the same woman, and this time he hugged her close, the pain and hurt so strong on his face that it stabbed at Bliss's heart.

"Whatever you saw troubles you, I can see it in your eyes."

How odd that he could read her face as easily as she read his. She wasn't ready to share her visions of him and another woman just yet. She wondered if she would ever be ready, but, then, that was nonsense. Her destiny was written, and she must follow it whether it included Trey or not. It was simply the way of things, and she could not bemoan it—or so she tried to convince herself.

"A vision too obscure to understand," she said.

"Not all visions are clear?" he asked, tearing the piece of cloth he needed and beginning to bandage her arm.

No one ever discussed her visions with her. They seemed afraid to do so, which left her feeling alone much of the time. She could not believe how easily Trey talked about the subject or that he was interested in doing so.

"Some are a challenge to understand," she said.

"But you embrace them anyway, don't you?"

"I really don't have a choice. It is hard to ignore them."

He finished tying off the strips of cloth he used to keep the bandage in place. He turned his head, his eyes meeting hers. "That must be a terrible burden."

There was something in the blue and green hues of his eyes that captivated. She couldn't quite explain it, wasn't sure what she saw, she only knew that it held more power than anything she had ever known, and, for a moment, it frightened her.

"At times," she said, turning her head to glance at the fire.

"You're tired and no doubt hungry."

"More so one than the other," she said.

"Regardless, you'll need to eat to keep up your strength, or so says my mum," he said with a laugh, "though her cooking was not easy to stomach."

His laugh brought a smile to her face. And she wondered how he had deduced that she'd be more tired than hungry. Then again, it would seem the more reasonable choice after all they had been through today. Still, his strong intuitiveness nagged at her.

Her yawn was another indication that the long day had caught up with her.

"The only strength left me is sleep," she said.

"First, a piece of bread and cheese to sustain you," he cajoled, searching through the sack.

He found the items and, after setting them near her side, moved to sit behind her. He slipped his hands ever so gently beneath her back and lifted her to sit between his spread legs and rest in the crook of his shoulder. He then reached for the food and split it between them, his one arm remaining firmly around her.

He took the liberties of a husband, sitting them intimately together and making no apology for it. Of course he was her husband, though the truth of it was that their marriage had not been consummated, so one could argue their union was not recognized.

And so she said after a nibble of cheese, "This is all so strange."

"It seems natural to me."

"It is natural to wed someone, unaware that you did, to do all you can to keep your unexpected bride safe, and to tend her when she foolishly falls down a hill?"

"The force of the arrow caused you to stumble; foolishness had nothing to do with it," he said. "And as for keeping you safe, it is no chore, though I didn't keep my bride safe enough, or she would never have tumbled down the hill."

"These are troubling times in the Highlands— the winds of change blow heavily, leaving debris and hardship in their path. You protect me when it is not your duty—"

"You can argue that point all you like, but it *is* my duty, and I will see it done."

"You have another duty that comes first," she reminded.

"I need no reminder that I serve the true king and will see him safely seated on the throne. I am well aware of what my duties are and where and when I am needed. And how do you know that I am not on a mission and that being wed to you provides me with the excuse needed to accomplish it."

She tilted her head to the side to study him. His eyes were as compelling as ever, and, before they could befuddle her senses, she said, "I have seen nothing to indicate that."

"And if that was the case, it is well that you don't." His finger pressed against her lips as soon as she opened them to respond. "Leave it be. And let this arrangement serve us well for now."

Bliss shrugged and pushed his hand away. "There is no harm in that. After all, how meaningful are vows when they are yet to be consummated?"

He rested his lips near her temple, and whispered, "I can rectify that very easily."

"Why?"

The simple question brought a smile to his lips. "Need I explain?"

"Aye, please do," she said.

"You're serious?"

"Of course I am. Why consummate vows you never plan to honor?"

His expression darkened. "I would honor my vows."

"Because you consummated them, not because of love?"

He shook his head. "You're complicating things."

"Love does that; it complicates."

"No it doesn't," he argued. "Love is simple."

She laughed. "You are a fool if you believe that."

"I not only believe it, I lived it," he said with a thump to his chest. "I once loved deeply, and it was not complicated. She loved me, and I loved her. There was no question about it. No need for concern. Love was there in our hearts, in our actions, in our words. Nothing could take it from us, nothing but—death."

He moved her gently aside, stood and walked around to the other side of the campfire, and sat.

"I am sorry for your loss," she said, "though I

know those words bring little comfort. I truly am sorry. I cannot imagine your pain."

"There is no healing it," he said, stretching out on the blanket and pillowing his arms beneath his head. "A wound to the body heals given time. The pain fades and returns no more. Not so when you lose someone you love. You think the pain gone, then it surfaces once more and hurts all over again."

She could not stand to see the suffering in his eyes, and so she said what she sensed. "Your pain will go away and never will you feel it again."

He turned on his side, his eyes locking with hers. "Promise."

"Aye, that I can promise you."

"How can that be?"

"I do not know," she said. "I cannot explain it. I can only tell you that it will come to pass."

"Soon?"

"Aye, soon," she said, and felt a stabbing pain to her heart.

"I wish I could believe you, but the only way for my pain to go away is for Leora to return to me, and she can't. She's dead." He dropped back on the blanket. "Sleep and rest so that we can get an early start in the morning."

Bliss eased herself down on the blanket, her arm paining her. She lay there trying to heal her wound, but found it difficult to concentrate. Her thoughts continued to return to Trey and what she had sensed. How could his pain ever heal when the woman he loved was dead? Of course he could find love again, but would that heal his old wound or simply make it easier to live with?

An icy shiver ran through her, and she shuddered as another vision assaulted her. This time she saw only the blond woman. She was reaching out, calling for Trey, tears streaming down her cheeks, begging him to help her.

She heard herself whimper and felt her body shudder again, but try as she might, she could not escape the vision. She was trapped, just like the woman.

Her whole body jolted, and she was yanked out of the vision so sharply that she cried out.

"I've got you. You're all right," Trey whispered in her ear as he held her snug against him.

She realized then that he lay stretched out beside her. His warmth flooded her and began to chase away the chill that seemed to run deep into her bones, and she didn't want his arms, so hard with muscles, ever to let her go.

She was grateful he lay wrapped around her. She had never experienced a vision like that before. Never had she felt trapped in one. The visions came suddenly, and often without warning, and left just as suddenly. But never, ever had a vision trapped her.

She shivered with fear.

Trey gently stroked her back. "You're safe. It's all right."

"No, it's not," she said, pressing her face in the crook of his neck.

"Why? Tell me what frightened you," he urged.

She slowly eased her head back to look up at him and was grateful for the concern she saw there, but more so for the indomitable strength she forever saw in his eyes. He made her feel safe.

"Tell me," he urged again.

"I was trapped," she said softly.

"Where?"

"In a vision." She shivered again, and he instantly pressed his lips to her brow.

"I pulled you out," he said, and kissed her cheek. "You are safe, and I will see that you stay that way."

She grasped hold of his shirt. "I have never been trapped in a vision. If you hadn't pulled me out, I don't know how I would have gotten out."

"Tell me about this vision."

She shook her head. "No, I do not want to get pulled back again."

He pressed her cheek to hers. "It's all right. You don't have to say anything. And if you were to get pulled back in, I would pull you free again. So do not worry."

"How would you know I was trapped—how *did* you know I was trapped?"

"I didn't know. I thought you suffered a bad dream. But I know now, and I know what to do, grab hold of you and hold you tight."

Bliss cuddled closer though she was already firm against him. She needed to feel his thick muscles pressed against her, feel his warmth, and share his strength, his courage. She didn't want him to leave her side. She wanted him right there beside her all night. But how did she ask him to stay?

With courage, she said, "You'll stay with me tonight?"

"I had no intentions of going anywhere. It is in my arms you'll be sleeping tonight."

She placed a gentle kiss on his cheek. "I am grateful."

"I am here for you, *wife*, whenever you need me."

Chapter 6

Trey and Bliss woke with the sunrise and were on their way. Trey would have preferred Bliss rest in his arms, but that wouldn't have been a prudent decision. Once the two soldiers were missed, others would be sent. It was inevitable that they would run across the king's soldiers again. And the more soldiers, the more victory favored them.

He wished they hadn't had to rush. He liked waking up with Bliss wrapped in his arms, her head tucked in the crook of his shoulder. She seemed to belong there.

Where Leora once rested.

The thought had only now crept up on him. Unusual, since Leora had been first on his mind every morning he had wakened, since her death . . . how long now?

He shook his head. He had faithfully counted the passing days, as if hoping he would somehow reach the end of his misery. Had that been today? Had sleeping wrapped around Bliss made a difference? Had feeling connected to another woman helped heal his pain?

A sudden memory sprang up that chilled him to the bone. He recalled meeting an old woman, a seer he thought, though he learned later that she was believed a witch. She had pertinent news of Reeve's wife, Tara. She also had predictions for him, warning him that he would suffer great injury and that when he woke from healing, he would gaze upon the face of his future wife. He had shared all the information with his brothers, feeling somewhat of a fool for rattling on about gazing upon his future bride when he woke and learned it had been Bliss. He shook his head again. The seer had been so accurate; all her predictions had come true. How was it possible for a person to peer into the future like the seer did . . . like Bliss did?

"You debate yourself?" Bliss asked.

Trey sent her a questionable glance.

She smiled. "You keep shaking your head, stop, then shake it again. You must be debating something with yourself."

He grinned. "It's a good debate I often have."

"Who wins?"

He laughed and thumped his chest. "I do, every time."

Her laughter warmed his heart, a heart that, he could not deny, was beginning to feel again. And for the first time in what seemed a very long time, he wanted it to.

"Could we stop for a few moments?" she asked.

"Your arm pains you?" he asked concerned.

"My stomach," she said with a smile.

He nodded. "You're hungry."

"So are you."

"You know that?" He shook his head again. "You heard my stomach protesting."

She laughed. "Quite loudly though you were too deep in thought to pay heed to it."

A matter he had to rectify. He could not keep getting lost in his thoughts and fail to pay heed to his surroundings. It had already proven dangerous; he did not want it to turn fatal.

He found a spot beneath a towering pine that had shed enough needles to provide a nice cushion for them to sit on.

They shared the last of the food, having determined that it would take perhaps three hours or less to reach their destination. Then food and shelter would be no problem. Once finished there, they could start their journey to MacAlpin keep, where he could see she was kept safe.

"What is it that so often steals your thoughts?"

Her question startled him, especially since he wasn't prepared to answer it. But how did he avoid it?

"It does not involve the true king," she said, staring at him strangely.

"You intrude where not invited," he snapped, not wanting her to know his private concerns.

"My apologizes," she said, and turned her head away from him.

A twinge of guilt struck him, not for warning her about intruding on his thoughts but for snapping so sharply at her.

"There are things that are private," he said in way of an apology though he would not offer one.

He did not want her to know his every thought, and she had to realize that.

"I understand," she said.

He didn't like that she kept her head turned away from him. He reached out, his hand slipping beneath her chin to gently turn her face.

She avoided his eyes, and he didn't like it. "If you're angry with me, have your say and be done with it."

"I am not angry," she said her glance finally falling on him. "But it is difficult for me to avoid your thoughts when you so easily open them to me."

"You know all my thoughts?"

"Not all. Some come jumbled though I don't know why, while others are clear, as if you are speaking to me. I don't understand it myself. Usually, I sense or have a vision, or I hear a thought or two." She shook her head. "Not so with you. I have seen and sensed more than most with you."

"I cannot have you knowing my every thought. It could prove dangerous for you," he said, and difficult for him. What would happen when he got the urge to kiss her? Or his thoughts turned intimate. What then? "How do we stop this?"

Her surprised, steady gaze was enough to let him know that she had heard his thoughts. And there was only one thing to do. He cupped her chin, tilted her head up, and kissed her.

His kiss was as confident as his stance and his stride. This was a man who knew what he wanted, and he wanted her. The overwhelming sensation of his desire and the rise of her passion melted away any doubts that this was wrong.

Bliss did something she rarely did—she let herself be carried away. She surrendered to her senses instead of relying on them. Soon, nothing but the kiss filled her head. It was the most freeing feeling she had ever experienced. And she didn't want it to end; she wanted nothing more than to linger and enjoy it.

After bringing the kiss to an end, he teased her bottom lip with nibbles and in between asked, "Do you know what I'm thinking right now?"

"Befuddled," she murmured, her mind and senses dwelling on the kiss and his tormenting nibbles.

"My kiss bewildered you?" he asked with a prideful laugh.

"It did, it has, it does," she said, her rambling words proving truthful.

He laughed again, kissed her hard, and hugged her tight. "We have settled our dilemma."

Her mind had yet to clear, and so she asked, "How?"

"It is simple," he boasted. "I will kiss you whenever you sense too much about me."

The idea startled her though she could not say she opposed it. She did, however, want to know, "But do you want to kiss me?"

He laughed again. "It has proven successful already. You have forgotten."

She smiled. "I remember now. I sensed that you *wanted* to kiss me."

"And so I did, without objection from you."

"It was most pleasant," she said, "and gave my mind rest."

"Then since I *wanted* to kiss you, and you *wished* me to kiss you, we have no problem in how to settle this dilemma."

It seemed reasonable enough though she was concerned with where it might lead. But they would not be together long. Even though his intentions were to return her home with him, she had different plans. She would go to her home and remain there with her people. They would protect her, and it would give her time to think about Trey. Nothing made sense when it came to him, not her vision, not her knowing, nothing, and she needed to make sense of it before she lost all sound reason and did something unwise.

"For now," she said. "But time may show us otherwise."

"What do you mean?"

"It is up to time; it is not for me to say."

"You speak in riddles," he said.

"It will make sense soon enough."

He shook his head. "You confuse."

She laughed. "It is the way I often feel."

He stroked her cheek. "How difficult it must be for you."

No one had ever cared how she felt. What mattered was what she could tell people. What they wanted to hear. What they needed to know. Her grandmum had told her that she would be condemned more than revered. And that life would prove difficult for her unless . . . she was lucky enough to have someone understand and love her for who she was.

She could not help but wonder if Trey could be that man.

"Sometimes more than others," she answered. She thought he would kiss her then, he leaned in close. But a noise startled them both, and they jumped apart.

Trey's hand went to the hilt of his sword, and he cast a cautious glance around.

"Animals at play," she said.

"You know this?"

She pointed to two squirrels scrambling along the branch of a tree.

He shook his head and stood. "We have wasted enough time."

Was that what he thought of their time together—wasted? She knew before the thought was finished that it was not what he meant. He was concerned for her. It showed in his eyes and his touch. He reached out and took her hand as he always did, as if by simply holding on to her, he could keep her safe.

Bliss wasn't so sure. As much as she wanted to believe their time together would be over soon, and she could go home as planned, she didn't see it that way. What was it that would keep them together, at least for a time? And why did she try so hard to deny it?

He stood, reached down, and grabbed her around the waist, but before he lifted her gently to her feet, he asked, "How is your arm?"

"It heals well," she assured him. The little healing she had done on it had helped greatly.

He lifted her, settling her in front of him, his

hands remaining at her waist. "We need to be on our way."

She was growing much too accustomed to his touch. His hands were always there to help her, and she found herself relying on him. It seemed strange, yet so right.

"Aye, I agree," she said. "A storm will break soon enough."

"There isn't a cloud in the sky." He smiled, though as they took a few steps, the first gray cloud raced overhead, and others soon followed.

Bliss shivered, not from a chill but the portent of the darkening sky.

Trey kept close watch on Bliss as they made their way along a well-traveled path. He had thought to travel the woods rather than a worn path, but with the terrain rough and her wound so fresh, he felt in the end it would only slow them down.

He also wanted to reach her friend's before the storm broke, and so the well-traveled road was a quicker route. Or perhaps it was he who needed the familiar road, feeling in unfamiliar territory with Bliss.

She was different in many ways and yet so familiar in others. When he had kissed her . . . his groin had tightened, a common enough reaction, and yet he had thought only on the kiss, nothing beyond that. It had been—he almost laughed aloud, for the kiss had been magical just like Bliss herself.

But how to deal with magic? Women could be complicated creatures on their own; add magic, and what then? There was much besides the kiss to consider, and the only way he could conceive of making sense of it was to pursue it. And he truly did look forward to the pursuit.

The weather did not favor them, rain starting to fall when they were not far from their destination. By the time they arrived at her friend's cottage, they were nearly soaked through.

A sharp crack of thunder heralded them through the door, and they both stood silent after first glance. The cottage was empty.

Trey went to the fireplace and after examining the half-burnt log and ashes, said, "This has been cold for some time." He grabbed kindling from the nearby basket and soon had a fire going.

Bliss moved close to the hearth, rainwater dripping from her cloak and down her face from her wet hair. She held her hands out to the heat, her eyes fixed on the leaping flames.

Trey remained silent though deep in thought. Had her friend died because of their delay? If not, where could she have gone? Bliss would surely blame herself if anything had happened to the woman.

He wanted to comfort her, and so he reached out to take her hands in his. He was stunned when she not only pulled away from him but turned and walked away. He could well understand her upset, but her rebuff disturbed him.

"Bliss, you—"

She didn't turn around, her back remained to him, and she shook her head and, with a snap of her hand, warded off his words. He bristled at her sharp dismissal. He offered comfort and help, and she rejected both. He turned around, hunched down and stoked the fire, the flames heating his annoyance.

Damn, but he was irritated. He didn't want her to shoulder this responsibility alone. He had had a hand in their delay. It wasn't entirely her fault.

He almost jumped when her hand came to rest lightly on his shoulder. He looked up and grew even angrier though this time with himself. She looked exhausted, her face pale, and she shivered.

"Thank you," she said, "for remaining quiet and giving me the time I needed to *sense* what had happened to my friend."

He felt like kicking himself for his foolishness. He had allowed his own misgivings to interfere when his only concern should have been for her. How many times would he need to remind himself that she was unlike other women? How long would it take for him to truly get to know his *wife*?

"She is well?" he asked standing and reaching out to slip her wet cloak off her shoulders.

"She was too ill to leave on her own. My people have taken her to my cottage and will look after her until my arrival."

"Two days at least to get there," he reminded, draping her cloak on the back of a chair near the fire.

"She is in good hands and should do well until I arrive though I feel that she will need to stay with my people or perhaps seek shelter with yours. She should not live alone any longer. Dolca needs family."

"She is welcome in my home," Trey assured her.

"No doubt she will be," Bliss said with a shiver.

"You need to get warm," he said, reaching out to rub some heat into her arms. His hands met wet wool. "And you need to get out of those wet clothes."

"As do you," she said, grabbing a handful of his shirt and squeezing the rainwater from it.

"We're a good pair," he said with a laugh. "Wet—"

"Tired."

"And hungry," he finished.

"Dolca should have food about, and she might have left a garment behind"—Bliss grinned—"though I daresay none that would fit you."

"Then I will just have to go naked until my garments dry." He quickly slipped out of his shirt, leaving his chest bare.

Bliss's cheeks burnt red, and she hurried over to the single bed tucked in the corner of the one-room cottage. She grabbed the blanket folded at the bottom and tossed it to Trey. "That should do nicely."

"It embarrasses you to see me naked?" he teased.

Bliss grinned from ear to ear, walking over to him. "It embarrasses me to think what I would do if I saw you naked."

Her response stunned Trey speechless.

"Now turn yourself away from me as you strip naked so that I don't do anything foolish," she said, and gave him a slight shove.

It took Trey a moment to regain his senses and realize that if it was a game she played with him, he'd join in the play. He grabbed hold, his fingers closing tightly around her wrist, and drew her nearer.

"I beg you . . . be foolish," he said with a challenging gleam in his eyes.

Chapter 7

Bliss wasn't sure how to respond or how to escape a folly of her own making. All reason failed her, and when she felt the drops of rainwater trickle down along her neck and into her already soaked blouse, she stuttered, saying what made the most sense to her. "I-I am wet."

He smiled and rested his cheek against hers to whisper, "Ready for me then, are you?"

She jumped away from him so fast that she stumbled and would have fallen on the bed if Trey hadn't grabbed her around the waist.

"Eager to get me into bed?"

She struggled to escape his embrace, shoving at his chest, her hands meeting hard, damp muscle . . . and a scar. She ceased her struggle, recalling his injuries, and her hand stroked along his chest over a scar that had proved difficult to heal. She had recalled Tara, Reeve's wife, detailing the trouble she had in stitching it. It had healed well though it would take time to fade. He let her go when her hand slipped over his shoulder, and she moved to walk around him.

She stopped, her hand traveling down the length of another scar. Bliss had wanted to lay her hands upon it when she had been helping to heal him, but Trey had remained on his back in bed, mostly sleeping, and, not wanting to disturb his rest, she had never gotten to lay her healing touch on it.

But she could now.

"Be still," she whispered softly, "and let me touch you."

He made no move to object, he remained still, though she could hear his breathing, the rhythm a bit faster than usual. She set to work, heat radiating from the center of her hand as she ran it slowly over the scar. The heat from her touch poured into him like warm liquid that was meant to heal. She retraced her path over and over, slowly and meticulously covering every inch of the nasty scar.

She did not realize how long she worked, and it wasn't until she felt herself grow weak that she stopped and stumbled backward. Her hand reached out to grab Trey's arm, but her fingers barely grazed his muscle.

Bliss thought for sure she would tumble to the ground when suddenly Trey's hand slipped around her waist and scooped her up against his warm body. Weary, she rested her head to his chest.

"You are weak, I can feel it," he said with alarm.

"Tired, that's all," she assured him.

"And wet."

Her head snapped up, recalling his earlier remark, and at that moment sensed clearly that they were destined to consummate their vows. The thought thrilled and frightened her all at once.

Her worry subsided, for now, when he said, "You need dry clothes."

She agreed though she would prefer not to leave his arms. She was so comfortable in his embrace, and the more comfortable she became, the more she ached to remain there.

"Get dry," he said, easing her down to stand. "We'll eat, then get a good night's rest before leaving for your home in the morning as long as the weather proves agreeable."

She walked over to the bed without comment and reached under the blanket. She recalled Dolca keeping an extra linen shift tucked away there. Sure enough, she found it and turned to instruct Trey to keep his back to her.

She twirled her finger, indicating to him to turn around. "Privacy please."

"Why? You are my wife," he said with a wicked smile though he laughed and did as she requested.

Bliss hurried out of her wet garments and into the shift. It fit fairly well, though with no sleeves and minus her stockings, she turned cold fast. She hung her garments near the fire as best she could and remained in front of the flames warming herself, then let Trey know she was finished.

He gave her one look and was quick to wrap the blanket she had earlier thrown to him around her. "That should help ward off some of the cold."

"What of you? This blanket was to keep you warm."

"It will when we crawl in bed together."

His remark didn't surprise her. Now that she knew that fate intended them to make love, there would be no preventing it. It was only a matter of time. Besides, they were tired, it was cold, and it wasn't fair to assign him to sleep on the hard ground after what they had been through. And he no doubt would make certain to remind her that they were husband and wife. And there was no stopping what fate decreed.

He began to scavenge for food while Bliss continued to warm herself.

"Mostly roots and little vegetables, nothing more," he said. "And my stomach grumbles." He reached for his shirt.

"What are you doing?"

"We need food. I'm going to get us some."

"It's raining. The animals are no different from us. They seek shelter in a rainstorm."

"We will see." He laughed and struggled into his wet shirt. He walked over to her and rested his hand on the back of her neck. "Keep warm, rest, and I will return soon."

She didn't know why she asked, "Promise?"

His eyes darkened to a deeper shade of blue, and he frowned, as if her words upset him. "You are my wife. I will not leave you."

The thought slammed into her hard, and she gasped just as he settled his mouth on hers. She had no chance to enjoy it, the sense that one day he would walk away from her so overwhelmed her that it twisted in her stomach like a sharp dagger.

"Good, I leave you breathless for now," he said with a grin. He gave her another kiss though it was quick. "Rest, so you will be ready to feast."

When the door shut behind him, Bliss dropped

down on the nearest chair. What she sensed had changed things for her. How could she lose her heart to him if in the end he walked away? She was relieved she had sensed this early on, for now she could protect her heart.

She shook her head. How would she do that if they were destined to make love? Her knowing, her visions, they all confused her, and she wished she hadn't seen anything. She wished that fate had simply placed her hand on them and guided without showing her anything. For once, it would be nice to live as others did, not knowing what life would bring but embracing all it had to offer.

Bliss heard the lift of the latch and was surprised that Trey had returned so soon. The door sprung wide open, and so did her eyes.

"A fire and a woman to keep me warm."

Bliss didn't need her skills to tell her that she was in trouble. The man who kicked the door shut behind him had made his intentions clear with his words, but his leering look alone would have told her the same.

The rain had done little to wash the stench off him, he and his garments in need of a good washing. Grime stuck to his knotted, long hair and craggy face even though it was obvious from his dripping garments that he had walked a good distance in the rain. It had done little to wash away the filth. Dirt caked thick beneath his nails, but the worst thing was his size. He was big and wide and much too strong to defend against.

The only weapon she possessed was her knowing, which would have warned her of his approach if she had not allowed herself to get lost in her worries over Trey.

Stop, you need to concentrate. She was grateful for the silent warning and paid heed to it.

Her hand flew up when he took his first step. "I am a seer and was expecting you—"

She paused and waited, for a moment worried that she had not cleared her muddled thoughts fast enough, but her knowing did not fail her. "William of Longee."

He stopped dead. This time it was his turn for his eyes to grow wide.

His fear washed over her like a rushing wave, and she shivered at the unexpected force. Many believed seers were witches and, therefore, feared them, though they sought their powers, and not always for good reason. William obviously feared seers, and that could prove advantageous or deadly.

When his hand pulled a dirk from a sheath at his waist, Bliss worried that it was the latter.

Trey was soaked and annoyed. Bliss had been right, the animals had sought shelter from the storm, and there was not a single one about. He wondered if there was ever a time she wasn't right. And would it do him good to pay heed to her words more often?

He had been about to give up and return to the cottage when he had come upon a stream, and the heavens had taken pity on him and seen to it that he caught a fish. It would feed him well enough, but he needed another for Bliss. The heavens must not have agreed with him, for now he was having trouble catching another.

With the rain continuing to soak him through, he was about to give it a few more minutes when he was suddenly hit with the overwhelming urge to hurry back to the cottage. His heart began to pound in his chest so badly that he thought it would burst. Something was wrong, very wrong. Bliss was in danger, he could feel—it twisted at his gut and turned his blood cold. He took hold of the lone fish and rushed through the woods, hoping he wasn't too late.

He shouldn't have left her. These were dangerous times, and vigilance was called for more often than not. She might be able to sense things, but did it help her defend herself?

The more he thought, the more anxious he became and the more he believed that Bliss was in trouble. He rushed through the woods, paying no heed to the pouring rain, his feet pounding the muddy ground. He stopped abruptly when he drew near the cottage and gave a quick glance around. No one lurked about, and no horses were tethered to the trees. Still, the sense of dread fell heavy upon him, which meant that the threat had to come from within the cottage.

Trey rushed forward, his heart hammering in his chest and fear gripping his heart like never before. He burst through the door and found Bliss sitting alone at the table.

After shutting the door and making sure the latch caught firm he approached her. He slapped the fish, then his hands down on the table, and said, "What happened?"

"You sensed danger?" she asked, appearing perplexed.

"Aye, I did, strong and hard and I raced back here to find you alone and yet—" He shook his head. "What happened? I know something happened."

She nodded. "It did. I had an unexpected visitor in your absence, but he's gone now and won't be returning."

His heart stopped slamming against his chest, and his fear ebbed though not entirely. "Who was he and what did he want?"

"You're dripping so much rainwater that fish may just come back to life."

"Then he too will be just as interested to hear what you have to say."

She gave a chuckle and shook her head. "You need to get out of those wet clothes first."

He shed his garments quickly and without care and stood stark naked in front of her.

She pulled the blanket from around her shoulders.

"Don't," he ordered stopping her. "I did what you requested. Now it's your turn."

"You'll chill," she said, flustered, and again attempted to offer him the blanket.

"My annoyance heats me."

She kept her glance on his face. Now and again it slipped to his chest though she quickly retrieved it. "William of Longee was his name, with little manners, a foul stench, and large in size."

He felt his anger mount and wondered how she

was able to defend herself against such a man. He didn't ask; he waited for her to continue.

"He thought me and this cottage a welcoming sight. Once I told him I was a seer, he changed his opinion and drew a dirk."

A low growl rumbled in Trey's chest.

Bliss hurried her tale. "I sensed potential trouble—"

"Potential? The dirk made his intentions perfectly clear. He intended to do you harm."

She shook her head. "Nay, he feared me and only tried to protect himself."

"You defend him?"

"As I learned more about him, I felt sorry for him. He was a man who misunderstood fate, and so he labored under misconceptions. He believed love treated him badly when in essence he had failed love."

"You talk in riddles."

She stood and walked around the table, her eyes on his face the whole time and remaining so while she tucked the blanket around his waist.

Trey didn't object. He was chilled as she had warned, and he worried that his body would soon react not only to her lovely features but more so to her courage.

"That's better," she said with a pat to his chest. "Now where was I?"

He grabbed her around the waist and hoisted her up to sit on the edge of the table in front of him, planting his hands on either side of her, restricting her movement.

"Love," he reminded.

"Aye, love," she said. "Poor William didn't believe strongly enough in it. If he had, he would not have suffered so senselessly. You see, he believed the woman he loved stopped loving him, when it was her family who kept her locked away from him, not thinking he was suited for their daughter. Her love, however, was strong, and she waits these many months for him to rescue her . . . she *believes* in their love." She grinned. "And now he does too. He's gone to rescue her."

"In a rainstorm when night is nearing?" He shook his head. "Insane, and only someone in love would do something insane."

"You understand," she said, her grin growing.

"I do; I loved strongly once and would have done the same."

"But are you ready to love again?"

Chapter 8

Bliss regretted asking the question, his hesitancy and the dazed look in his eyes having answered it for her. And she regretted being trapped, unable to maneuver herself away. She would have preferred some distance from him right now.

She wasn't surprised when he turned the question on her. What better way not to answer.

"What of you? Are you ready to love?"

"Aye, I am," she said, and with the need to step away from him so great, she gently pushed his arm out of her way, jumped down off the table, and walked around to stand in front of the fire, "though I don't know if love is ready for me."

"It eludes you?" he asked.

She turned with a flourish to face him. If he would not answer her question, she would no longer answer his. "What eludes me is that fish."

He seemed reluctant to end their conversation, but he did, turning his attention to cleaning the fish. Love was discussed no more, and well it shouldn't be. Times were difficult enough in the Highlands and would grow worse before they settled, and Trey was an intricate part of it all. There was no time for love, only survival, the most likely reason fate had brought Trey to her. And hadn't fate let her know that he would eventual leave her. Their marriage was not a marriage at all, and what a folly to allow herself to think that her situation was anything other than what it was.

If she would stop these foolish musings and concentrate, there was a good chance she would learn what fate truly intended her to know.

Bliss was relieved when Trey stepped outside to discard the fish scraps and rinse the stench of fish off him. The cottage was small, and it felt like they were on top of each other most of the time. Or was it that his presence dominated the snug room?

For a lean man, he could fill a space, but, then, his shoulders were broad, and he carried himself with such distinction. He was not the type to blend with a crowd, but rather stand out.

And he was magnificent naked.

Her cheeks flamed red. Whatever was the matter with her? Why couldn't she get him off her mind? This brief time alone could serve her well if she concentrated.

She went to the bed and stretched out, forcing her eyes closed, forcing her mind to quiet, inviting fate in. Soon she was lost in the crackling sounds of the fire, the heat that wafted around her, and the delicious scent of the cooking fish, which had her stomach grumbling. Content, she drifted off into a light slumber.

Trey finished, the air having grown more chilled and forcing him back inside, a place he wasn't sure he should be at the moment. Bliss was just too tempting, and her beauty wasn't the only thing that played havoc with his passion. She was strong and confident, and damned if he didn't find her strange abilities fascinating. She was different, and that difference challenged him.

He entered the cottage with a sense of anticipation though it faded when he saw Bliss asleep on the bed. He walked over to her. She was stretched out in peaceful repose, her arms at her sides. He drew the warm wool blanket up over her and tucked it gently around her, then quickly stepped away.

He busied himself with cooking the fish, though he attended it more than necessary. He had to do something to keep himself busy or else he just might crawl into bed with Bliss and—she wouldn't remain sleeping for long.

Frustrated, he ran his fingers roughly through his hair and paced in front of the hearth.

He could attempt to convince himself that it was lust, nothing more than pure, simple lust. It was obvious that they were both attracted to each other. Before, when he had stripped naked in front of her, he had seen how she had struggled to keep her eyes focused above his waist. He, however, had no qualms in baring all to her. Or did he hope that she would reciprocate and do the same?

He hunched down and poked at the fish a bit too hard. A morsel of meat fell loose and toppled off the heating stone to be quickly devoured by the flames.

"Be gentle, or there will be nothing left for us."

Trey jumped up and turned, not having heard Bliss approach, and nearly knocked her over. It was she who reached out and grabbed his arm to steady herself though he was quick to put a hand to her waist.

"I thought you were asleep."

"A rest, that is all." She smiled. "Besides, the scent of the fish is much too tempting."

It wasn't the fish that he was hungry for though his stomach thought differently, grumbling loudly.

Bliss laughed. "You are just as hungry."

"That I am," he said, his thoughts far from the fish.

"Let's sit in front of the hearth and eat," Bliss suggested, getting the blanket from the bed. With a quick shove to Trey's chest to move him aside, she placed the blanket over the rushes on the earth floor in front of the fireplace.

She plopped down and reached her hand up to him. "Join me."

He did, folding his legs as he lowered himself opposite her. With the slip of his dagger, he carefully removed a portion of the fish, blew on it gently to cool it down, and placed it in Bliss's hand. He then did the same for himself. He was glad the food filled his mouth, for words escaped him at the moment.

Her simple touch had given him a shock though it wasn't the touch itself that had surprised, it was the image that assaulted him. It was quick and vivid, so very vivid that it had stunned him. He blamed it on his musings. He had been thinking of nothing else but Bliss. So why wouldn't he have been struck with an image of them making love. And Lord had it feel good, the silky softness of her body, the eagerness of her touch, the heat of her kiss, the frantic beat of his heart, the swell of his desire, and the love that had radiated between them.

He almost choked on the piece of fish in his mouth.

"Are you all right?" Bliss asked anxiously.

Trey held up his hand while he covered his mouth to clear his throat.

Love. Where had that come from? And yet he had felt it strong and hard, pulsing through them both. It was fantastic and frightening all at once, and damn if he didn't want to feel it again.

"Are you sure you're all right?" she asked again.

He lowered his hands. "I'm fine. Piece of fish got stuck."

She smiled, and he could have sworn he heard a tinkle of laughter. Did she know? Had she seen the same? Had it been her vision he had caught a glimpse of?

"Delicious," she said with a lick of her lips.

Was she talking about the fish or the vision? Or was he simply going insane?

If it were madness, then he might as well enjoy it. He reached out, slipping his hand around the back of her neck, drew her near as he leaned forward, and kissed her.

It was as if an ember that was soon to die was suddenly sparked and set aflame. Heated passion raced through them, turning the kiss more eager than either expected. Trey wanted nothing more than to scoop her up, carry her to bed, and make love to her.

Love.

The word resonated in his head like a tolling bell and was enough for him to end the kiss, though reluctantly. He knew he should say something. You don't kiss a woman and turn silent afterwards, but words failed him. Besides, what did he say? I believe I could be falling in love with you though we don't know each other well, and I'm not sure if I can ever love again because, you see, the woman I loved with all my heart died.

He turned his face to the flames, guilt rising to trouble him. He wasn't even sure what he felt guilty about. Did he feel as if he betrayed the love Leora and he had once shared? Or did he feel guilty for wanting to make love to Bliss?

"You loved her very much, didn't you?" Bliss asked softly.

He could not deny the truth. "I did. I loved her more than anything." He shook his head. "You knew I thought about her?"

"Nothing more than a reasonable assumption on my part," she said. "Also while I was healing you, I felt emptiness within you that only the loss of a love could create. At times it had me fearing that you did not want to live."

"There were times I didn't," he admitted. He turned his head for a moment, the vision of Leora's death so clear that he could still smell the blood and hear his own raging screams echoing in his head.

"But you knew you were needed here," she reminded.

"I had a duty to my king, otherwise—" He shook his head. "I would have welcomed death."

"You would be selfish and die rather than pay homage to such a love by loving again?"

"You think me selfish for loving so strongly?" he asked, annoyed.

"I think you selfish for choosing death over love. Love may hurt, but it also heals, and it never leaves you. It is there with you always, waiting for you to trust in it once again. Are you ready to trust love again?"

He answered honestly. "I don't know."

She smiled and nodded. "This is good. You did not say no."

Surprisingly, he smiled, and it made him feel good, not only the smile but his answer. He hadn't said no. Hadn't thought about saying no. Perhaps he was on the verge of trusting love.

A wicked wind suddenly ripped at the cottage, spiking the flames and rattling the door.

"Is that fate knocking?" Trey teased.

"If it is, will you answer it?"

"I believe I already have," he said leaning close to kiss her gently.

They returned to eating the fish and spoke of love no more, not that they wouldn't again, but enough was said for the moment. Time was needed to think and sort through what seemed like a maze, at least to Trey.

When they finished eating, they sat in comfortable silence before the fire, Trey wrapping his arm around Bliss and she tucking herself close and resting her head on his shoulder. Both were lost in similar thoughts about each other and love. Could it be possible? Could love have struck them hard and fast? Had fate a hand in it?

Trey rested his cheek to the top of her head. He relished the simple moment with Bliss. It felt right, and he wanted to linger in it. He wasn't sure what tomorrow would bring, but he was ready to explore possibilities. And while he was anxious to take her home, he was also eager to spend time alone with her.

Bliss yawned. "We need to get sleep so that we will be fit to continue our journey."

He hugged her close before standing and helping her up. "I'll bed in front of the hearth."

She laughed. "That's nonsense. The ground is cold even with the rushes. We'll share the bed."

"That might not be a good idea."

"Would you force yourself on me?"

"Never," he said as if insulted that she asked.

Bliss shrugged. "Then what is there to worry about?"

"You wound me, woman," he said half-jokingly. "You're telling me you don't desire me?"

Bliss smiled and stepped closer, to teasingly trace circles on his bare chest, as she said, "This is not the time or place for us to make love."

He grabbed her hand and yanked her up against him. "But we do make love, don't we?"

"It seems to be our fate."

"When?"

"I don't know," she said.

"Soon. It must be soon," he said with a grin.

"It will come to pass no doubt. But what will follow I do not know." Bliss slipped out of his grasp, though, took his hand, and walked to the bed.

They climbed in, and Bliss rested her back to Trey's chest. It was the only way they could fit in the narrow bed, unless they lay on top of each other . . . not a wise choice.

Bliss was asleep in no time.

Trey wasn't. He lay there, his eyes wide open and unable to sleep.

It pleased him to know that they would make love though he had already assumed they would. The attraction was strong between them and could not be denied or avoided. What troubled him was her remark about not knowing what followed. He certainly knew what would follow.

They would remain husband and wife.

Chapter 9

They left early the next morning. Bliss had woken before Trey and thought it prudent that she slip out of bed before he stirred. Not that she wanted to. She had been comfortably snug in his arms and wished she could have remained so. But she had felt her desire for him spark, and though she knew their coupling was inevitable, she wasn't ready just yet. She didn't know why. It simply didn't seem the right time.

Disappointment was evident in his eyes when he woke and found the spot beside him empty. He had looked even more frustrated when he had seen her standing in front of the hearth fully dressed. He had been quick to don his garments after that and hasten them on their way.

They had spoken little since then. Busy thoughts, and no doubt similar ones, had kept them both occupied, though Bliss had noticed how vigilant Trey had remained, keeping a watchful eye on their surroundings. She didn't need her ability to know that he had no intentions of being caught off guard again.

And this time he wasn't.

He whispered to her, "Someone follows."

"Aye, it's Roan, and he'll join us soon enough."

"You knew? And what keeps him from making himself known?"

"Once we stepped on Pict land, we were watched. Our people are cautious about our safety," she said. "He'll show himself soon enough."

"Is there anything else I should know?"

The thought came suddenly. "Aye, I believe I am needed." Bliss hoped it wasn't in regard to her friend Dolca, for she sensed it was serious. She grew anxious as she waited for Roan to appear since, try as she might, she could sense nothing beyond that. She only knew the news was not good.

"You're worried," Trey said. "Is it your friend?"

She had no time to respond. Roan appeared and hurried toward her. She let go of Trey's hand and rushed to meet the tall Pict halfway.

"What's wrong?" she demanded, her hands grabbing his forearms.

The vision hit her hard, *a young lad laid out in final repose*.

"I'm too late," she said, her heart swelling with sorrow for the lad who could have been no more than five years.

"Nay," Roan said. "The lad, Philip, sleeps and will not wake. He took a tumble while playing, got a good gash on his head, and soon after collapsed and has not woken since."

"I must go and see if I can help him," Bliss said. "But there is Dolca to consider."

"The women tend her, giving her your special brew. She rests comfortably, and her cough has subsided."

"I am relieved to hear that, and now we must go immediately to the lad, Philip."

"There is a problem with that," Roan said.

"What problem?" Trey asked, stepping alongside Bliss.

She had sensed him standing behind her, leaving her and Roan to talk. But with a problem at hand, she would have expected nothing less than for him to step forward and protect her.

"The lad isn't a Pict. His father, Albert, ventured into Pict territory specifically in search of you," Roan said with a nod to Bliss. "He begged for your help. Albert and his wife Teresa had been blessed with their son after many years of marriage and all hope of having children gone. They cannot bear losing Philip, their only child."

"I see no problem," Trey said. "Bliss tends all people, Pict or not."

"It's where the child lives that presents the problem," Roan said. "He lives north of the Pict borders, and, recently, a large contingent of the king's men has established a camp in the area between Pict territory and Albert's farm. He had managed to avoid them on his way here, keeping to the deep woods when possible. Just as he reached Pict territory, he spotted a troop of the king's soldiers and wasn't surprised to see that they were headed in the direction of the camp."

"It appears King Kenneth is getting ready to attack from the north," Trey said.

"You must go and warn your family," Bliss urged.

"And you?" he asked and answered. "You will go to heal the lad." He looked to Roan. "Can you send someone to take the news to my brothers?"

"If that is what you wish," Roan said. "Or perhaps you would prefer to take this news yourself. My men and I can get Bliss safely to the lad."

"And if attacked?" Trey asked. "Will you retaliate, thus declaring war on the king?"

"The Picts will have no choice but to join in the fray sooner or later," Roan said. "We cannot continue to stand apart from it."

Trey rested a hand on Roan's shoulder. "Then choose the right time. Besides"—Trey removed his hand and wrapped his arm around Bliss—"I protect *my wife*."

Bliss had not wanted her people to know of their strange union. Marriage was sacred to the Picts and never taken lightly. Few, if any, ended their marriages willingly, death being the only thing parting husbands and wives permanently.

Roan broke out in a grin after a moment of shock passed. "What wonderful news. The Picts will surely want to celebrate this special union."

"There is no time for celebration now," Bliss said. "Too many are suffering, and no doubt more will with war on the horizon."

"What better time than for all to know that you have wed a MacAlpin. They fight for the true king, and when he takes the throne, our people and land will be safe once more."

Bliss hadn't considered what her marriage to Trey could mean for her people. Of course it would help them. In order to be a true king of Scotland, one had to have been born of a Pict mother and, therefore, the true king would protect his people.

How foolish of her not to realize the significance, and perhaps it made clearer the reason fate had brought Trey and her together.

"Not if we don't get news of this troop buildup to my brothers," Trey reminded. "Time is needed to alert those who will fight at our side to prepare for battle."

"I will see to it," Roan said.

"Also, I would prefer to deliver the good news of my marriage to my family, but do advise them that I will return home as soon as I can."

Bliss was relieved that he chose not to spread word of their union to his family. It would only complicate matters, and it was complicated enough already.

"I could send men to follow you discreetly and help only if necessary," Roan said.

"And if something happens that provokes the king, it could place your people in harm's way. And that I will not do," said Trey.

"This is all right with you?" Roan asked, turning to Bliss. "All will be well?"

She understood what Roan wanted from her . . . a vision that foretold the outcome. Unfortunately, one was not available to her. She had yet to see what would be.

She shook her head. "I see nothing—yet though I sense your hesitancy. I can tell you there is no need for you to worry. Things will go well for you."

"What of you?"

"It has always been difficult to see things for myself, but since I told Willow I would see her again, I can only assume all will go well."

Roan smiled. "That eases my worry." He looked to Trey. "I have no doubt you will take care of your wife. You are an honorable man, and you battled death and won."

"With Bliss's help," Trey reminded him.

"Then it appears you two were meant to be," Roan said. "Now it is time for us to be on our way. "Stop at Maude and Thumble's cottage; food and extra garments wait for you there. And be careful. Danger now lurks everywhere."

Bliss gave Roan's hand a squeeze. "Your journey will be a safe one."

"Stay safe, and I will see you both soon," Roan said, and was gone as swiftly as he had appeared.

Bliss could not help but ask, "Are you certain you wish to do this?"

"Are you certain you need to ask that question?"

"What of your family? They need you with them now."

"They need me to find out all I can about the king's troops that are forming in the north," he said. "If I hadn't stumbled upon you and wed you, we would have discovered too late what the king was planning. The best thing I can do for my family is to find out all I can about the king's plans and return home with that information."

It did make sense, and his duty to the true king did come first.

"And there is my wife to protect," he said. "And a child to save."

"Aye, we must get to Philip," she said, and though he did not need to remind her that he would continue to protect her, it pleased her to hear it.

Maude was as short and wide as Thumble was tall and slim. To some they might appear an odd couple, but no one could doubt they were a loving pair. Their eyes glowed with happiness when they glanced at each other, and they were forever holding hands. In the fifteen years they had been married, they never had children though the menagerie of ill animals that found their way to them, and often remained after getting well, were like family to them.

"He's a fine-looking man," Maude said with a grin and a nod toward Trey, who stood outside the opened, cottage door talking with Thumble.

"He is a good man," Bliss said, though she avoided referring to him as her husband. She didn't want to hear any well-wishes for a happy, fruitful, and long life when their marriage was nothing more than . . .

Her thought drifted off. This was not the time to wonder about her marriage.

Maude had insisted on adding more food to an already full sack once she had learned that Trey would be taking the journey with her. She was just about done when she asked, "Could I ask a favor of you, Bliss?"

"You have an animal that does not heal, and you are worried about him," Bliss said, having sensed Maude's concern upon entering the cottage.

The plump woman smiled, her full cheeks blushing. "You have so much to see to that I did not want to impose, but this little fellow just will not get well." She walked over to a basket near the hearth, a cloth partially covering it. She reached down and scooped up a bundle of fur, cradling the baby rabbit in her cupped hands.

Bliss brought her hands to her mouth, closed her eyes a moment, then opened them and rubbed her hands together before cupping them and holding them out to Maude.

The woman gently handed the tiny rabbit to Bliss.

Bliss knew as soon as she held him that he would not survive. No amount of healing would save his life; it was his time to go.

She looked to Maude, and said, "I'm sorry, but there is nothing I can do for him. He will pass before night falls."

Maude got teary-eyed. "I was afraid of that. Thumble reminds me that I must learn that I cannot save all creatures, that some are not meant to live."

"I can tell you that he suffers no pain and will die peacefully."

Maude forced a smile. "I am glad to hear that." She reached out and took the small ball of fur in her hands and cradled him close for a moment before returning him to his comfortable nest in the basket.

"I must go," Bliss said. "I wish I could have been of more help—"

"Nonsense," Maude said, "you do what you can do, and you do more than your share."

Bliss gave her a hug, and the two left the cottage to join the men.

Trey reached out to her as she approached, and she took it, slipping her hand around his.

"Ready?" Trey asked, and Bliss nodded.

"I gave the directions to Trey that Albert gave to me," Thumble said. "His place is a day's journey from here, if you keep a good and steady pace."

"Blessings be with you," Maude said.

"And to you," Bliss replied, and, with a smile and a wave, she and Trey took their leave.

The weather had chilled considerably, and Bliss was grateful she had changed garments. She hadn't expected her own garments to be waiting for her at Maude's cottage, but someone had fetched her green, warm wool skirt and blouse and blue shawl, and she had quickly exchanged them for the clothes she had worn.

"The terrain is rocky and hilly in a good portion of the area where we travel, with a scattering of woods here and there. We will need to be careful of our steps and of being seen," Trey advised.

"I will do all I can to help," Bliss said.

"More than your share."

"You heard what Maude said to me?"

"I caught a word or two, her words confirming what I already knew. You do more than most. Like now, placing yourself in harm's way to help a lad."

"How could I not help?"

"That's what I mean. The thought of not helping someone never enters your head. Not even when the situation proves dangerous for you. Not many would do that."

"I cannot help who I am, nor would I change myself," Bliss said proudly.

"I wouldn't want you to change," he said. "You're perfect the way you are."

His compliment fluttered her stomach. Most men wanted her to change, but then Trey was not most men. And she liked him just the way he was.

"Do you sense anything about the lad?" he asked, as they walked.

"No, and that troubles me. He looks as if he sleeps."

"You've seen him in a vision?"

"Aye, but I see nothing more."

"What does that mean?" Trey asked.

"I'm not sure. The lad could be close to death or trapped in sleeping death."

"A man in our village fell into a sleeping death for three months before he finally died. Can you save anyone from such a horrible fate?"

"I don't know; I have never come across one."

He squeezed her hand reassuringly. "I will help any way I can."

She expressed her appreciation, all the while thinking how different Trey was from other men. Her skills didn't threaten him.

He was actually interested in them.

Chapter 10

Nightfall wasn't far off, and with it came a chill. Their travel thus far had proved uneventful, and Trey preferred it to remain that way. He wanted to get Bliss to Albert's farm and see her settled safely. Once he was sure she was out of harm's way, he would need to go and scout the area where the king's troops were gathering. Then, once he had the information he needed, he'd return for Bliss.

He hoped it would take only a few days, but not knowing how long it would take to heal the lad or to gather the necessary information made it difficult to judge. It could possibly be a week or more. And once done with this, they would need to return to see how her friend fared, and only then could they head home.

Another time, all this delay might have irritated him, but not now, not since wedding Bliss.

He almost grinned. He still found it amusing as to how he found himself wed. And that it did not bother him in the least. It wasn't that he hadn't planned on marrying. He wanted children and would have eventually found himself a woman to wed. It was that he hadn't planned on falling in love, didn't think he ever would or could again. That he was actually even considering the notion brought a smile to his face.

It broadened when he realized that he was feeling that familiar, pleasant tug of falling in love. He hadn't truly thought it would be possible. He had thought all chances of loving again had died along with Leora.

"You are happy about something," Bliss said.

He leaned down and gave her lips a quick kiss. "I'm pleased to be here with my wife."

She laughed. "Pleased to be forced into a marriage, are you?"

"No one forced me; I consented."

"Without realizing it."

"It was necessary," he said.

"Only for the moment, and why did you tell Roan we are wed?"

"I thought I made it clear. You're my wife, and I protect *my wife*."

"My people will expect my marriage to last," she said. "They will assume I knew, in advance, the man who was to be my husband."

"Perhaps you did."

Trey felt a catch in her rhythm, as if she missed a step, though righted herself fast enough. Had she known? Was there something she wasn't telling him and why? Though that answer proved easy, at least now that he had gotten to spend time with Bliss. She would have never wanted him to know what fate had written for them. She would want him to discover it on his own, and he was certainly having a grand time doing so.

"Time will tell," she said softly.

"Time or fate?" he asked, and, not needing a response, said, "Nightfall is near upon us; we must find a spot to stop."

It didn't take long for them to find a place and make camp. With no trace of the king's soldiers all day, Trey wasn't concerned that any lurked nearby. He built a campfire, and Bliss placed the blanket close and laid out some food.

He marveled at her confident movements. She knew what she was about and didn't hesitate. She made choices and didn't think twice. To her, her path was clear, and she walked it with confidence.

"Tell me more about your knowing," he said after joining her on the blanket and sharing in the small feast.

She shrugged. "There isn't much to tell, since I barely understand it myself. I only know it is part of me and always has been. And I follow where it takes me."

"Don't you fear that some would claim you a witch?"

"Thus far I have not had that problem, but then, when people are ill and in need, they will reach out to anyone they feel will help them. My healing skills have proven true; therefore, no one speaks a harmful word against me. Besides, I am already considered a pagan, so no doubt I am whispered about."

"Do you ever wish you didn't have such skills?"

"When I am overburdened by it at times, the thought has crossed my mind, but to be honest, I don't know if I could live any other way. It is what

I have known all my life. To live differently might be more of a burden, though we all carry some sort of a burden. Tell me of yours."

He looked at her oddly.

"The woman you continue to love, but lost."

He wouldn't deny the truth. "I do still love Leora, I always will."

"And so you should, but something troubles you about the loss."

He should have realized that spending time with Bliss would leave open the possibility of her seeing and sensing things about him. He could choose not to discuss certain things with her, and he knew she would respect his choice. Yet she talked openly with him, so shouldn't he do the same with her?

He thought on it a moment more and felt the old pain begin to surface. Memories could tear at the heart. He supposed that was why he had worked so hard to keep them locked away. He hadn't wanted to ever feel that horrific pain again.

She reached out and rested her hand over his where it lay on his thigh. "If you prefer not to discuss it . . ."

Though her touch was light, it felt warm and comforting, and, oddly enough, the painful memories began to subside. And he suddenly felt the intense urge to tell her, share the memory in hope of finally laying it to rest.

"Leora and a couple of the women in the village would forage the woods for roots and plants for Etty, our cook. She loved the woods and would often go off on her own though I preferred she didn't. But she had always insisted there was nothing to worry about. She was on MacAlpin land and safe."

Trey slipped his hand from beneath hers and laced their fingers together. He felt the need to hold on to her. "One day, two of the women came screaming back to the village that a marauding band of warriors had attacked them, felled the other women, and was headed our way."

He stopped a moment, the day suddenly vivid in his mind and the pain rising up to choke him. He cleared his throat and continued. "Reeve and I and several warriors rode out immediately, while Duncan and Bryce remained behind to defend the keep in case it was an attack. I spotted Leora on the ground; blood covered her garments and splattered across her face. I knew she was dead and was just about to reach her when the marauding band emerged from the surrounding woods. We fought, but they were too many. We had to pull back and return to the keep. It was hours before the battle ended, many of the marauders dead, while others ran off."

He turned to stare at the flames and to find the strength to continue. He had never discussed this part with anyone though it had haunted him all this time.

"Once it was over, Reeve, my brothers, and several of our warriors rode with me so that I could get Leora's body and give her a proper burial. When we got there, her body was gone." He swallowed hard. "We found animal tracks and parts of her bloody garments, but we could not find her body."

He turned silent and continued to stare at the flames. "Her death was bad enough, but not being able to bury her?" He shook his head. "I should never have left her. I should have protected her even in death."

Bliss squeezed his hand. "You did what you could."

He shook his head again. "Nay, I should have done more or died trying."

"She would not have wanted that."

He turned angry eyes on her. "The other women survived, and each one of them told me how she screamed my name, screamed for me to help her."

"I'm sorry for your pain, but it is imperative that you let it go."

"How?" he asked, though to his ears he sounded as if he begged.

"Open your heart. Let it heal and forgive yourself for something fate has decreed."

"Fate plays foolish games," he said angrily.

"At times necessary ones, though more often than not, we do not learn that until later."

"What happened to Leora was not necessary."

"Someday you may think otherwise," she said.

"Never," he spat. "Fate is cruel, and I will never forgive her for this."

"Be careful; you may regret those words," she warned softly.

"I regret not having been there for the woman I love, but that will never happen again," he said adamantly, not wanting to discuss it any longer. "Time to sleep. We start early tomorrow. And we sleep beside each other to stay warm."

Trey was glad Bliss didn't object. He needed to wrap himself around her tonight and keep her snug in his embrace. He wanted to crush her up against him, feel the heat of her body mingle with his, feel every breath she took and know she was safe in his arms.

Bliss lay content, pressed against Trey. She understood his need to keep her close and her own need to be close to him. She had felt his pain as strongly as if it had been her own. She had seen through his eyes the whole horrid scene and had felt the swell of guilt that rose to strangle his heart and turn it away from love.

As much as she wished to heal his pain, she knew she couldn't. He was the only one capable of healing his hurt, and, until he understood that, he would suffer.

"You sleep?" he whispered near her ear.

"Nay, not yet."

"Neither do I."

She caressed his hand where it lay over her waist. "Yesterday is gone, Trey, look to tomorrow, for each new day we have is a blessing."

He turned her so quickly that her head spun, and she had no time to clear it, for his lips came down on hers and claimed a kiss that sent shivers racing clear to her toes. The warrior was in this kiss, his strength, his courage, and his determination. And she knew then and there that he was determined to love her.

And that would take the most courageous warrior, for he would have to let go of his guilt and fear and learn to love again.

His hand drifted down over her backside, while his kiss trailed down along her neck, and he nudged her up against him, his leg wrapping around hers to draw her even closer.

Pressed against him so tightly, she could not help but feel his desire, or perhaps he intended it so. Perhaps he wished her to know he wanted her and waited to see if she felt the same.

And, of course, she did. She had found her passion for him sparking when they simply held hands or when he smiled at her; and certainly when he kissed her, desire soared like a roaring fire within her. But at the moment his need for her had come right after they had spoken of Leora, his old love. If she surrendered to Trey now, it would be to help him erase the memory of Leora.

His kisses and touches continued, and it was difficult not to surrender to them. She ached to reach out and explore him as he did her, but if she did, it would seal their fate. They would make love, and she did not want her first time with him to be in the shadows of his old love.

She caught his face in her hands and brought her lips to his in a tender kiss.

He shook his head. "I know what that kiss means."

"You do?" she asked with a gentle smile.

"Aye, it means we go no further."

"Do you understand why?"

"Leora stands in the way."

"Come to me when she is gone, and I will not deny you."

"Promise?"

"You have my word," Bliss said.

"That is good, for I will hold you to it, but for now I will hold you beside me while we sleep."

"I would like that," she said, and snuggled against him, resting her head on his chest.

"You feel good in my arms."

"I like being here."

"We make a good pair; perhaps fate knows what she is doing."

"Are you telling me that you are changing your mind about fate?"

"Let's say I'm considering it and will give it time," he said.

"It is a start," she said on a yawn.

"Sleep, a busy time lies ahead for us."

He fell asleep before she did and though she could feel sleep creeping around the edges, it failed to lay claim to her. Her mind was much too busy with fleeting images, and, try as she might, she could not make sense of them.

The blond woman refused to leave her mind. She lingered there in pain and longing, calling out to Trey. She seemed unable to find any peace.

Somehow, Bliss would need to find a way to help them lay their love to rest.

Chapter 11

They reached the farm by late afternoon the next day without incident. Albert and his wife rushed out of their sizeable cottage to greet them. It was age or worry or perhaps a mixture of both that wore on Teresa's face. Tears spilled from sad, wrinkled eyes, and when she took hold of Bliss's hand, Bliss caught a glimpse of the woman she had once been: jolly, weightier, and far fewer wrinkles. Teresa clung tightly to Bliss, repeatedly thanking her for coming to the aid of her ill son.

Albert was stoic though his eyes glistened with unshed tears. Gray generously peppered his brown hair, and deep wrinkles lined his lean face.

Trey and Bliss were ushered inside, and though they were offered drink and food, it was obvious the couple hoped Bliss would see to their son first.

And she did.

"Time for that later, I would like to see Philip now," Bliss said.

The relief on the couple's faces was obvious, and Teresa hurried to draw back a curtain that separated the two-room cottage. Bliss and Trey followed, and Albert trailed behind them. Once in the room, Trey stepped to the side. He did not want to interfere with Bliss's healing. He simply wanted to make sure she remained protected.

He tucked himself into the corner of the small room, giving the parents and Bliss their privacy.

The lad lay in a bed far too big for his meager size. He looked asleep though lifeless, and thus appeared laid out in a deathly repose. Teresa ran her hand lovingly over her son's forehead. He was a cute little lad, with brown hair and a round, pale, angelic face. Trey's heart went out to the woman. He could not imagine the pain of seeing your only child lying there as if in death.

"He was playing, fell and hit his head, got a good gash he did to the back of his head, but I cleaned it up and it seemed fine—" Teresa stopped, her voice breaking. She cleared it, and continued. "Then, a few hours later, he collapsed in a dead faint and hasn't woken since."

Bliss placed a gentle hand on the woman's arm. "Let me see what I can do."

Teresa scurried out of her way and into the arms of her husband, who held her tight.

Trey could see that they were attempting to draw strength from each other . . . and hope. He wondered if Bliss would be able to help or if it was too late. He kept to the corner shadows, not wanting to disturb his wife yet wanting to be there if needed. How he could help he didn't know, he just knew he had to be there for her.

Bliss looked like an angel, her blond hair falling softly around her face as she hovered over the lad before sitting beside him on the bed. She gently took his small hand in hers and shut her eyes. She sat there, not moving, and after several moments, Trey began to worry. She was as still as the lad, and he suddenly feared for her.

He recalled how she had gotten stuck in a vision, and he had pulled her out. Did she need him to do the same now? He waited since she was not in distress, but if she didn't emerge soon, he would place a firm hand on her shoulder or take her in his arms if necessary.

He was relieved when her eyes opened, and she laid the lad's hand down at his side. But when she stood, she wobbled, and he didn't hesitate—he was at her side in an instant, wrapping his arm around her and drawing her against him.

"Are you all right?" he whispered.

"I need a hot brew," she said with a shiver.

Trey helped her into the other room, Teresa hurrying out before them and Albert following behind. Trey helped her to a chair at the table and drew another chair close so that he could sit beside her. He took her hand and when he felt it cold, he worried.

It didn't take long for Teresa to brew a hot drink for Bliss, and as she placed it in front of her, she said, "Please tell me of my son."

Bliss wrapped her hands around the heated tankard and shivered. "There is nothing to tell at the moment. I must spend more time with him, then I will know more."

"Can you save him?" Albert asked with a catch in his throat.

Trey could see she was reluctant to answer, and

he wished he could help. The only way he could do that was . . . he took hold of her hand. He wanted her to know he was there for her.

Her fingers threaded with his tighter than he had ever felt them do before. She was looking for extra strength, and he gave it to her with the slight squeeze to her hand.

"I'm not sure, but I would like to try," Bliss said.

"Yes. Yes, please try," Teresa begged.

"We are grateful for any help you can give Philip," added Albert.

Bliss nodded and took several sips of the brew before saying, "I need a moment of fresh air, and then I would like to start the healing process."

Trey didn't give anyone a chance to object or delay Bliss's request. He stood, not letting go of her hand, and said, "I will go with you."

He saw that she was relieved by his action, but before they walked out the door, Bliss turned to the parents, and said, "Please talk with your son while I'm gone and tell him that the woman with the blond hair is here to help him."

They looked perplexed but nodded vigorously.

"What's wrong?" Trey asked when they were a few feet from the cottage.

"Philip is trapped. I do not know where." She shook her head. "My grandmum talked about the sleeping dead and how difficult it was for them to escape it."

"You are not in danger helping the lad, are you?"

"I do not know. I have never had the opportunity or misfortune to run across this before."

He wanted to take her and leave, and if it were

anyone other than a child, he would have done so, whether she protested or not. But he could no more leave that child than she could. His only recourse was to protect her.

"What can I do?"

She smiled. "Thank you. I was hoping you would ask."

"You could have asked for my help."

"I did when I grasped hold of your hand."

Trey nodded. "I will remember that, now what can I do?"

"I need you to remain near my side, and after I close my eyes and begin to work, if I grow at all agitated, you must grab hold of me and call me back."

"I'll demand you come back," he said empathically.

"Will you now?" She smiled sweetly.

"You'll not escape me that easily, *wife*."

She pressed her cheek to his, and whispered, "I hope not."

He grinned and gave her a quick kiss. He enjoyed the banter and play of falling in love. A give-and-take, a push and pull, a catch of the heart, and, damn, but wasn't he glad to be sharing it with someone once again.

They hurried back into the cottage, and Trey did as Bliss had instructed. He kept an eye on her as she sat beside Philip, holding his hand, though she had begun with her usual ritual of placing her cupped hands over her mouth, then rubbing them together before laying her hands on the person, in this case holding Philip's hand.

He had no intentions of leaving her side until this was done one way or the other. The problem, however, was that the information on the king's troops could not wait indefinitely. If the lad's healing was prolonged, Trey might have to make a choice, and there truly was no choice to make. He had given his word to help the true king, and he could not renege on it, not when it meant the lives of so many.

He hoped it would not come to that, for it would be difficult to leave Bliss even though he knew she would urge him to go. She would understand that his duty to the true king came first and she would tell him not to worry. But he would worry all the same, leaving her on her own.

He pushed the troubling thought from his mind. Until the time came, he would not waste thoughts on it. Bliss needed him now, and he would be here for her while he could.

Supper was a silent affair that evening. It appeared no progress had been made with Philip, and so all were somber. Bliss looked exhausted, yawning much too often during the meal. So when all was done, Trey suggested they retire and get up early so that Bliss could resume her healing.

No one objected, and Albert and Teresa retired into their son's room, having fashioned a sleeping pallet on the floor so that they could remain near him. Trey and Bliss got to share Philip's narrow bed, but that was all right with Trey. It meant they could sleep snuggled together.

Bliss turned to rest in his arms when he joined her in bed, and her head went to rest on his chest.

He could feel that something troubled her, and so he waited, his hands gently massaging her back.

"I don't know if I can save him," she whispered.

"It's in fate's hands," he said, hoping it would help.

She sighed. "That's what I'm afraid of."

Trey comforted her throughout the night, her sleep fitful, and when she woke, she went immediately to Philip's side. It continued like that for several days, and Trey began to worry about her, and his need to find out about the troops.

It was settled for him when Albert returned from a neighboring farm the next day, having gone to return a tool he had borrowed for too long, and when he arrived home his face was pale as freshly fallen snow.

He walked into the room and, with a flick of his hand, summoned Trey to follow. Trey was reluctant to leave Bliss, but Teresa had assured him that she would watch over her.

"What's wrong?" Trey asked when he and Albert stepped outside.

"A large troop of king's soldiers passed by Thomas's farm and wiped him clean of what little livestock he had and what food he had stored for the winter. And"—Albert stopped a moment as if he couldn't believe what he was about to say—"They took Thomas, leaving Mary on her own with their two young daughters. They told him he was to serve the king and that other troops will be arriving soon."

"I need to see where they camp for myself," Trey said.

"Too dangerous," Albert said, shaking his head.

"But necessary."

Bliss and Teresa came out of the cottage and walked over to them.

"You need to leave, don't you?" Bliss asked.

Trey nodded, feeling torn with leaving her behind.

"I must go with you," Bliss said.

"No," Trey said with a finality that had all eyes turning wide. "You have Philip to see to."

Bliss turned to Teresa and took her hand. "I have done all I can for your son, I can do no more. The rest is up to him."

"I feared you would say that," the woman said, with tears gathering in her eyes.

"Nay, do not fear, keep hope strong and do not give up," Bliss said. "I will return in a few days' time and see how he does."

"Promise?" Teresa asked, grabbing Bliss's hand.

"Aye, I promise." She gave the woman a hug, and Teresa had a difficult time letting Bliss go, but she finally did. She turned to Trey. "I will get my things, and we can be on our way."

Trey took hold of her arm and walked a short distance away from the couple. "You're not going with me. It's too dangerous."

"It's too dangerous for me to stay. And we have no time to argue. We must leave now."

"Why?"

Bliss didn't answer, and she hurried over to Albert. "Hide some of your food and what livestock you can. The soldiers head this way, and if they don't find something, they will destroy your place."

Albert paled once again. "I cannot leave my wife and ill son."

"No, you cannot," Bliss said. "That is why we must make it appear that you are too ill to join the troops."

"What do I do?" Albert asked.

Trey, with Teresa's help, worked to hide some of the animals and food, while Bliss worked on Albert. She rubbed ash under his eyes until the area appeared gray and sunken. And she pricked his neck and arms with pine needles to make it appear that he had a rash.

"Make certain you cough more than talk with them and stumble once or twice. They may not even take any of your food or animals for fear all is contagious."

"How can we ever thank the both of you?" Teresa asked.

"Stay strong," Trey said. "The true king will soon rule."

Trey and Bliss were off in a rush, having a good portion of open land to cover before they could reach the protection of the woods. They remained cautious as they traveled, keeping alert and keeping their pace quick.

Hours later, when they were finally in the bosom of the woods, they stopped to rest.

"We need to scout the area where the king's troops are gathered and see for ourselves how many await his order," Trey said.

"You can see for yourself, but you will learn more from the two we meet."

"What have you seen?"

Bliss shook her head. "It is what I sense though I can tell you no more."

Little by little, Trey understood Bliss's abilities and at times how frustrating it must be for her, not completely understanding them. But at this moment he was grateful for whatever information she could provide.

He was about to ask if they would meet the two soon, but realized that when she sensed or saw nothing more, there was no point in questioning her. She'd have no answer.

"Do you know exactly where the king's troops gather?" she asked.

"From what information Roan and Albert supplied, I can only surmise their location, and if I am right, then the king has made a foolish move."

"I was thinking the same," she said. "This terrain is not hospitable, and have you seen that snow is already heavy on the mountains?"

Trey nodded and looked out over the landscape, Glen Affric rising in the distance and snow covering more than the peaks. "Aye, I have. Winter will strike hard this year."

"Making it difficult for the king's troops to maneuver," Bliss said.

"A king who does not even know his own kingdom is ill prepared," Trey said.

"Then surely King Kenneth will fail."

"Do you see that?" Trey asked anxiously.

Bliss turned her head away for a moment, and Trey wondered what she didn't want him to see, for to him she wore her thoughts in her eyes and her expressions. He took gentle hold of her chin and turned her to look at him.

"What's wrong?" he asked, and the answer

came to him before he could respond. "I forever ask if you sense or see things. I expect too much of you."

"Most do."

That angered him, for he didn't want to do what others did to her . . . want . . . more than give.

"I am sorry," he said. "I admire your skills and the courage it takes to deal with them. Though they intrigue me, you intrigue me more. There is so much more to you than your abilities. You care about helping complete strangers, and you give of your skill to any who ask. And I should know better than to always ask, for I am your husband, and with me it should be different."

He kissed her then, not a light kiss or an apologetic one, but one filled with love.

Chapter 12

*L*ove.

It was an exquisite feeling though Bliss wondered if Trey experienced its power as much as she did. Was it just another kiss to him, or did he feel the overwhelming punch that love had delivered?

She didn't want the kiss to end, but then she never wanted his kisses to end. His kisses not only sparked her passion, they brought her mind some rest, and that was a precious gift.

"Kissing you is so very different than any kiss I have ever experienced," he said after he ran his lips gently over hers one last time.

"How so?" she whispered.

"It consumes me and I feel . . ."

Bliss knew his words trailed off because he wasn't quite sure how he felt, and that meant he needed to discover the depth of love that she had felt.

Trey shook his head. "I cannot say for sure."

"In time," she encouraged, and gave his cheek a kiss. "Now we must not dally any longer."

"But I so want to dally," he teased, and nibbled at her lips.

She chuckled and shook her head. "As much as I wouldn't mind dallying, myself, we cannot. It is time for us to move on. A troop approaches."

They didn't hesitate. Trey quickly looked around, and with no refuge in sight, he chose the only thing left to them . . . the trees.

Bliss wrapped her arms around his neck, and, after he grabbed the lowest branch, she wrapped her legs around his waist. He climbed the branches with little effort and found a solid spot where they could perch. Once wrapped around each other and braced snugly in the crevice where two thick branches and the tree trunk met, they waited.

It wasn't long before a sizeable troop on horses rode right beneath them. Their gait was steady, not at all rushed, almost overly confident. Bits of conversation drifted up through the branches and the leaves that had yet to fall.

Bliss smiled at the snippets of chatter she caught.

"Gave his son the sickness, he did."

"Don't want none of his food."

"Glad we left fast."

So Albert had fared well; she was pleased.

The chatter continued.

"Too far north."

"We'll battle the snow before we battle foe."

The soldiers seemed to have their doubts as to the king's decision to send them north just before winter. Not a good tactical move to their way of thinking and one that could cost many soldiers their lives.

The voices drifted off as the last of the soldiers passed beneath them.

Trey cautioned silence, and Bliss saw why when a lone soldier appeared several minutes later. He meandered slowly, his attention on the road. No doubt scouting to make certain no one followed. After he finally vanished from sight, Trey climbed down from the tree, bringing them effortlessly to the ground.

"I need to follow their trail," he said.

He had not included her. He obviously worried over her safety, but then she worried over his. Wasn't that how it was when it came to love?

She was about to argue, wanting to help him, when she realized it would be best for her to remain behind. She couldn't say why; she only knew it was the right thing to do.

So she did what was best for them both. "I can wait here for you if you think it more prudent."

His smile hinted at relief, and he took hold of her hand. "I must find you a safe place to hide."

She gave a quick glance around and, finding what she searched for, pointed a short distance away. "That formation of rocks, I'll take shelter behind them and wait there for you."

He appeared reluctant to leave, and she was not surprised at his reluctance after learning of what had happened to Leora. She now better understood his need to protect.

"Go," she urged. "I will be fine." She gave him a light shove, and he reluctantly left her side.

"I will return," he said after taking only a few steps and casting a quick glance over his shoulder.

She nodded and turned, not wanting to watch him walk away, and made her way to the cropping of rocks.

Aye, he would be back for her, and love would grow between them . . . and intimacy. She smiled at the thought and looked forward to it. The more she got to know Trey, the more easily she fell in love with him. He was such a good, caring man and one she could rely on without worry or doubt. And that appealed to her more than his fine features and lean body.

She laughed and shook her head. That wasn't completely true. She favored his good looks and his attractive body. She couldn't keep from smiling though it didn't seem right to feel lighthearted and carefree at the moment, but she couldn't help it.

Love was teasing her heart, and she was enjoying every part and parcel of it.

Bliss stopped abruptly and listened. She heard stirring behind the cropping of rocks. She waited and sensed . . . then knew. A man waited there.

Trey made his way cautiously through the woods, traveling parallel to the path the soldiers had taken. He had limited time to view the troop encampment. Lingering too long could get him caught since there probably would be sentinels around the camp. And no doubt, scouts roamed about. He had to survey the area quickly and be gone.

Besides, he didn't want to leave Bliss unprotected too long. She did carry a weapon of sorts, her knowing. But it would do her little good if caught by a group of soldiers, and that was what he feared.

She was vulnerable no matter what way he

looked at it. And it tore at his gut that he had to leave her alone in the woods.

He didn't need to get too close to the camp to judge troop buildup, and the closer he got, the more of a chance he would take of getting caught. So he kept a safe distance, and when he came upon a tall pine tree, he knew it would give him the view and safety he needed.

He climbed it with haste though cautiously, and, not far from the top, he found himself a good perch that gave him a clear view of the troop encampment. There he waited and watched.

It was larger than he had expected, and seeing the preponderance of archers there was no doubt that preparation was being made for battle. The question was when would the king strike?

Or perhaps the question was that the prophecy was about to be fulfilled.

When summer touches winter and the snow descends, the reign of the false king begins to end, four warriors ride together and then divide, among them the true king hides, when he meets death on his own, that is when he reclaims the throne.

Just before he had come upon Bliss, the weather had been unnaturally warm and now it was cold and no doubt snow would soon fall, fulfilling part of the prophecy. Missions had divided him and his brothers. And despite the buildup of troops, the fact that more troops were yet to arrive meant that an attack was not imminent. But why would King

Kenneth be foolish enough to wage war in winter? Or did he believe it would be tactically beneficial since neither Trey nor his brothers would expect an attack from the north, especially this time of the year?

Whatever the answer, he was glad he had happened upon the information. He and his brothers could now make sure that they were prepared. Or perhaps attack before King Kenneth did.

Having learned what he needed to know, Trey was ready and eager to return to Bliss, but as he reached the lower limbs of the tree, he heard voices and instantly stilled. He listened but could only hear snippets, and he didn't like what he heard.

It seemed a sentinel was being placed right beneath the tree, and the other two soldiers with him were debating the wisdom of the spot. He hoped the older soldier won the debate since he thought it a foolish choice, but the younger one was adamant.

Trey waited, knowing that once the sentinel was alone he would have no choice but to attack and take his leave. But if he did that, he would alert the encampment to the presence of an enemy. No doubt contingents of soldiers would be sent to find the culprit, and that could prove difficult for the few farmers who lived in the area.

It was a dilemma for sure, and so he waited, though not patiently, hoping the older soldier would win, and the three would move to a different location.

He grew more irritated, and when, after a few moments passed and there was still no decision made by the quarrelsome two, Trey had no choice but to rest against the thick tree trunk and temper his impatience. It would do no good to let the soldiers know that someone watched. It could possibly force King Kenneth to take action before he planned to, and Trey did not want that.

And so he waited and waited when suddenly . . . he sat forward. He sensed something was happening with Bliss, and he couldn't be sure if it was good or bad. And that frightened him. He had to get to her. He had wasted enough time, hours to be exact, and it would take at least another hour to return to her.

Where are you, Fate, now that I need you?

Suddenly, the quarreling stopped, and he could only hear grumbling. When Trey peered through the branches he saw the three soldiers walking away.

Had fate heard him and answered?

Perhaps so, and without hesitation, and as soundlessly as possible, he lowered himself to the ground and hurried off. He kept a fast pace, worried that night would fall before he was able to reach his wife.

He didn't understand this sudden ability to sense when she needed him, or that she was in danger, but he was pleased with it. He liked that he was so attuned to her. It gave him more peace of mind.

He was relieved that he was making better time than he had expected, daylight having yet to give way to nightfall. He would need light, if for some reason he needed to follow her tracks—he stopped abruptly, realizing he had reached the very spot where he had left her.

With cautious and silent steps, he approached the cropping of rocks where she had said she would wait for him. Something wasn't right, and he wasn't surprised to find that she was not there. He was, however, surprised to see a bloody piece of cloth that looked to have been torn from her skirt.

He took a deep breath and gave thought. Was the blood hers, or had she come upon someone who had been injured and required help? But where would she have gone? And why would she leave the spot where she had said she would wait?

He cast a cautious glance to the ground and saw two separate and distinct footprints. One he knew belonged to his wife and the other was large and deep, and no doubt belonged to a sizeable man. He didn't want to think she was in danger. And there were no indications in the footprints that there had been a struggle. She could have merely come upon an injured person, but why then would she go off with him?

Knowing his wife the answer came easily . . . someone needed her help.

His gut twisted with worry regardless of whether she willingly followed the man or not, and he started following the footprints. He would find out what happened though, more importantly, he'd find his wife.

It took until dusk for him to find the campsite and at first glance he knew he had no worry. He strode into camp, taking in the sorrowful scene surrounding him and keeping a keen watch for his wife.

There were at least a dozen farmers, all with injuries, some more serious than others. It didn't take long to realize that the soldiers had simply dumped the farmers they had collected as soon as they had sustained a wound.

Many looked with pleading eyes at him, no doubt recognizing him as a MacAlpin warrior, and it troubled him that they had suffered for the true king.

Trey came to a halt when he spied his wife bent over a man prone on the ground, holding his hand. She released his hand to rest on his stomach, stood and turned as he approached, and his heart tore in two when he saw her eyes glisten with unshed tears. He rushed to her side.

"Trey," she said on a sigh, and threw her arms around him.

He hugged her tight and he saw that the few nearby farmers nodded, as if in some way it gave them hope that they too would soon be reunited with their loved ones.

Bliss looked up at him. "I couldn't save him. I tried, but it was too late."

He wiped at the single tear that trickled from the corner of her eye. "You not only heal those you don't know, but you mourn for them as well. His family will be pleased that he did not die alone but that a loving hand held his."

"They all need healing," she said with a sigh.

"You cannot mean to heal them all?" he asked with concern.

"Of course I do," she said, and took a step away.

"It's too much. I forbid it."

Bliss smiled and shook her head. "A foolish choice of words for sure."

Trey knew they were before they had left his mouth, but he hadn't been able to stop himself. He was worried for her and wanted to protect. But she didn't need his protection right now; she needed his support.

He rectified his error. "What do you need from me?"

Bliss stepped close and kissed his cheek. "That's the husband I"—she stopped abruptly as if catching herself then finished—"I know."

Trey had the distinct feeling that she intended to say I love, and the thought gladdened his heart. "What do you want me to do?"

"Help me to see how bad the wounds are so I know whom to tend first."

He nodded, and soon they were going through the camp, examining and ascertaining who was in need of immediate care. Bliss took a moment to introduce Trey to Burnell, the farmer who had bravely ventured away from camp in search of help. He had suffered a gash to his arm that had left it painful for him to use. Bliss had had to clean the wound, then bind it with cloth from the hem of her blouse. The healing she had done on it had given him movement without pain.

The big farmer had been grateful and pleaded for her help at the camp.

Once Bliss began to tend the injured, Trey, with Burnell's help, got two campfires going. Then he went in hunt of food for the men, knowing that what little food he and Bliss had would never be enough to share with all of them. He caught enough game for the men to feast on, most not having eaten in days. And the delicious scent of the roasting meat brought smiles to many faces.

It wasn't until well into the night that his wife finally finished with the last of the wounded.

She joined him by the fire and before he could hand her a tender piece of meat, she said, "You gave Burnell instructions on how to get to the MacAlpin keep?"

He hadn't yet. Though leave it to her to know that was his intention. He could never walk away and leave these farmers without help.

"I intended to do that later as well as reassure them that we will do what we can to locate their families and see them safe, though some may have already taken refuge in the MacAlpin village."

"Two of the men cannot travel for a couple of days, and even then, they will need carriers to transport them. I do not think it is wise to linger here, but we have no choice."

"Burnell and I have already talked about posting guards."

Bliss yawned and rested her head on Trey's shoulder. "After I finish helping these men, I must return to see Philip."

"I need to return home as soon as possible," Trey said.

She lifted her head. "You learned what you needed to know?"

"Aye, and my brothers need to know as soon as possible."

"Then go now," she insisted.

"No," he said firmly. "I will not leave you. My brothers will at least learn from Roan of the troop buildup and prepare for attack. It is just that I cannot be away much longer."

"Then once we reach my cottage, you must go."

It made sense that he should do just that, but the thought of leaving her wrenched at his heart, and he didn't know if he would be able to walk away from her. But he had a duty, and that duty came before anything else, of which she reminded him.

"You are duty-bound to the true king. You must not forget it."

"I am, but I am also duty-bound to my wife"—he held up his hand to stop her retort—"I will honor both . . . and hear no more about it from you."

She smiled. "You really must learn to choose your words more wisely."

Trey grinned. "And you must learn to be *obedient*."

Bliss's warm breath whispered across his ear as she said, "As you wish, I will be obedient, especially in bed, though I much prefer to be . . . *wild*."

"Forget obedient," Trey said, and took her in his arms and kissed her.

Chapter 13

Bliss wished that they weren't sitting in the middle of a camp of injured farmers, or perhaps it was good they were. Trey's kiss tingled her senseless and had her wishing for more, a good reason to end it since it could go no further. So she did, and quickly, though with much reluctance.

She could feel the desire that sizzled between them; it heated her skin and made her wet all at the same time. She ached to make wild love with Trey, and if they were alone, she had no doubt that they would. How one simple kiss could stir such crazy passion surprised her and made her curious as to the depths of desire that would be ignited if they hadn't stopped.

It also continued to surprise her that, in such a short time, they had grown more and more attracted and attached to each other, but it shouldn't have. Her grandmum had told her how her mum had fallen in love with her da as soon as she laid eyes on him. Grandmum had detailed how Bliss's mum had burst into the cottage one day and announced she had just met the man who would be her husband though he had yet to speak with her. If her mum had fallen in love that fast, couldn't she? But her mum had chosen her husband, whereas fate had chosen Bliss's.

"I wish we were alone," Trey whispered with a kiss to her temple.

She had no intentions of denying the obvious. "As do I."

They both grew silent, their thoughts the same. They wondered when this torture would end and they would finally make love.

No further words were exchanged. They simply stretched out on the blanket that Trey had laid on the ground by the fire. He tucked his cloak around them once she was snuggled against him, and they both reluctantly, and with some difficulty, went to sleep.

Bliss woke a bit disoriented. She was cold and it was dark and Trey . . . was gone.

She sat up abruptly and saw that everyone still slept and then recalled Trey telling her that Burnell and he had discussed posting guards. He had probably volunteered for the late-night post, not trusting the wounded to remain as alert as he would.

For a minute, she thought to go to him, but that wouldn't be fair. Her presence would only interfere with his duty, and she had already interfered enough. She wished she could see the future more clearly for herself, but it was a senseless wish, and she knew it. She would only be shown what she was meant to see . . . no more.

She sighed as she stretched out on the blanket, and, in no time, she drifted off to sleep.

"Help me! Please help me!"

Bliss heard the pitiful plea but could not see who made it, the mist too thick. "Where are you?" she called out.

"Not far. You must help me, I beg you. I never meant it to be this way."

"Keep talking so that I can find you," Bliss said.

"You must hurry, please."

"I'll find you. I promise I'll find you," Bliss said.

Suddenly the woman was there and she grabbed hold of Bliss. "You can't have him. I won't let you. He's mine. He belongs to me."

The blond woman grabbed hold of Bliss, her fingers digging into her arm, and, try as she might, she couldn't break free.

"Let go of me," Bliss demanded.

But the woman didn't, she kept tight hold of her, and no amount of struggling freed Bliss. But it didn't stop her from trying. She fought and continued to fight to break free.

Farmers usually rose with the sun. With so much work to be done before nightfall, one had to rise with the break of dawn to have enough time to complete all the daily chores. So Burnell relieved Trey just as the sun came up.

Trey was glad to see him. It wasn't that he was tired though he yawned repeatedly; he knew there was no time to sleep. He intended to hunt again for game so that the men could eat and grow strong. He approached the campsite and immediately saw Bliss in distress. She looked to be struggling, as if fighting someone in her sleep. He hurried to her side, grabbed her, and gave her a shake before he took her into his arms, held her tight, and demanded that she come back to him.

"Come back to me, Bliss. Do you hear me? Come back to me *now*," he said adamantly.

It took two more good shakes before her eyes fluttered open. They widened even further as Trey spoke to her.

"Damn, but you frightened me. I thought I wouldn't get you back."

"I was stuck," she said breathlessly.

"I do not like the thought of your being stuck someplace where I cannot reach you."

"Neither do I." She slipped her arms tightly around his waist.

Damn, how did he protect her from her dreams?

"You cannot," she said.

He hadn't spoken aloud, which could only mean . . .

"Sometimes the words in your head sound as clear as the words from your lips," she explained.

"This will take getting used to," he admitted.

"For us both since I don't wish to intrude on your thoughts."

"But I wish to intrude on your dreams. I don't like seeing you struggle in your sleep, knowing that you are stuck in a dream and that I cannot possibly reach you."

"You do reach me, and that is what matters."

"Tell me of this dream that haunts you and attempts to imprison you."

She shook her head. "I don't wish to recall it right now."

It wasn't lost on Trey that this was the second time she had refused to share her dream with him. He was beginning to wonder if she didn't *want* to share it and if her reluctance had anything to do with him.

She was upset, so he would not insist though eventually they would have to discuss it. He needed to know about that dream and why it upset her so and why she had such a difficult time escaping it.

Bliss unwrapped herself from Trey though she would have preferred to remain in his arms, at least a little while longer. The warmth, comfort, and contentment she felt when he embraced her always overwhelmed her. It was as if she had come home, found the place she was meant to be, though it wasn't a place . . . it was a person.

Her husband.

Was this part of falling in love? Finding peace and solace with your mate?

"Are you all right?" Trey asked.

Concern was heavy in his voice, and his hands remained on her waist, as if he had no intention of letting go until he was certain she was well. She loved that he cared and worried over her and that he would always see her safe . . . another wonderful part of falling in love.

Bliss smiled. "I am fine, and it is time for me to see how the injured are doing."

"And I must go hunt."

Her smile suddenly faded, and she grabbed his

arm, squeezing it. "We must leave no later than tomorrow morning."

"Do you see more troops headed this way?"

She shook her head. "A band of mercenaries."

"To join with the king's troops?"

She nodded, then shook her head. "Yes and no . . . I'm not sure. But I don't want to take the chance of placing these injured men in more danger."

"Agreed," he said. "I'll tell Burnell we must make ready for early departure on the morrow. Do what you can to prepare the injured."

He gave her a quick kiss and took off. It dawned on her how often he kissed her that way, as if it was the most natural thing for him to do, as if he was her true husband. She had no time to linger on the thought, too much to do, but she could not help but think how lovely it was to have a loving husband.

The sun that had risen bright and bold was later devoured by heavy clouds and crisper air. Bliss intended to tell Trey that another fire was necessary to help keep the men warm. She wasn't surprised when he built one without her having said a word. They thought much alike, or perhaps he was more attuned to her thoughts than either of them realized.

The day wore on, with Bliss busy attempting to heal the more serious injuries enough so that they would not worsen with travel. She knew her zealous efforts would leave her tired, but with a bit of rest, she would feel refreshed soon enough.

Bliss barely had time to exchange even a few words with Trey throughout the day though he sent a smile her way often enough.

By nightfall, all in the camp were exhausted, and after the food was eagerly eaten, the men drifted off to sleep, all except Trey. He had the first watch.

Bliss lay next to the fire, her cloak and blanket wrapped tightly around her. She missed Trey's warmth, his solid embrace, and his hard chest, which so often pillowed her head. She had grown accustomed to sleeping beside him, snuggled in his arms. And she could not imagine ever sleeping alone again.

He had in a short time become necessary to her, and though the thought caused a moment of fear, it also brought pleasure. To think that he would keep her warm, love her, and grow old with her filled her with joy.

But would he? Or was this a momentary episode created by fate. But for what purpose?

It had been much easier to accept fate's ways when she was alone, but not so now that there was Trey. She would miss him terribly if they were to part.

She shook her head, not wanting even to imagine the possibility. The hurt would be . . .

How had Trey ever survived losing the woman he loved? Just the thought of Trey's parting wrenched at her heart. She had felt a mere moment of his horrific pain when he had told her about Leora's death. And while her pain ceased with the telling of the tale, his had not.

It continued to linger with him, along with memories, some good and some unbearable.

She would be asked on occasion to help heal the

bereaved, and sadly, she always had to refuse. Her grandmum had taught her that only time and the love of family and friends could help them.

Bliss stood taking the blanket with her and went to where Trey sat just on the outskirts of the campsite.

"Your steps are so light I barely hear them," Trey said, as she approached.

She plopped down beside him, threw the blanket around them, and cuddled close. "My intentions were not to surprise you but to seek warmth."

His arm went around her waist and drew her closer. "Truth be told, I wouldn't mind some myself."

She slipped her arms around his waist and rested her head to his shoulder. "Then you don't mind if I stay here with you?"

"I'm glad you're here, though I must keep alert to my post."

"I did not come to seduce you," she said with a soft laugh.

"You can seduce me any other time you would like to," he encouraged with a squeeze to her side.

She laughed again. "I've had no experience at seduction and wouldn't know where to start."

"You seduce me every time you look at me."

She lifted her head from his chest and stared at him bewildered. "I do?"

"Aye, you do. Your eyes need only settle on me, and I'm thinking things that . . . distract me."

She chuckled. "Such power. What will I do with it?"

"Nothing at the moment, though feel free any other time," he said. "Right now I'd prefer we sit quiet so that I can listen for unwanted company."

Bliss understood, for passion was beginning to stir within her, the knowledge that she had the power to excite him so easily excited her; but he was right—now was not the time.

She rested her head to his shoulder once again, and he tucked the blanket more firmly around them. The night had turned cold, but she was snug in his warmth. She listened along with him to the silence. Nothing seemed to stir tonight; the forest was at peace. And so was she.

It wasn't long before her eyes drifted closed, and she fell asleep.

Bliss woke with a start and sat up abruptly.

Trey jolted up beside her. "What's wrong?"

It took a moment for her to realize that they were in front of the campfire. Last she remembered . . . she cocked her head and stared at him.

"I carried you here after Burnell took over guard duty."

She had slept soundly and without dreams, unusual for her, but a sudden sensing had woken her. "We must get the men ready to leave at first light."

"What's wrong?" Trey asked, standing along with her.

"If we wait too long to leave, our paths will cross. If we leave as light breaks on the land, we have no chance of crossing paths."

Trey nodded and went to work rousing the men. Once told their sunrise departure was necessary to avoid confrontation with mercenaries, the men got busy. Carriers had been fashioned the day before for two men who were too seriously injured to walk.

When the glow of the rising sun was seen on the horizon, the group departed. Bliss led the way, knowing that certain areas had to be avoided. It was a strenuous morning for all. The men, though weakened by their plight, remained determined by the chance to see their loved ones again.

It was late afternoon when they came to the area where it was necessary for Bliss and Trey to part ways from the group of farmers.

Burnell stepped forward. "We are grateful and in your debt for all you have done."

"Arrive at my home safely, and your debt is paid," Trey said with a smile and a firm handshake.

Bliss shook her head. "It is too long a trip not only for those more seriously wounded, but the others who begin to heal. You will need to stop and rest at least two days, and I know the perfect place where you will find help. You will stop and rest with my people . . . the Picts."

Burnell turned a doubtful glance to Trey.

"I have met the Picts. They are good people and will welcome you."

"Aye, they will," Bliss said, and reached for Burnell's hand, turning it palm up. "Sentinels guard our land. When one approaches, you tell him you have a message from Bliss, their healer. He will hold out his hand and you will draw this symbol on it with your thumb." Bliss drew a cross and pressed her thumb in the center. "He will then help you."

Burnell nodded and once again thanked them, as did the others who filed past them as the small band of farmers continued on.

When the last one had disappeared from sight, Bliss turned to Trey ready to continue their journey to see how Philip fared.

"Something wrong?" she asked when he saw how strangely he stared at her.

"The symbol you drew. Draw it for me," he said, and held out his hand.

Bliss obliged, drawing a cross and pressing her thumb in the center.

"What does this symbol mean?"

"It is a symbol my people use to let our kind know that it is safe to trust the one who knows it."

"There are no words that accompany it?"

"A Pict will sometimes attach a message to it," she said.

"How do you know the message is from a Pict? Couldn't an outsider who knows the symbol also add a message?"

"The Picts deliver their message in a special way that is never discussed with outsiders."

"So if I asked you to explain—"

Bliss shook her head. "I couldn't."

"What if I recited a message that accompanied that symbol? Could you tell me if it was sent by a Pict?"

"That I could do."

"Good," Trey said with a nod. "The message was 'When two are one, it will be done.'"

"Aye," Bliss said with a smile, "the message was from a Pict."

Trey looked shocked. "Mercy's mother gave her that message, which means—"

"Mercy is part Pict. You did not know that?"

"You did?"

"Of course, as soon as I met her I knew," Bliss said. "Besides, I know Mercy's grandmum. She's Dolca, the woman who is in need of healing."

Chapter 14

Trey didn't move, even though Bliss started walking. He couldn't believe what he had heard. It had stunned him to see Bliss draw the symbol that Mercy's mother had drawn on her hand before they had parted and her mother had died. And it had shocked him even more to learn that Mercy's mother had been a Pict.

Could that have some connection as to why Mercy's mother had been in possession of the piece of hide, symbols on it that made reference to the true king's birthright? And there was still the burning question . . . who had stolen the hide from the keep and given it to Mercy's mother.

"Are you coming with me?" Bliss called out.

Trey shook his head, confused, and hurried to catch up with her.

"The answers you seek will come in their own time," Bliss said, when he caught up to walk alongside her.

He was about to ask her if she already knew the answers but held his tongue instead. If there was something she could share with him, she would.

And he couldn't continue to constantly seek answers from her like everyone else.

He would be the one to give to her, not constantly take.

He did, however, say, "Dolca must be Mercy's father's mother, since Duncan made mention of Mercy's mother's mother being dead for some time now."

"Aye, you're right."

Trey hoped to learn more, but Bliss spoke before he could.

"You will meet Dolca when we reach my village. I am sure she would be happy to satisfy your curiosity"

"Does that mean you do not wish to say any more on this matter?"

"You have not reached for my hand since joining me," she said. "This news you have learned has upset you."

Trey had not even realized he had failed to take her hand. It had become an instinctive reaction when walking beside her to reach for her hand. But his mind had been so focused on what he had inadvertently discovered that he hadn't even thought of holding her hand.

She took his hand before he could rectify the matter, and he was glad she did. Her hand joined tightly with his, as if letting him know that she didn't intend to let go, and that was fine with him.

"What questions can I answer for you that will help ease your troubled thoughts?" she asked.

He had so many that he didn't know where to begin or what was relevant. Until he finally said,

"Mercy will be pleased to have found her grand-mother, and Duncan will be pleased for her."

Bliss grinned. "Aye, that is the most important thing of all . . . family reuniting. Just think of what Mercy will learn about her family."

And think of what secrets he and his brothers might learn from it.

"No more questions?" Bliss asked, Trey having remained silent.

"Not at the moment," he said, though there was a burning question that he wished answered, but he kept it to himself. "With so many soldiers in the area, it's wiser that we remain alert. We should reach Albert and Teresa's farm tomorrow by mid-morning if we keep a good pace."

They walked in silence for several minutes before Bliss finally spoke. "Ask the question that torments you."

Trey shook his head. "Are you forever in my thoughts?"

"Perhaps it is you who is in my head, for I hear only the most persistent ones."

"I have no such powers like yours."

"Not so. I believe many people have the ability; they simply do not pay heed to it."

He was about to disagree, but her words stopped him.

"That matters not right now. My concern is that something troubles you, and I wish to help ease your burden."

Leora was not as thoughtful as Bliss.

The unexpected thought stunned him, for he had always assumed that any woman would pale

in comparison to Leora. And he suddenly realized
that simply was not so. It seemed that his concerns
were Bliss's concerns. She not only worried along
with him, she offered to help ease his worries.

Leora had often told him that he could talk with
her about anything, even his missions, if he wished.
She would not betray his trust, but he never did.
He would never take the chance of putting the
true king in harm's way. And she had never realized when his thoughts troubled him though she
had been quick to share whatever troubled her, and
frequently.

This time spent with Bliss had him seeing Leora
differently. Not that it changed his love for her, but
it made him see that perhaps she wasn't the perfect
woman he had thought her to be.

He realized then that Bliss could be hearing his
thoughts, but she had said that it was the most persistent ones she heard, and this thought was new.
It worried him that his thoughts were so available
to her.

"I hear nothing at the moment if that is what
concerns you," she said.

And it concerned him even more that she should
say that as he thought it. She had been nothing but
honest with him, and so it was his decision whether
to trust her word or not.

He didn't hesitate; he trusted her. "I do have a
concern."

"Tell me."

Again he didn't hesitate. "Do you know the
identity of the true king?"

She didn't hesitate as well. "I do."

Trey felt a burden descend on him like never before.

"You worry that if I should be captured I would reveal his identity, leaving him vulnerable," she said.

Damn, if she didn't know his very thought.

Bliss stopped and stood in front of him. "I have known the true king's identity for some time. I have never spoken of it to a soul, and I have no intention of ever revealing it—under any circumstances."

"Torture can reveal truths as well as lies," Trey said.

She smiled. "I am a seer and therefore what I say is taken as my word."

Trey chuckled. "Are you telling me you would lie?"

"I would do what I must to protect the true king, for I know he will keep my people safe."

Trey caught her chin with his fingers. "It is a heavy burden you carry."

"You carry it as well."

He shook his head. "It is different."

"Why?"

He stared at her a moment as if the answer was obvious. He was a man who could defend himself; she was a woman who . . . knew more than most.

He grinned, leaned down, and kissed her before whispering, "You best me more often than not."

It was her turn to chuckle. "It is easy to do."

His arm snaked around her waist and pulled her close. "Be careful, woman, or the warrior in me will rise to defend."

"Promise?" she said, pressing her cool cheek to his.

"You tempt fate."

"Fate drew us together, so I but give her what she wants."

"She wants me to kiss you," Trey whispered, his lips almost touching hers.

"My thoughts, not fate's," she murmured, and kissed him.

Their kiss was hungrier than usual . . . hungry for more than just a kiss. It stole the breath and ignited passion that lay so close to the surface.

Arms wrapped around each other, bodies drew near, and hands touched places that neither objected to. It was an aching frenzy that drove them until finally a sound of footfalls intruded, and they broke apart, Trey shoving her behind him and drawing his sword from its sheath, ready to defend.

A hare sat a few feet away, staring at them with wide, round eyes, and, with a twitch of its nose, it hurriedly hopped away.

Trey returned his sword to his sheath and turned to take Bliss's hand. "We need to be on our way as much as I'd prefer not to."

She held his hand and walked alongside him in silence, and he wondered why. Usually, she would have a comment or at least a smile, but, instead, she appeared deep in thought. What was she thinking? Could he possibly sneak into her thoughts?

It was as if a bolt of lightning struck him.

She wanted to make love with me.

The thought actually turned him hard, and he silently swore. Damn if he didn't want the same, and to know that she was willing only made him harder. He'd love to throw a blanket on the ground and consummate their vows here and now, but it was not a good time or place.

Danger could lurk at any turn, and he had to keep her safe. Making love to her might satisfy his lust, but it would do little to protect her. Besides, it wasn't lust he was looking to satisfy, and that was something he himself had to understand. He wanted more from Bliss and their unusual union.

He was beginning to realize that love played a larger part in what he was looking for than he would have thought possible. He had believed that he would never love again, at least not the way he had loved Leora. But time changed things, as did life, and he was finding that it just might be possible to find love again, and a stronger one at that.

"What troubles you?" he asked with a squeeze of her hand.

She smiled along with a brief laugh, and he was glad to see it.

"Roles reverse, and you worry over me," she said.

"As husbands and wives do, so share your troubles with me."

She shook her head. "It is nothing."

"Nothing or something, I want you to share it with me."

She looked over at him and when their eyes connected, she laughed and once again shook her head. "You already know."

He grinned. "Did I get it right?"

"You tell me," she said.

"You want to make love with me," he said without hesitation.

"I see that secrets will be impossible with each other."

While he had been annoyed that she could know his thoughts, he didn't at all mind knowing hers, at least at the moment.

"There is no need to keep it a secret that you want to make love with me," he said. "I want to make love with you."

"It is a good feeling, a good thought, and one I enjoy thinking on. It frees me from sensing and visions, and, for a while I simply feel my own feelings; and I never realized how precious that could be. In a sense, you bring me peace."

"I'm grateful that I can do that for you." He grinned. "And believe me when I tell you that I can consistently keep your thoughts occupied."

She smiled. "Promise."

"I give my word, *wife*. I shall keep your musings busy with thoughts of me . . . and pleasure."

He felt her shiver, and his own body did the same. Somehow . . . was it fate? They had become more husband and wife than they had realized, and he was not at all opposed to it. He actually found himself more and more liking the idea.

They traveled on in relative silence, only exchanging a word or two. It was imperative that they see this done. Now more than ever, Trey didn't mind delaying his return home. He had a reason to go to Pict territory. He needed to meet Dolca and talk with her, and he needed to see that she returned to his home, with Bliss and him.

Clouds and cold settled early over the land, forcing Trey and Bliss to stop for the evening earlier than planned. A fire was necessary to chase away the cold that was settling into their bones, and food was required to fill their hungry stomachs.

Of course, the idea of making love to her remained strong in his thoughts, his body also reminding him since every time he looked at Bliss, he felt a catch to his groin. He had to keep reminding himself that now was not the time or place, but damn if he didn't want to ignore his own words of warning.

They found a place to stop and feasted on a rabbit that Trey had been lucky enough to snare. Soon after, they cuddled on a blanket in front of the campfire though sleep eluded them.

Trey tried not to think about her body pressed so intimately against him though it was hard not to. Her full breasts lay hard against his chest, and the junction of her thighs nestled nicely against his groin, which responded instinctively.

He grew hard, and there was no stopping it. She had that effect on him, and it had been worsening lately. It could be because he ached to be intimate with her and because he knew she felt the same way. Nothing like a willing woman to grow a man hard.

If, however, it had been only lust he wished to satisfy, he could well have had his way with her by now. And that was the reason he presently fought his desire for her. He wanted something special with her, something memorable.

She cuddled her face in the crook of his neck, her warm breath tickling and heating his skin all at once, not to mention what it was doing to other parts of his body.

He should push her away, but he didn't want to. He wanted her right where she was, tight up against him, where he could feel her nipples harden and poke at his chest. And smell the scent of her, so rich and ripe with desire.

"You need to turn away from me," he said suddenly, and eased her away from him.

She shivered. "But I am cold, and you make me warm."

He took hold of her chin. "And you make me hot. Now turn around and keep your back to mine."

She wrinkled her nose in disappointment but didn't argue with him.

He draped his arm over her waist, though he kept a space between their bodies. They didn't utter a word, and, finally, after some time, they both fell asleep.

Bliss woke with a start to find Trey's hand gently exploring her body. While his touch was intimate, it also explored, as if he wanted to get to know every part of her. His fingers lingered just beneath her breast, his hand slipping beneath to cup her and squeeze ever so gently. His thumb rubbed across her nipple several times, turning it hard, then he teased the tip with light strokes.

She stayed as she was, eager to see what he would do next, eager for him to continue. His hand slipped down over her stomach and splayed across it. It remained there, not moving, and for a moment Bliss feared he would go no farther . . . and she wanted him to.

He had brought her body to life. It was as if she was fully alive for the first time, her feelings foreign but ever so delightful. Tingles raced through her, and though the night was cold, she felt hot.

His hand began to move, once more slipping farther down until it came to rest between her legs. His thumb soon settled over a particular spot and began massaging it with just the right pressure. A sensation began to spread deep inside her until she found herself squirming against his touch and felt herself begin to pulsate between her legs.

Her breath caught when his fingers slipped down into the folds of her skirt and rubbed at her wetness.

It drove her insane with the want of him, and she knew that she didn't want to wait any longer. She wanted her husband to make love to her here and now, under the night sky, with a sliver of a moon and only a few twinkling stars, and the stillness of the night surrounding them.

With a smile, she turned around in his arms to surrender and was shocked to find him asleep.

Chapter 15

Trey wondered what was wrong. As soon as he woke, he knew that Bliss was annoyed, more than annoyed; she seemed angry. His suspicions were confirmed when he realized she stayed out of his reach when they began their journey for the day.

It was obvious she didn't intend for him to hold her hand. He only wished he knew what disturbed her and if he was to blame, though he had done nothing but fall asleep, dream about her, and wake up.

So what had gotten her in a snit?

It just wasn't like her to be annoyed at something and not speak her mind. She had encouraged him to do so when troubled, so why, when something obviously troubled her, didn't she speak to him about it?

She walked ahead of him, and where usually her steps were light, she now more stomped.

"Women," he mumbled.

She spun around. "You have something to say, speak up."

She looked ready for a fight, and he had no intention of obliging her. He simply shook his head.

She turned with a huff and almost stumbled. He was at her side in an instant, his hand reaching for her arm.

She slapped it away. "I can manage myself."

Trey stepped back, surprised by her terse response.

She continued walking, and he thought it wise to remain walking behind her. When she was ready, she would talk with him and let him know what had her angry. He wished he could sense the problem, but he couldn't. So he would wait.

Bliss almost stumbled again, and, again, she pushed him away.

She was not watching her steps as keenly as she usually did, and so she suffered for it, but he had no intention of warning her to pay attention.

When she tripped the fourth time, he didn't bother to offer assistance, and she swung around and glared at him.

"You would let me fall?" she accused.

Trey had had enough. He marched over to her, grabbed her around the waist, and yanked her up hard against him. "Now you will tell me what has you so agitated that you snap at me like a harping wife."

She poked him in the chest. "You left me tormented, and it haunts me."

He shook his head. "What do you mean? I've done nothing to you."

She gave him a hard shove, and he released her. She stepped away. "Aye, you're right about that. You did nothing."

He went to take hold of her again, and she pushed his hand away.

He would have none of her rejection. He grabbed her around the waist once more though this time he tightened his hold on her. "I will not let you go until you explain."

Her eyes ignited with fury, but it wasn't anger he saw in them; it was passion.

"You touched me, made me ache for you, and left me wanting. And now that ache will not leave me."

He shook his head. "I would remember touching you."

"How could you?" she said, shaking a finger at him. "When I turned around in your arms, you were asleep and I"—she shook her head—"I was left aching for you."

He stared at her, bewildered. He didn't recall touching . . . suddenly he remembered. "I thought it was a dream."

"It wasn't," she said, her voice turning soft. "You touched me like I've never been touched. You made me feel things I've never felt, and you made me want you like I'd never thought possible."

He ran his finger gently along her cheek. "I am so sorry. I never meant—"

Her face drained of all anger, though passion still stirred in her eyes. "I am the one who should be sorry. I don't know what happened to me. I woke angry at you and feeling unsettled. Instead of talking with you, I wanted to . . . ."

"Punish me?"

She pressed her hand to his chest, and said softly,

"No, I wanted you to finish what you started, but . . ."

"Found it difficult to ask?"

She nodded. "I do not know why. We have talked about many things, and yet I couldn't bring myself to . . ."

"Ask me to make love to you?"

"I know we are destined to make love, and now is not a good time or place, but why not tell you how I feel?"

"Because you think there is nothing that can be done about it, yet your passion still stirs, and you suffer. It is difficult when passion insists on being satisfied and left untended," he said. "You should have told me."

She shrugged and sighed. "What difference would it make? We must—"

He swung her up in his arms before she could finish.

"What are you doing?"

"What I should have done last night . . . satisfy that ache of yours."

Bliss was torn between her desire for him and guilt for being petulant and causing them to delay their journey. He had a mission, and she had ill people to tend. Why ever had she reacted so badly? It wasn't like her, yet . . .

She ached for what he could offer, and that ache refused to go away. Every time she looked at him, she thought of last night and how his hands had brought her such pleasure. But was now the time?

He had information he had to get to his brothers, and she had an ill child to tend. She should not be thinking of herself.

"We can't do this," she said, as he walked to a more secluded area of towering pines.

"Aye, we can," he said as if there would be no changing his mind.

Sound reason battled with desire, her body traitorously siding with desire and using every weapon it could to win. Tingles raced through her in anticipation, turning her nipples hard, and she was already moist. She wanted him, but then she had wanted him since last night. The ache had not gone away. It had kept her awake most of the night. Until, finally, after what little sleep she did get, she woke annoyed and grew more annoyed when she saw that Trey had not been affected by it at all.

She had wanted to scream, rail at him, then make love with him, but that hadn't happened. Instead, she had been petulant, like a child who had not gotten her way. And worse . . . she hadn't cared.

Now, however, she did care. Trey was willing to put aside everything to tend to her here in the middle of the forest. A thrilling thought that excited her all the more, but . . .

"We have no time for this," she insisted, fighting her body for control.

He kissed her quick. "It shouldn't take long. A deep lusty kiss, intimate touches, and you will explode with pleasure."

"And what about you?"

"When I lie between your legs for the first time, it won't be for a short rut. I intend to take a full night making love to you."

Why did he have to say that? Her body went wild with thoughts and vivid images that provoked even more traitorous reactions, her nub pulsating so hard that if he simply touched her, she'd burst with pleasure.

"Though don't think I won't enjoy what I'm about to do to you," he said with a smile.

He would take pleasure giving her pleasure.

The thought warmed her heart, not to mention other places it heated. And it also brought her to her senses. As much as her body wished him to pleasure her right now; she wished for them to share it.

She placed her hand to his chest. "I don't want it this way."

Trey stopped and cast a questioning glance at her.

"I want a full night of making love with you."

"But—"

She pressed two fingers to his lips. "It is what I want."

"Are you sure?"

"Aye, most definitely," she said while ignoring her body's pleas to be satisfied.

Trey hesitated, his questioning look telling her that he didn't quite believe her.

She reinforced her wishes by saying, "Please, Trey, it is what I want."

"But not necessarily what you need."

"Perhaps, but it is what I want."

He placed her gently on her feet, and, with a

tender touch to her face, he said, "I will give you this, but you will give me something in return. And I will have your word on it."

She was hesitant to ask, "What?"

"The next time I touch you intimately in my sleep, you will wake me so that I may finish what I start."

She smiled. "I promise."

"Good," he said, and was about to kiss her but stopped.

"It is better you don't," she said. "My desire for you has yet to fade, and I worry that it never will."

He grinned. "I wouldn't mind having a wife with that problem."

She laughed and took his hand and, with a tug, started them walking. "You may tire of my ever-burning passion for you."

"Somehow I don't think so," he said with a laugh.

Soon their pace increased, and they talked no more. With quick, guarded steps and glances, they turned cautious to their surroundings. But it was their eagerness to be done and on their way to Bliss's home that told the true story, for both knew it would be there where they would make love and possibly seal their vows forever.

As Trey and Bliss approached Albert and Teresa's farm, they both paused with worry. There was no one about, and, for a moment, it looked as if the place was deserted.

Bliss turned to Trey. "Hurry."

Bliss wasn't surprised when Trey ran in front of her, shielding her against any possible harm, but it wasn't necessary though she'd let him see for himself.

His hand was about to draw his sword when the door was flung open, and he stumbled to an abrupt stop.

Philip stood there with a smile, though quickly leaned against the doorframe.

Bliss ran past Trey, her arms stretched out to the lad.

Philip stretched his thin arms out in return, obviously too weak to run to her.

As soon as she reached the lad, she hugged him tight.

"I did it, I did it," he said. "I woke up just like you told me to," he said, and hugged Bliss even tighter.

"I knew you could do it," she said, and gave his hair a tousle.

Teresa stood behind her son, a huge smile on her face, but worry in her eyes, and hurried them all into the cottage. "He woke soon after you left, talking endlessly about Bliss, who helped him find his way home. He is just now getting around, though I tell him he must rest."

"I rested enough, I did," the lad said with a laugh.

Bliss sensed that Teresa was eager to talk with them but not in front of her son. "Philip, let me help heal you some more, while your mum feeds Trey. His stomach has been rumbling since morning."

Trey grinned. "Especially knowing what a tasty cook your mum is, I couldn't wait to get here."

She knew he'd understand her intentions, and Philip took her hand, eager not about the healing but to show Bliss the wooden animals his da had carved for him.

Trey kept his voice low, and Teresa filled a bowl with soup that brewed in the cauldron in the fireplace.

"Where is Albert?" Trey asked, taking a seat at the table.

Teresa placed the bowl in front of him and sat. "He gathers the few animals we have. We plan to leave tomorrow and seek protection at the MacAlpin village. It grows too dangerous. Another troop passed here and, thankfully, kept away, seeing Albert. But his ruse can't last long, and with war on the horizon . . .

Tears gathered in her eyes. "We both fear, now that Philip grows well, the soldiers will take him."

Trey rested a comforting hand over hers. "You've made a wise choice. Tell me where Albert is, and I will help him ready the animals while Bliss helps you."

Teresa grabbed tight hold of Trey's hand. "Albert fears the soldiers passing and seeing that we prepare the animals and cart for departure. He has a spot in the woods where he makes everything ready for us."

Trey nodded and continued to listen as Teresa detailed the directions.

"Explain to Bliss and make ready yourself. You leave today."

Bliss and Philip entered the room shortly after Trey left.

"He does well," Bliss said, placing a gentle hand on Teresa's shoulder. "He also tells me that you are leaving here."

"We go to stay with the true king for a while," Philip said happily, and plopped down on the ground in front of the fire to play with his wooden animals.

Teresa nodded, her tears near to spilling.

"Let me help you get ready for your journey," Bliss said.

Teresa stood and wiped at her eyes before any tears could fall. "I'm grateful for the help."

Bliss smiled, knowing the woman expressed her gratitude for much more.

They worked together, gathering what was necessary, packing food in baskets and sacks, taking what bedding they could and what little clothes they had.

The door burst open suddenly, and Teresa was quick to stand protectively in front of her son. Trey entered with a young girl no more than six years draped in his arms, looking as if all life had drained from her.

"That's Mary's oldest, Deryn," Teresa said, and hurried to draw back the curtain to the other room.

Trey was quick to place the young girl on the bed and step back as Bliss hurried forward to tend her.

"What happened?" Teresa asked her husband as he stood in the doorway, Philip clinging to his leg with a look of fear.

"She suddenly appeared in front of us, and Trey caught her as she collapsed."

Bliss studied the young child and, as soon as she laid a hand on her forehead, knew that exhaustion had claimed her. But she also felt strength and determination, so Bliss wasn't surprised when, after only a few minutes of healing, the child woke.

Her eyes sprang wide. "My mum and sister are sick. They need help." She began to cry. "I didn't want to leave them, but I didn't know what to do." Tears streamed down her face.

"It's all right," Bliss assured her. "We'll go help your mum."

Deryn sat up. "I'll go with you and help."

Bliss took the young girl's hand. "You need rest, so you can help your mum and sister when we bring them to you."

"You'll bring them here?" Deryn asked eagerly.

Bliss would not lie to the child. She needed the truth so that she would feel safe. "Albert and Teresa are leaving here today, and you will go with them."

Deryn shook her head, tears continuing to run down her pale cheeks.

Bliss squeezed her hand gently. "Listen to me, Deryn. You were a brave girl for walking here all by yourself. Now you must be brave and go with Albert and Teresa while Trey, a brave warrior and I, a healer, go to help your mum and sister and bring them to you."

Deryn sniffled. "Promise?"

"I promise," Bliss said.

Trey stepped forward. "And you have my word as a warrior."

Philip eased his way past everyone and offered Deryn his wooden cow. "You can have this, and we can play together while you wait for your mum."

Deryn smiled and took the cow.

Leave it to a child to make another child smile, Bliss thought.

Deryn and Philip played on the bed while the adults all gathered in the other room.

"We'll get the last of your things packed on the cart along with the children and see you on your way," Trey said. "Then Bliss and I will go see to Mary and her daughter."

"What if Mary—"

Bliss stopped Teresa before she could finish. "Do not worry. We will bring them both to you in time."

While Trey hurried them to finish, Teresa gave the last of the soup to the children, with a chunk of bread. She then saw to dousing the fire and making sure the last of what they would need was given to her husband and Trey to put in the cart.

With directions given to Mary's farm and a route to MacAlpin village mapped out, one that would hopefully avoid any soldiers, Trey and Bliss waved good-bye, though not before the little girl had reminded Bliss of her promise.

"Tell me. Do you sense anything about Mary and her daughter," Trey said, as they turned and walked in the opposite direction.

"They grow worse. We need to hurry."

Chapter 16

It took them an hour to reach the farm, and, once Trey was certain no soldiers lurked about, he and Bliss approached the cottage. Trey insisted on entering first. An unpleasant odor gave him pause and as soon as he saw the two prone bodies on the bed, the mother's arms around the small girl, he thought the worst.

Bliss pushed past him. "They're not dead; they're ill and need tending."

Trey watched for a moment as Bliss went to work on the two. Then he said, "I'm going to scout the area and see if it is safe to stay here."

"You don't have to. There are none nearby and none expected just yet."

No wonder she was able to keep herself from harm when alone. She knew when and where it was safe to travel. How remarkable to have such power . . . and what a burden.

"Can you get a fire started and get me water from the rain barrel outside and set it to boil in the cauldron?" she asked, nodding at the large black pot hanging from a hook in the cold fireplace. "I need to set a broth to cooking while I clean and help heal them."

Trey and Bliss both went to work.

While he got a fire going, Bliss filled two buckets with water. When she began to tend the woman and child, Trey stepped outside and told her to let him know if she needed help.

He spent the time looking around the farm. It was obvious after only a few glances that there was not enough food for the woman and two girls to survive on. The soldiers had stripped them of all animals and what food they had harvested. The few winter plants left untouched would never be enough to sustain them. And from the look of the woman in the bed, she was a petite thing without the strength to endure on her own.

Though Bliss had assured him that no soldiers were about, his warrior instincts warned him about always remaining alert. He dropped onto an old wooden bench he thought might collapse from his weight, but didn't. It sat close to the door, and he wanted to be near if Bliss should call out for help.

She was an amazing woman, whose skills were sought after by many, and, when needed, she would go where necessary without question. Now, however, she was his wife, and he did not want a wife of his traipsing off wherever fate would send her.

How would he keep her safe? And he didn't want her away from him for too long; he would miss her far too much.

Miss her?

The thought that he would miss her put a grin on his face. It was no chore spending every moment with Bliss. Whether they talked, kissed, touched, or were silent, he enjoyed it all.

Even more than I had with Leora.

The sudden thought didn't upset him as it once would have. Perhaps he was finally able to lay Leora to rest and live again. He hadn't admitted to anyone how lifeless he had felt since her death. It was as if a vital part of him had died along with her, and only now was it resurrecting.

He hadn't even realized how deeply her death had affected him until Bliss came along. Being with her, feeling for her, had filled that empty void, that pit of darkness he had come to accept and live with.

He had thought it was his lot in life to continue on as he had, feeling nothing and not wanting to. Bliss had changed all that.

He grinned and shook his head. Damn, but he was grateful that she had. And now . . . he didn't know what he'd do without her, and he didn't want to find out.

She was his wife, and he planned on keeping her his wife.

The door to the cottage opened, and Trey stood.

Bliss stepped outside and discarded a bundle of bedding to the side. She took a deep breath and rolled her shoulders back before stretching her arms to the sky.

"Mother and child?" he asked.

"Come see," she said, and preceded him through the doorway.

Trey stood amazed at the woman and child sitting up in bed, their faces still pale. But a hint of color stained their freshly washed cheeks. They wore clean garments, and a clean blanket covered them. The cottage even appeared brighter though perhaps it was the pleasant scent of bubbling broth that made the difference.

Trey introduced himself to Mary, and the little girl, who could be no more than four years old, proudly announced, "Allena."

Trey bowed gallantly. "I am most pleased to meet you, Allena. You are feeling better?"

She nodded, smiled, and cuddled up to her mother.

"I can't thank you and Bliss enough for sending my daughter Deryn to safety with Albert and Teresa," Mary said, her voice surprisingly strong.

"You and Allena will be joining her when you are well enough to travel," he assured her, and looked to Bliss.

"With some hot broth and a good night's sleep to give them strength, I would say we could leave tomorrow."

"I don't know what is in that broth," Mary said with a smile and a tear in her eye, "but I feel strong already."

Allena nodded to let everyone know she felt the same.

Trey didn't bother to tell Mary that it was Bliss's touch that had healed them so quickly though he wondered himself over their rapid recovery. Most times Bliss's healing had taken longer, but this . . . this bordered on miraculous.

A chill ran through him. Were her powers far greater than he had known?

Bliss filled a tankard with some broth and handed it to Trey. "To warm you and keep you strong."

With a grin, he leaned down, and whispered in her ear, "I'm not strong enough for you?"

She smiled sweetly at him. "I'm thinking you will soon need extra stamina."

"Then you better drink some yourself, so you can keep up with me."

"Have no fears," she whispered, "for I will far outlast you."

"A challenge?"

She chuckled. "A knowing."

He found himself speechless, and she smiled as she turned, though stopped suddenly. Her body swayed slightly, and her hand shot out to grab the table. He reached out, his arm wrapping around her waist as he placed his tankard on the table. Then both his arms settled around her, and her head came to rest on his chest.

"What's wrong?" he demanded.

"Just tired," she assured him.

He didn't believe her for one minute, and he sensed that she knew that. Her next words proved him right.

"We'll talk later."

Which he knew meant when we're alone, so he let it be . . . for now.

He kept his arms around her until she was ready to leave them, and when she moved to slip away, he let her though he reminded in a whisper, "Later."

She nodded and returned to healing mother and child.

It wasn't until later that night when all was quiet, Mary and Allena asleep, that he and Bliss had a chance to speak.

They had moved the table and chairs to make room for their blanket on the ground in front of the fireplace. No flames were needed to warm them; their bodies snuggled close did that for them.

Trey kept a firm arm draped around her waist, her back snug against his chest, and his leg resting over both of hers. A wool blanket covered them.

Contentment washed over him, and he wondered if it wasn't only his own he felt. Bliss rested contentedly in his arms though he could tell she was fatigued. He didn't know how he knew it, he simply did.

"You are bone-tired," he said against her temple after kissing there.

"More than usual, but that is the way of it when I attempt to heal quickly."

"It robs you of strength? The reason you almost collapsed earlier?"

"Nothing to worry about."

"But it is," he said. "You give too much at times."

"When necessary, I give more than usual, and this situation warranted more," she said, her last word caught on a yawn.

How did he argue that with her? She was right, this situation did warrant more. Mary and her daughter needed to get well as fast as possible so that they could leave the area, which was growing ever more dangerous.

"What of your strength? You share it with others, then leave yourself exhausted. How then do you manage the journey?"

"Sleep will heal me well enough."

"I remember seeing you sitting in the chair beside my bed sleeping."

"I wasn't sleeping. I was talking with you just as I did with Philip," she said. "You are a brave warrior, but your heartache kept you from fighting as strongly as you could have. I had to get past your sorrow to help you heal well."

He was curious. "Did you sense my sorrow?"

"Your sadness was so great that I felt it as if it were my own. My own heart hurt for yours, and I wished there was something I could have done. But such heartache is for fate to heal, not me."

"But you have helped heal my heartache," he admitted.

Her hand slipped over his, where it rested at her waist, and locked fingers with him. "You finally want it to heal, and so healing has begun. I have learned through the many healings I have done that those who not only wish to get well, but have a strong reason to get well, heal much faster than those who have surrendered to their illness . . . surrendered to death."

"So in a sense, Mary and her daughter helped your healing along because they both had a reason to live?"

Bliss nodded while she yawned. "Mary's determined to see her daughters safe, and hope is alive in her heart that her husband will return to her. Allena misses her da and worries over her sister, so she fought to live for them."

He was silent a moment, then asked, "I felt as if I had nothing to live for after I lost Leora. Why then, when I was so close to death, didn't I die? And I don't believe fate had anything to do with my living. So what then kept me alive?"

"Something just as powerful as love."

"There is nothing more powerful than"—he shook his head—"hate."

"Your hate for those who took Leora from you gave you the will to live though, at the time, you didn't know it," she said. "A warning . . . leave revenge to fate. She has a way of balancing things in time, and though it may take us a while to realize it, in the end we are aware of the wisdom of her ways."

"I don't need fate fighting *my* battles for me."

"Perhaps it's not *your* battle to fight, but *hers*." She gave his hand a squeeze. "Right now I battle to keep my eyes open. I must sleep."

"Surrender to sleep," he urged, and wrapped himself more snugly around her.

"And will you surrender to fate?"

Trey waited and let sleep claim her so he wouldn't have to answer. He was a Highlander warrior who fought for the true king of Scotland. Surrendering was not in his blood; he would fight to the death.

And someday he would find and kill the man or men who took Leora from him.

Bliss walked alongside Mary, her steps filled with strength that Bliss lacked. She hadn't been surprised at the woman's quick recovery. As soon as she had started to heal her, Bliss had felt her determination to get well and protect her family. While it had taken more of her strength than usual, it hadn't been difficult. Mary's courage had helped tremendously.

"He will be a good da," Mary said, with a nod to Trey.

Bliss smiled. Trey walked ahead of them, with Allena perched on his broad shoulders. At first she had been apprehensive about it, but he had cajoled her into it, and now, after traveling over an hour, she giggled with delight.

"Aye, he will make a good da," Bliss agreed and couldn't help but think of having children with him. A daughter who would have her abilities or perhaps a son who would? A large brood they would have for she doubted she would be able to keep her hands off him. The urge to make love with him never left her, and she worried that it never would, or perhaps the worry was that they would never have the chance to make love.

Fate had predicted otherwise, and she should not doubt fate, so why worry? Or was her worry that they would make love, for then it would seal their vows and it would be that much harder to end their marriage.

Why did she continue to think their marriage would end? Her knowing had not indicated it would, yet she had this nagging doubt. What caused it? Could it have something to do with the way the blond woman haunted in images and dreams?

She felt a catch to her chest. It was time to admit that she knew the identity of the woman in her visions. She had realized who the woman was when she had insisted that Trey belonged to her. It was Leora.

The only thing she couldn't understand was why, with Leora dead, she fought for Trey?

She had slept fitfully last night, thanks to Leora, though she had been grateful she had not gotten stuck in her dreams. The woman would simply not leave her alone. She was either begging for help or warning Bliss that Trey belonged to her and that Bliss could not have him.

She wondered if perhaps it was Trey who kept her close in death, refusing to release her and let her rest in peace.

"You are lucky to have such a good man," Mary said. "My Thomas is a good man and a good da." She got misty-eyed. "The girls so miss their da."

Bliss got a sudden image of the injured farmers they had helped. There had been one man who had been seriously injured with a wound to his side. She had feared he wouldn't make it, but he had fought hard. He had been determined to live. It would take time, but Bliss knew that he would heal.

"Thomas does not have the fine features of your man," Mary said. "But he is handsome to me just the same. He stands only a head over me and is heavy with muscle." She laughed. "He often hoists

a girl up in each arm, and they squeal with delight
as he kisses their cheeks repeatedly."

"By any chance had he suffered a broken nose
one time?" Bliss asked.

Mary's eyes popped wide. "How did you know
that?"

"I wondered because Trey and I came across a
group of farmers who had been abandoned by the
soldiers because of their injuries. There was a man
among them who is similar in features as you have
described, and I wondered . . ."

"My Thomas? You saw my Thomas? Did he not
tell you his name? He would—" She gasped. "He's
hurt and cannot speak?"

"This man suffered a wound to his side that in
time will heal, but he was not well enough to tell
me who he was."

Mary sighed with relief. "My Thomas would
have been wearing gray leggings and a brown
tunic with a gray shirt, the cuffs frayed. His right
ear would have a chunk missing from it, an acci-
dent when he was but a lad."

Bliss nodded. "That sounds like the man I tended."

"Where is he now?"

"I sent the farmers to my people . . . the Picts.
They will look after them until they can be moved
to the MacAlpin village."

Mary frowned, and Bliss knew why. She was
torn between going to help her husband and seeing
to her daughter.

Bliss reached out and took hold of her hand.
"Don't worry. I'm sure you all will be reunited very
soon."

Mary calmed some though her eyes remained misty.

As soon as Bliss released Mary's hand, her senses were bombarded with warnings. She hurried up alongside Trey, and whispered, "Soldiers draw near."

Chapter 17

Allena was quickly handed over to her mother, and Bliss walked a few feet away to talk with Trey.

"How many?" he asked.

"Too many for you to battle on your own," she advised.

"We'll have to hide—"

Bliss didn't let him finish. "No time to find a hiding place." She grabbed a handful of dirt and turned it palm up close to his face and blew.

He coughed and sputtered and rubbed at his burning eyes. "What the—"

She grabbed his arm. "Don't argue; do as I say." She took the bedroll off his back and shook the blanket open, then draped it over his head. "Keep your head down and cough frequently when the soldiers draw near."

She tugged at him to follow her back to Mary and Allena. "We must appear sick," she said, and did the same to Mary as she had done to Trey though she didn't wrap a blanket around her. She smeared dirt on Allena's cheeks, and it wasn't necessary to make her eyes red as fearful tears were already beginning to do that.

"Say nothing, just cough and keep your heads bent," Bliss ordered, and did the same to herself, her eyes turning red and watering as the first soldier appeared.

Bliss stepped forward, her head slightly bent, her shoulders slumped and in between coughs, she begged, "Help us . . . please."

"Back away," the soldier demanded.

"Please," Bliss said, reaching out to him with her dirt-covered hand, to which she added a slight tremble.

"Be on your way," he ordered sternly and pointed to his right. "I'll not have you crossing paths with the soldiers."

"But—"

The soldier moved his horse closer to Bliss. "I'll not contaminate my sword on your putrid blood, but I will have a skilled archer take aim if you do not move on." With that said, he gave her a kick, sending her sprawling to the ground.

Bliss's first thought wasn't of the pain that tore through her chest but of Trey. She feared he would not contain his anger, and so she scrambled quickly to her feet though the pain robbed her of breath.

She nodded repeatedly and shuffled over to Trey and Mary and, with great effort, managed to say loud enough for the soldier to hear, "We must move on."

Mary bobbed her head and coughed. Even Allena gave a cough though she kept her head tucked in the crook of her mother's neck, Mary hugging her tightly.

Trey's head didn't bob, and his cough sounded more like a snarl. Bliss was quick to wrap her arm around his back and give a pat, hoping it would reassure him that she was fine even though she wasn't. And she worried that he just might sense the truth and jeopardize their safety though that would be a foolish move, and Trey was not a foolish man.

They walked slowly though their feet wished to take flight and run from potential harm. That their cautious actions proved wise was made obvious when the large troop became visible through the trees as they made their way through the woods away from the soldier.

Mary gasped though quickly turned it into a hacking cough, and they heard the soldier Bliss had spoken with yell, "Keep your distance from the sick peasants."

Bliss felt the muscles in Trey's back grow taut beneath her hand, and, once again, she gave it a pat, hoping to calm him.

It took time to pass the long line of soldiers, which seemed never-ending, and it wasn't until hours later that they finally felt safe enough to stop for a rest.

As soon as they did, Trey threw off the blanket and turned to Bliss. "How badly did he hurt you?"

"You showed remarkable restraint," she said rather than answer him.

"He kicked you awfully hard," Mary said, Allena clinging to her leg.

"How badly?" Trey repeated more firmly.

"It hurts to take deep breaths"—though she quickly added—"but I will work on healing it."

Trey swore beneath his breath. "You need rest."

"He is right," Mary agreed.

Bliss shook her head. "I appreciate the concern"—she stopped a moment to catch her breath—"but we all know that the longer we linger"—another breath—"the more danger we place ourselves in."

Trey gave an angry growl and walked away, his fists clenched.

"He knows you are right, but his love for you overpowers reason, and he battles with it," Mary said with a bittersweet smile.

Bliss pulled a small sack from the other rolled bedding and handed it to Mary. "Allena must be . . ." She rested her hand on her chest.

"Go and comfort your angry warrior. Allena and I will be fine."

Bliss didn't hesitate and walked over to Trey. He paced between two trees, his hands still fisted at his sides and his eyes an angry blue, like the sky before a storm.

When she was near enough to him, he stopped pacing and reached out to gently draw her against him. His hands went to rest at her waist, and he lowered his brow to hers, closing his eyes as he did.

"I cannot stand to think of you in pain." His frustration came out in a hard whisper.

She attempted to reassure him. "I can heal myself."

He opened his eyes and shook his head. "Where will you find the strength? Your sleep was restless last night, which means you didn't get the rest you should have. You need time to regain your strength so that you can heal yourself."

"We have no choice."

"Do you know what it took not to rip that soldier off his horse and kill him?"

"Love."

He shook his head again. "Love was the furthest thing from my mind."

"I have not the breath to explain," she said, needing to maintain what strength she had left to heal herself.

He cupped her face. "We make camp here so that you can rest."

"We can't," she said, and walked away from him. She had to get them moving. She had to get home. Only there, in the safety of her people, could she heal herself properly.

"More danger?" he asked, catching up with her.

She took his hand and rested it on her chest. "I need to get home."

She didn't need to say any more. Trey walked over to Mary and Allena and hoisted the little girl onto his shoulders.

"We need to keep moving. We need to get Bliss home."

"My daughter Deryn?" Mary asked anxiously.

"I'll send someone to see that your daughter reached the MacAlpin village safely," Trey said. He then turned to Bliss. "You will tell me if you need to stop and rest."

Bliss nodded, relieved that no one would attempt to speak to her as they traveled. She would use the quiet time to begin healing herself. It would depend on their pace, but if they could maintain a good one, with few or no stops until nightfall, and they left with the first light of dawn, they could reach her home—

"We could possibly have you home by mid-morning tomorrow," Trey finished as if reading her thoughts.

The day wore on endlessly for Bliss. Her attempts to heal herself faltered at times, the pain interfering with her focus. She had hoped she would have at least eased the pain, but all the walking had only served to worsen it.

When it came time to stop for the night, Trey and Mary would not allow her to do anything, and so she took the time to sit and heal. By the time she was ready to stretch out beside Trey on the blanket in front of the campfire, she was feeling better . . . that was until she lay down.

She gasped for breath from the pain, her hand clawing at Trey for help. He sat her up so swiftly that everything around her spun for a moment. It took several minutes to regain normal breathing.

"It is too painful for you to lie on the hard ground, isn't it?" he asked.

She nodded and saw that Mary looked at her with concern from the opposite side of the fire, Allena asleep and cuddled against her.

Trey didn't hesitate; he moved to sit behind her and reached out to ease her into his arms.

She shook her head and pointed adamantly back and forth between him and the blanket on the ground.

"No, I am not going to lie down and sleep while you sit up all night." He waved her to him. "Now come here to me."

She shook her head again.

He grinned. "Shaking your head will get you nowhere. I'll have my way."

She jutted her chin out stubbornly.

He leaned closer to whisper, "I need you in my arms. I need to feel your warmth. I need to hear your heart beat against me. I need to know you are safe. Won't you satisfy my need for you?"

She sighed, his words so lovely that they stole her heart. She didn't object when his arms wrapped around her and gently drew her into them.

"Find a comfortable spot against me," he said, "and I will see that you stay there throughout the night."

That he would so unselfishly give up a restful night's sleep so that she could sleep without pain was another reason among many others that made her see what a wonderful, caring, unselfish husband Trey would be to his wife.

She did as he asked and, surprisingly, found herself more comfortable than she thought she would. Still, she felt guilty that she should rest so peacefully while he sat cradling her all night.

"Do not worry about me," he said, once she was settled. "I am where I want to be."

He leaned down and kissed her lightly. "A brief kiss, or else I might excite you," he teased.

"Too late."

He laughed. "How easy it will be to keep you in my bed."

"It will be hard to get me out."

He laughed again, and she couldn't help but laugh herself . . . a mistake. It sent a stabbing pain through her, and she gasped.

"Easy," he urged, and stroked her cheek with a gentle hand.

His touch soothed and helped ease her pain, and her eyes fluttered closed.

"I'll take care of you. I'm right here, I'll always lo . . ."

Her mind had gone fuzzy, and she repeated aloud what she was sure she had heard him say, "I love you."

Did Bliss say what he thought she did?

"It is so gratifying to see two people so much in love," Mary said with a smile before closing her eyes and snuggling closer around her sleeping daughter.

Trey stared down at Bliss, sleeping peacefully in his arms. Love certainly poked at him though he had yet to acknowledge it. But why? Did Leora still haunt his heart? Did he feel guilty for allowing himself to feel again?

He gently lifted a strand of Bliss's blond hair and carefully tucked it behind her ear. She was such a beautiful woman and in so many ways. He grinned. He loved waking up and seeing her face first thing in the morning. He loved holding her hand when they walked. He loved her smile, which seemed to brighten even the most dismal day; he loved her unselfishness; and he truly loved the passion for him that forever burned in her light blue eyes.

He chuckled quietly. He had no choice but to finally acknowledge what he knew from the very first. He loved Bliss, loved her more—

He shook his head. It wasn't possible, but his heart told him differently. He loved Bliss more than he had Leora. There was so much more to Bliss than there had been to Leora, and it made him wonder why he had fallen in love with Leora in the first place.

There was no point in lingering in the past anymore. Nothing would change it, and finally, in almost a year's time, he was ready to let it go. He felt the urge to feel, to love . . . to live again.

He leaned his face close to hers and finished what he had stopped himself from saying, "I will always love you."

Chapter 18

Trey was never so relieved to see the Pict sentinels drop from the trees when they crossed into Pict territory. True to her nature, Bliss inquired, through labored breath, to see if the farmers had arrived yet, and when she learned that they hadn't, she attempted to speak again.

Trey stepped forward. "Bliss has been injured, and speaking only worsens the injury."

The men looked at her with concern.

Trey was quick to reassure them. "She will heal, but she needs the rest to do so. And she will never rest if she continues to wonder why the farmers have yet to get here."

One of the Picts said, "I'll take some men and see what keeps them and offer whatever help is needed."

Bliss smiled her appreciation at Langward, a young Pict warrior.

"Has Roan returned from seeing my family?" Trey asked.

"We expect him home in a few days," Langward answered.

"Dolca?" Bliss asked.

Trey gave no time for an answer. He scooped her up. "After you heal yourself, then you can heal others." He looked to Langward. "Would you see that Mary and her daughter Allena are given food and shelter?"

Langward nodded. "Of course."

Then Trey walked over to Allena, held in her mother's arms, her skinny arms wound tightly around her mother's neck. "These are good people, Allena, and they will help you and your mum. You have nothing to fear. And I will be nearby if you need me."

"Promise," she asked, wide-eyed.

"I am at your service, m'lady."

Allena giggled.

Langward escorted them away, and Trey, familiar with the area, went straight to Bliss's cottage.

"I should at least—"

"Have the sense to know that you are useless to others if you have no strength to heal."

He shoved her cottage door open with his shoulder and walked in. He sat her on her bed, and ordered, "Stay there."

She smiled and nodded.

He shook his head. "Why is it that I think you are only placating me?"

Her smile widened, and she continued nodding.

He hunched down in front of her and grinned. "Move, and I'll strip you bare and remove all your clothes from the cottage so you have no choice but to rest beneath the covers of your bed."

She rested her warm hand on his cheek. "Would you join me?"

His groin tightened, and he could feel himself grow hard. He jumped up and walked to the door, though he stopped, turned, and pointed at her. "When you are well, nothing will stop me from making love to you." And with that he walked out the door though not before grumbling that he was going to get firewood.

Bliss sighed and carefully stretched out on the bed. There was some pain but not as much as when she had lain on the hard ground. She was relieved to be home, safe in her cottage, where she would have no trouble healing herself.

There was peace in her home that she always found comforting, and it seemed even more so now that she was not alone. Not that being alone had bothered her, but knowing Trey would return shortly, build a fire, and look after her made her feel better already.

And, of course, here was where he would make love to her for the first time. The thought tingled her senseless, and she lingered in the pure pleasure of anticipation.

You must heal first.

Leave it to her grandmum's voice to remind her.

Grow strong. You will need strength.

She sensed a warning in her grandmum's voice and wondered over it, though not for long. Her eyes began to flutter shut, and, try as she might to remain alert to her grandmum's advice, she couldn't. Sleep quickly claimed her.

She woke to a delicious scent of something bubbling in the cauldron in the fireplace and an empty cottage. She didn't have to wonder where Trey was . . . she knew. He had gone to find Dolca and talk with her. She hoped he would find the answers he searched for though she sensed he was not meant to know all the answers . . . yet.

Feeling refreshed from her nap, she took the time to heal herself. With quiet and focus, she hoped she'd be healed in no time . . . preferably a few hours.

She chuckled at how eager she was to make love with Trey. But had she given enough thought to the consequences of her decision? Did she realize that to her people, it would bind him more tightly to her than any document could?

Of course, as she had told him, there was always the exchange of a few words that could end their marriage. But it was not as simple as reciting a few words. There had to be meaning behind them; they had to renounce their love for each other. And where at first she had believed it would be no problem, now it was different.

She loved Trey, and she could not in all honesty stand before him and renounce her love for him. It wasn't possible.

She shook her head to clear it. She couldn't think on this now. Now she needed to focus and heal herself. She tried for several minutes and grew frustrated. All she could think about was Trey's joining her in bed tonight and what a mess she was, covered with sweat and dirt.

Careful to ease herself off the bed, Bliss gathered clean garments and a towel, then grabbed her white cloak off the peg by the door and draped it around her. She would heal herself while bathing in the water hole she was so fond of using.

Few used it but her, for they believed it magical and were afraid of its powers. There was a similar thought about her abilities. While her people respected her skills and accepted her, there was also an inkling of fear many harbored, and so that was why her cottage sat removed from the others. It brought her people peace, and she didn't mind the solitude at times.

It had grown colder since their arrival, and with the sky a dull gray, they could very well see a few snow flurries tonight. She hurried along and made her way inside the cave. She was thrilled upon reaching the luminescent pond. She discarded her clothes and boots, grabbed one of the soap chips she always kept stashed in a crevice in one of the large rocks that bordered a section of the pond, and stepped into the water.

She sighed, the water warm and welcoming. She walked farther in and sunk down until the water reached her neck. She would focus on some healing first, then wash herself thoroughly and heal herself some more. Then, if she was feeling well enough, she would swim. She loved to swim here. Her grandmum had taught her when she was young, and it had always helped ease her worries.

She got to work, scrubbing her hair first.

Trey sat across the table from Dolca in a small cottage. He was impressed with the woman. Though older with signs of age, she appeared young and vibrant, her bright green eyes more like those of a young, inquisitive lassie. Petite and slim though regal in stature, she gave more the appearance of nobility than peasant. And her mass of pure white curls refused to stay contained on top of her head, several stubborn ones falling loose around her face and neck.

She had graciously welcomed him when he had knocked on her door and introduced himself. She had invited him to join her for a hot brew, and he eagerly accepted, anxious to speak with her.

He had asked as to her health, not wanting to bother her if she wasn't feeling well, but she had assured him she was recovering nicely and feeling quite fit.

She asked with tender concern about Bliss, and Trey explained what had happened and how Bliss was at this moment healing herself.

"She'll go to the cave," Dolca said. "The water is good for her there and will aid in her healing."

"The cave?"

Dolca explained to him where it was and how it was strictly for Bliss's use though sometimes she would take people there and let them make use of it. "A good place for her to be now," Dolca said.

Trey nodded, glad he had learned of it.

"You have many questions for me," she said with a smile. "But I am not sure if I have the answers you seek."

Trey's first question was obvious. "You are Mercy's grandmother?"

She smiled and nodded. "I see that Bliss has told you. She realizes it is time for the truth."

"What is the truth?"

"While I would love to share it with you, I believe it is for my granddaughter to hear first."

"I can understand that," Trey said, "but perhaps there is a question in regard to the true king that you can answer now."

"I will do my best."

"Why would your daughter, Mercy's mother, have been in possession of a scrap of hide that pertains to the true king?"

Dolca didn't answer directly. She seemed to pause in thought before she finally spoke. "The truth is best left for those who need to know it."

"You know more about the true king than you share," he said, his own revelation surprising him. "How?"

"It is safer for the true king that I do not answer that."

Though bursting with questions and curiosity, Trey knew that the older woman would say no more, and while he wished she would, he understood that she did so to protect the true king. And he could not argue with that.

"I think it is time I met my granddaughter," Dolca said with a smile. "May I accompany you and Bliss when you return home?"

"I would be honored to have you travel with us."

"It will be good to see Mara again."

"You know my mum?" Trey asked.

"We are old friends. She visits me from time to time."

That bit of news surprised him and for some reason nagged at him, as if somehow it should connect something, but he didn't know what. Though it did bring a question to mind, and so he asked, "Does my mum know that Mercy is your granddaughter?"

"She knew only that I had a granddaughter."

"You've never met Mercy?"

"Briefly, when she and Duncan happened by my home one day," she said. "I knew who she was right away. She resembles her mother though I also saw some of her father in her."

"But you said nothing?"

She shook her head, and her face saddened. "It wasn't time yet." She reached out and rested her slim hand on his arm. "I know you are anxious to hear more, but let it be for now. As I've advised, it is best for the true king."

Trey nodded. He had been taught the importance of keeping information private until the time was right, and so he would honor her request no matter how curious he was.

"We have spent much time conversing. Surely, Bliss must wonder where you are?" Dolca said.

He liked how wisely she had brought their time together to an end, by giving him a strong reason to leave.

He stood. "Thank you for your gracious hospitality, and we shall talk again."

Dolca gave him a nod, and he left.

His thoughts were heavy as he walked to Bliss's cottage. While he didn't learn as much as he would have liked to, he had learned something. His mum knew Dolca. Why that surprised him, he couldn't say. She had many friends, and sometimes would be gone a few days visiting with them. But for some reason the knowledge nagged at him.

It hit him just as his hand settled on the door latch. Just because Dolca had never met her granddaughter didn't mean that her daughter hadn't visited. And if his mum visited Dolca . . .

He shook his head. How could he think that his mum would be the one who had stolen the scrap of hide that was kept hidden in the solar and passed it on to Mercy's mum? It was a crazy thought that made no sense, yet he knew that it would continue to nag at him.

He entered the cottage, hoping that Bliss had woken. He was eager to see how she was feeling and to talk with her.

The cottage was empty, and, in a heartbeat, a chill of fear raced through him. Then he recalled what Dolca had told him about the cave and the directions. He smiled and left the cottage, thinking he could use a good swim.

He found the place easily enough and made his way to the belly of the cave though he stopped as soon as he saw Bliss. She stood waist high in the water, her hands stretched upward, her breast perfectly round, the nipples hard, and a slight bruise marring the creamy flesh just above her breasts.

His fists clenched, recalling how she had gotten the bruise, but the image soon vanished when she brought her arms down, her hands going to her mouth as in prayer, her eyes closing as she then pressed her hands to the bruise and healed herself.

Quietly as possible so as not to disturb her, but with every intention of joining her, he made his way to where she had discarded her clothes. His garments soon joined hers.

He stood completely naked at the water's edge. He wanted to join her, but he didn't wish to disturb her healing. He wanted her healed, and right now, since he didn't want to wait another minute to make love to her. He had waited long enough as it was, and this secluded cave was the perfect setting to consummate their vows.

"You are welcome to join me," she said, her eyes opening and her arms spread in invitation.

He didn't hesitate. He walked in and dunked himself to rid himself of some of the dirt before he reached her. His body glistened along with his long auburn hair as he rose out of the water and went straight to her.

His hand went directly to the bruise that looked to have faded even more than when he had seen it from a distance. He rested his hand upon it ever so gently. "Does it still pain you?"

"It is healing fast, and I have no doubt it will be gone by morning."

He frowned, not wanting to touch her until she was well, but aching to do so anyway.

She settled his dilemma, saying, "But the pain is mostly gone, a twinge now and then. I am well enough to resume my work."

He smiled and slipped an arm lightly around her waist before kissing her, a tender kiss that tempted. "Well enough for me to make love to you?" he asked, and kissed her again before she could answer though he truly didn't expect a response.

She responded, though not with words, her

arms going around his neck and her body pressing against his.

Damn, if she didn't feel good naked against him, and damn if he didn't like the feel of her hard nipples poking at his chest. And damn if he didn't want to feel more. His hand ran down over her round backside, and he eased her closer to him, settling her right against his hardness.

"You and I were meant to be," he whispered in her ear.

"Aye," she murmured. "Fate decreed it."

"No," he said firmly, and kissed along the column of her neck and smiling when he felt gooseflesh rise over her backside. "It wasn't fate." He moved to tease her nipple with his tongue but only for a moment. He brought his lips to hers once again and after a quick kiss, he took hold of her chin, and said, "It was love that brought us together. I love you, dear wife, and I intend to keep you."

Chapter 19

Bliss smiled and was about to tell him the same when a vision hit her.

Leora screamed frantically for Trey. "Bring him to me. Hurry and bring him home." Her screams turned to pleas until she sunk to her knees, tears streaming down her face.

It was difficult not to share in the woman's suffering, and even though the vision was brief, the pain lingered though something about it troubled her. Bliss's eyes finally fluttered open, and she was never so grateful to see Trey and realize that she was in the safety of his arms.

He had carried her closer to the water's edge though he had kept them partially submerged as he cradled her in his arms.

"Are you all right?" he asked anxiously, and held her even tighter against him.

"Being in your arms always makes everything all right though I am sorry."

"Why?"

"My vision intruded upon a very special moment for us."

"Through no fault of yours," he said. "Do you wish to talk about your vision?"

Now was not the time to discuss Leora's begging for Trey to come home. She shook her head. "Not now."

"Is there some reason you don't wish to discuss certain visions with me?" he asked. "Could they possibly have something to do with me? Something you don't want me to know?"

She would much prefer to discuss their love for each other though it would be much wiser and made more sense to discuss Leora now, before things turned intimate between them.

"I believe Leora is coming to me in visions."

His whole body grew taut, and Bliss thought it best to ease herself out of his arms. She sunk lower in the water, suddenly feeling more vulnerable than naked in front of him, and casually moved to deeper water.

He followed, and she was glad she could sense that he did so thinking she needed the cover of the warm water to chase away her sudden chill. She didn't want him to think that she was pulling away from him . . . or was she? Had the vision reminded her that there were things Trey still needed to settle?

"What does she want from you?" he asked.

She truly didn't want to tell him that Leora wants his help, wants him to return to her. It would only add to the guilt he already felt over her death. But she couldn't lie to him, either.

"It's as if she searches for you, calling out your name."

"She should haunt *me,* not you. I was the one who failed her."

"I don't get the sense that she feels you failed her."

"Then why torment you?" he asked.

Bliss shook her head. "It is she who is tormented though I'm not sure why. I wish I could make sense of it, but I can't."

"And so she continues to come to you."

"It is odd that she comes to me in visions," Bliss said. "The dead have always come to me in dreams, not visions. My visions are usually of things to come."

"Have you seen me helping Leora?"

Bliss hesitated, not wanting to tell him but having no choice. "I have seen her run into your arms."

"That would take a miracle, or perhaps I die and reunite with her."

"Do not speak such nonsense," Bliss snapped. "I have not seen your death."

"Perhaps you aren't meant to."

"Do you wish to die and be reunited with her?"

Trey reached beneath the water and slipped his arm around her waist as he moved closer to her. "At one time, aye, I would have. Now?" He shook his head slowly and gave her lips a gentle kiss. "I have found love, not merely again, but a far stronger love than I even knew existed. And I'm not giving it up."

Her arms went around his neck, and she kissed him, not gently but with an aching demand. When it ended, she went to speak but Trey pressed a finger to her lips.

"The only thing I want to hear you say is, 'it's time we make love.'"

She moved his finger away, and, with a teasing grin, said, "I need to tell you?"

He gave her a wicked smile and lowered his mouth to hers.

It was a kiss meant not simply to spark passion but to ignite a fire that would take hours to finish burning.

Their mouths fed hungrily on each other, the thirst so desperate it was not easy to quench. And while they tried to fill themselves, their hands began to explore. Her nipples hardened even more to his teasing touch, and he flared even larger when her hand settled on him and began to stroke.

They were not shy in their actions, each feeling familiar with the other. And though it was their first time together, it didn't feel that way. It felt as if they were long-lost lovers finally reuniting.

Bliss relished the feel of him, so thick and large in her hand, and was disappointed when he brushed her hand away.

"Your touch makes me want to explode, and I much prefer to explore first." He scooped her up then and carried her out of the water.

He stood her on her feet for only a moment and went to retrieve his cloak. He quickly spread it out near the water's edge and reached for her hand to ease her down before he stretched out beside her.

"I want to know every inch of you." And his mouth and hands did as they itched to do . . . explore.

She shivered at the gentleness of his touch and the strength of his taste. His lips nipped with a fierce love, and she had no doubt that he was laying claim to her. She belonged to him, and he belonged to her, and that knowledge fired the passion already racing through her.

He lavished kisses over every part of her, and just when she thought him finished, he found a new spot to explore intimately.

His tongue did absolutely wicked things to her and made her move with pleasure against his every touch and taste. It was as if he commanded her body, and she didn't at all mind surrendering to his tantalizing touch.

He knew exactly where to kiss, where to touch, where to linger. And when he finally slipped over her and into her, she wanted to scream with joy at the feel of him burrowing deep inside her.

"I am not hurting you, am I?" he stopped to ask.

"Aye, you are," she whispered.

He went to pull away.

She held tight to his arms. "You halted the exquisite pleasure you were bringing me by stopping."

He rested his brow to hers. "I would never hurt you."

An overwhelming sense of sorrow washed over her, and tears suddenly filled her eyes and spilled down her cheeks.

"What's wrong?" he demanded, and tried to move off her.

"No!" she cried. "Love me. Love me now."

He hesitated.

"Please, Trey, I love you."

He brought his lips to hers and, before he kissed her, he said, "And I love you."

They moved slowly at first, both in no hurry, both lingering in the moment that would seal their fate forever. Then their bodies began to require more, and they obliged, their tempo turning stronger, more demanding.

Bliss raised her legs and wrapped them around him and groaned as his rapid, strong thrusts grew even stronger.

She held tighter to the muscles that contorted in his arms, braced on either side of her, when, suddenly she felt propelled to the edge of some unknown precipice. Soon she would take that step, had to take that step, couldn't stop herself, and . . .

She screamed as she plunged into pleasure so exquisite that she never wanted to stop falling. She felt the exact moment that Trey joined her, and she tightened around him, wanting to fall along with him . . . and she did.

Her body tingled all over with the most exquisite sensation, and all she wanted to do was linger in every last tingle until there were no more.

"Are you all right?"

Bliss opened her eyes to see Trey braced over her, and she smiled, glad he hadn't slipped out of her yet and not wanting him to.

She smiled. "I have never felt better."

"Your tears . . . I have never—"

She grinned.

He shook his head. "This is not the moment I should be thinking such a thing."

"But you couldn't help it, for no women you have made love to have ever cried with joy."

"Coupled with, not made love," he quickly corrected as he moved to ease off her.

"Must you leave me? I love the feel of you inside me."

He smiled and kissed her. "I'll return soon enough." He slipped off her to rest alongside her.

She turned on her side. "You promised me the whole night."

"And I will keep my word," he said, and reached out to tuck her against his chest.

She rested her head there and listened to the rapid beating of his heart. He had yet to calm from their lovemaking, but, then, neither had she—her heart was continued to beat wildly.

"You do realize what this means," Trey said after a few moments.

"What?"

"That our marriage vows are sealed and cannot be broken. You are my wife and will remain my wife."

"Are you sure that is what you wish?"

"Like your knowing that you never doubt, this is my knowing that holds no doubt," Trey said, "and what of you? Do you wish to remain my wife?"

She smiled and traced circles on his chest. "I believe our hearts beat as one, and one cannot survive without the other. That is love, and I love you, so the only true answer would be . . . aye, I wish to remain your wife."

He lifted her, and she laughed with joy as he tugged her to lie across him.

A pain suddenly struck her that had her gasping for breath.

"Bliss," Trey cried out, fear tugging at him.

She pointed to the water and he had her up in his arms in an instant and hurried to submerge them both.

The warm water worked its magic, relieving the pain, and Bliss grew annoyed with herself. "I am a fool," she said.

"You are not," Trey argued. "If anyone is a fool, it is me for not considering your injury."

"I am healing just fine."

He scrunched his brow.

"I am," she insisted. "I need only to perform several healings close to one another, and I will be fine."

"I distracted you, so it is my fault, and I will not touch you again tonight."

Her eyes turned wide. "You can't mean that. You gave me your word."

"I caused you pain."

"You will cause me grievous pain if you do not keep your promise," she said, her eyes shooting daggers at him as her temper flared.

He looked about to laugh.

"Do not dare make fun of what I say. I have looked forward to this time with you, and I will not have the memory spoiled because I suffer a twinge of pain now and again."

"It was no twinge"—he stopped abruptly—"you looked forward to making love with me?"

"You did not realize that?" she asked, surprised. "I thought it apparent."

"That we were attracted to each other was definitely apparent, but that you actually looked forward to making love with me?" He grinned. "I but hoped."

She gave him a playful poke in the chest. "You tease me. You knew."

"Perhaps, though it was nice to hear it, to know that I was in your thoughts as much as you were in mine."

"That, I'm afraid, will only escalate. The closer we grow, the more easily it is for me to know your thoughts."

"I'm finding the same," he said.

"What, then, am I thinking," she challenged with a smile.

He nipped playfully along her bottom lip before kissing her senseless.

"Exactly what I was thinking," she said after her senses returned.

His hand cupped her breast, his thumb teasing the nipple hard. "And now you want me to make love to you again."

Her smile grew, then suddenly vanished. "You *aren't* thinking of making love with me."

"Not until you do another healing on yourself," he ordered. "And believe me when I say I'm showing remarkable restraint, for right now I want nothing more than to have you wrap your legs around my waist so that I can plunge into you and endlessly pleasure us both."

The image sent a tingle racing through her and an ache between her legs.

Trey shook his head. "Damn if I can't feel your

passion racing through me." He released her suddenly and put a bit of distance between them. "Be done with your healing," he snapped. "My need for you grows, and I have not the patience to wait."

The knowledge that he wanted her so badly that he had to walk away from her to stop himself from having her fueled her own passion beyond reason.

"Damn," he muttered again, and pointed at her. "Heal yourself now."

The intense passion rising between them wouldn't allow her to focus, and she knew it would be impossible to do any healing until . . .

"I can't," she said. "I can focus on nothing but my aching need for you."

He clenched a fist and pounded the water, sending it shooting up to splash his chest and face. "I will not see you suffer more pain." He turned to make his way to shore.

"Your absence will not matter. This ache, this longing to have you deep inside me needs to be satisfied so that my mind is clear enough to focus on healing."

He seemed to fight himself for a moment, his fist remaining clenched. And then he moved so rapidly that it startled Bliss, and she jumped, causing a pain to hit her and making her cringe.

She thought he would stop and keep his distance, but he didn't. His hands were suddenly at her waist, lifting her, and she instinctively wrapped her legs around his waist, her arms going around his neck.

"When this is done—"

"You can watch me heal myself," she said, and tried to kiss him though he didn't give her a chance.

He lifted her and, with a swift plunge, buried himself deep inside her.

She let out a gasp, and he captured it with a hungry kiss. She held on as he took charge, his body setting a frantic tempo and his hands at her waist helping her match it. The kiss ended as their breathing turned rapid, and she knew it wouldn't be long before they both exploded with pleasure.

She heard the groan building in Trey and felt herself once again near the edge, only this time, as the pleasurable fury erupted, she was propelled upward to explode over and over again.

They rested brow to brow, their breathing labored, their hearts pounding, and the last of their climaxes rippling through them.

"I'll never get enough of you," Trey said breathlessly.

"Good, for I'll never stop wanting you."

"Watch your words, or you'll turn me hard again," he warned. "And it is time to heal yourself."

"Then you'll grow hard for me again?" she asked.

He answered with a sputter of laughter. "I'm always hard for you."

"And I'm always wet for you."

He groaned and shook his head. "Enough." He eased her off him. "Heal yourself, then we will—"

"Make love again?"

He grinned. "All night as promised."

"I cannot wait," she said with the eagerness of one who had just been given a gift.

"I'd say be quick, but I want you healed, for what I have in mind will take stamina."

"You intrigue me."

"I will do more than that," he said, walking away from her. "I will teach you the many ways there are to make love."

Chapter 20

Trey woke in the cabin before Bliss the next morning and smiled, content for the first time in what seemed like forever. It was almost like waking from a bad dream that had been difficult to escape, and the thought made him realize how Bliss must feel when trapped in a dream or vision.

He wrapped himself more tightly around her warm, naked body and knew there wasn't anything he wouldn't do to protect her and keep her safe.

He had thought the same of Leora; to keep her safe, let no harm come to her, and he had failed horribly. He didn't want to fail Bliss. He didn't want to lose her as he had Leora. But as Bliss had so often reminded him, fate made plans that we didn't always like, and we certainly didn't understand.

What he did understand was that he could finally accept that Leora was gone and that it wasn't wrong of him to love again. And that's what Bliss and he had done all night . . . loved. It had surprised him to realize that making love with Bliss was far more satisfying than doing so with any woman he had ever been with, even Leora.

It was almost as if they were made for each other, they fit so well together.

He smiled again, pleased that guilt did not jab at him. It had been his constant companion for so long that he expected it to be with him forever. He was glad guilt had left him. He had let it eat away at him long enough. And he hoped that by releasing the past, he would also release Leora and that she would no longer haunt Bliss's visions.

She stirred in his arms, turning to cuddle chest to chest, and he welcomed the pleasurable connection. He settled around her once more, wishing they could stay here, at least for a while, and simply enjoy each other. But he knew that wasn't possible; he needed to get home.

Her arm slipped over his waist. She reached out to him in sleep, not doubting he'd be there beside her. They had grown accustomed to each other in a short time. Though what did time matter when it came to love?

One look, one touch, and love, or perhaps fate, took charge. Nothing you did afterwards mattered, for your fate was sealed. He grinned. It seemed that perhaps fate was wise in her ways, and he shouldn't argue or be angry with her. She had, after all, given him Bliss.

His grin grew when he felt the first nibble at his throat.

"You taste good," she whispered.

"So it would seem since you feasted on me last night."

She giggled. "I did make a glutton of myself, but it is your fault for being so tasty."

"Feast to your heart's content, wife, though"—he eased her on her back, spreading himself over her— "Right now I have a need to fill you."

"Good, for I feel empty without you inside me."

He was already hard, her warm body and teasing nibbles having thickened him. But her words hardened him even more. And when he reached down to stroke her, his hand met moisture. She was ready for him, and he hadn't even touched her. She seemed to always be ready for him, and that made him grow all the more excited.

He kissed her then while his thumb teased her nub, and her body moved eagerly beneath him. He didn't wait, he couldn't, and he knew that neither could she. He entered her swiftly and kept a hard, wild pace. It didn't take long for Bliss to reach climax, and it pleased him, for he had learned last night that he could easily bring Bliss to multiple climaxes, and the discovery had thrilled him. Her first climax was often the beginning of stronger ones to come, which made his own pleasure all the more satisfying.

He climaxed along with her second one, and soon after they lay flat on their backs, catching their breaths.

"Making love is definitely a benefit of marriage," she said when her breath no longer labored.

He laughed. "That depends on whom you wed. Not all husbands and wives are compatible."

She turned on her side to face him and sighed. "How sad for them. They will never know the wonder of true love."

He stroked her face and, for a moment, was

speechless. All he could think about was how lucky he was to have Bliss as his wife. "I am a happy man," he said, and ran his thumb over her lips, which were still plump from his kisses.

She nibbled at his thumb before answering, "And you continually make me a happy woman."

"And I will keep you happy for years and years to come." He punctuated each word with a kiss.

Their stomachs grumbled simultaneously, and they laughed. They were soon out of bed, dressed, and enjoying a breakfast of warm bread and honey. Trey startled when a rap sounded at the door though it had not disturbed Bliss. And why would it? People probably sought her help throughout the day.

She bid the person enter, and Trey moved his sword closer to his side just in case though he needn't have worried. That was until he heard what the young Pict Langward had to tell them upon entering.

"A troop of the king's soldiers has been seen on the borders of Pict and MacAlpin lands."

Trey stood, anxious to find out if Langward knew more, when he turned and looked to Bliss. She could possibly know more than the young Pict. He didn't have to say a word; she knew his thoughts.

"They go to join the others," Bliss said. "And hope to collect more men along the way."

Langward shook his head. "I don't understand why they would take men who do not wish to fight for them."

"So they cannot fight for the true king," Trey

said, "thus leaving fewer men to take up arms against King Kenneth." He looked again to his wife. "They presently pose no threat to my home?"

Bliss shook her head. "It is the men and lads in the outlying farms who need to worry."

"Once my brothers received my message about the troop buildup, they would have sent word to all the farming families to seek protection at the keep. Has Roan returned yet?" he asked of Langward.

"Not yet though we have sent men to the border to keep a watch. There is growing concern that the soldiers may attack Picts."

"They have never disturbed you before," Trey said. "Why would you worry now?"

Langward glanced to Bliss, as if she had the answer.

"Times are changing. No more will the Picts live separately from others. They will join force with the true king, and in the ensuing years, both people will blend until they are finally one. The Pict blood forever part of Scotland."

Another rap at the door had them all turning and Bliss bidding entrance.

It was Dolca, and before anyone could offer a greeting, she said, "The search party returns with the injured farmers, and some are in need of healing."

Bliss grabbed her white cloak from the peg, and Trey hooked the belt that housed his sword around his waist and followed Bliss out the door, Langward on their heels.

There was a bit of chaos when Mary spotted Thomas on the carrier and, with tears of joy, went running to her husband, with Allena in her arms.

Trey watched as Bliss made her way to Thomas, then stopped abruptly, turned, and grabbed hold of his arm. "Thomas continues to heal, but two Picts were injured defending the farmers against the king's soldiers."

She left his side so quickly that he grew dizzy. He stood for a moment, not happy with what he had just heard. It gave credence to why the Picts would side with the MacAlpins and proof that what Bliss had seen was true.

Trey took a moment to watch how Mary and Thomas rejoiced in their reunion. They hugged and kissed, and Thomas reached out for Allena, who had tears streaming down her cheeks. Trey only hoped that Deryn fared as well, that Albert and Teresa had managed to avoid the soldiers, keep Philip and Deryn safe, and be well on their way to arriving at the keep. And no doubt Mary and Thomas wished the same.

Trey conversed with several of the Pict warriors in regard to Roan's return. They were confident that Roan would have no trouble avoiding the soldiers and would arrive soon enough. Trey needed to know that his brothers had been made aware of the buildup of the king's troops in the region. If not? He had to return home immediately and inform his brothers of the news.

He would give Roan today to return. If he didn't, then Trey would need to leave for home at sunrise. He didn't want to, and he certainly didn't want to leave Bliss behind, but it would be dangerous to take her with him. Here, at home with the Picts, she would be far better protected than traveling alone with him.

The question was how did he prevent her from knowing that he might well need to leave her behind? He believed, actually he knew, that she would never agree to his decision. She would insist on going with him, and he refused to place her in such danger.

He watched from a distance as she worked on healing two Picts who had sustained injuries from their encounter with the soldiers. He worried that she had not fully healed herself, but then she had to have been healed sufficiently or she never would have been able to engage in such heated lovemaking as they had last night after they returned to her cabin.

Damn, but he loved her.

The thought hit him hard, like a punch to the gut. It stunned him to realize the depths of his love for her. He had convinced himself that he would never love again, or at least not as strongly as he had loved Leora. But here he was, madly in love with Bliss.

He saw her look up at him, and she immediately stopped what she was doing, stood, and hurried to his side.

"Do not even think of leaving me behind, for I will follow you. Nothing will keep me from being by your side," she said.

He snatched her around the waist and planted her against his hard body, then kissed her with such intensity that no one could doubt how much he loved her. When he released her, he saw that all around them stared in silence.

"I love my wife," he shouted for all to hear.

A cheer went up, along with grins and nods and shouts of wishes for a long life and many children.

"You have sealed our fate," she whispered.

"Nay, you did that the day you claimed me for your husband." He kissed her again.

More shouts and cheers rang out, and the somber mood that had arrived with the injured men changed quickly to one of joy.

"I will return home with you," she said.

"Only if it is safe," he insisted.

"Safe or not, I remain by your side."

"Don't argue with your husband."

"Don't argue with one who knows."

"What do you know?" he asked.

"More than you," she said, and gave him a quick kiss before hurrying to return and tend the injured men.

He stood staring after her and wondered what she knew. And couldn't help but think over her words.

Safe or not, I remain by your side.

Would he not be able to keep her safe? Would he again fail a woman he loved?

He had no ability to see the future, but he knew one thing. He would protect Bliss with his life and gladly give it to keep her safe.

Chapter 21

Bliss grew teary-eyed when she saw Thomas reunited with his wife and daughter. The three hugged, the little girl refusing to unwrap her arms from around her father's neck, as if by holding on to him, she'd keep him from ever leaving again.

She watched Trey approach them and knew he was reassuring them that Deryn, their brave little girl, was all right and that they would be reunited with her soon. He made his way through all the injured men, stopping and talking with each one and offering what comfort and reassurance he could.

Her people were impressed with him and happy for her. Well-wishes continued to come to her as she continued to heal the men. And though she was happy—how could she not be with Trey's boisterous declaration of love—something troubled her. She couldn't quite tell what it was; but something wasn't right.

She wished she could see what it was that nagged at her; but no visions came, nor dreams; she had only her senses to rely on. And they were strong enough for her to be cautious. Whatever it was, she didn't feel it would be long before it made itself known.

Time wore on as the group settled and fed. She had little time to sneak a peek at Trey now and again, he being just as busy. That all changed as soon as Roan arrived. They both left what they were doing and immediately went to him.

He looked worn and apprehensive, and so Bliss suggested they retreat to her cottage to talk. Silence accompanied them, and not a word was spoken until Bliss had set food and drink in front of Roan, and she joined both men at the table.

"It doesn't look good," Roan said with a shake of his head. "It is one thing for King Kenneth to dare travel across MacAlpin land, but to travel the Pict border in such force?" He shook his head again. "It is a sign that tells me that our truce with the present king is fast coming to an end."

"My brothers—"

"Are well aware of what is going on," Roan assured him. "Duncan and Reeve had already sent scouts out and knew of the soldiers' movements though they were surprised of the news I brought. And they eagerly await your return."

"Do you know if a couple, Albert and Teresa, traveling with two children, Philip and Deryn, have reached the safety of the MacAlpin village yet?" Bliss asked.

Roan nodded. "Aye, they were lucky and passed the troop of soldiers without being seen. They were not far from the village when I met up with them. By now, they should be safe."

Bliss was glad he had confirmed what she had already sensed.

Roan turned his attention to Trey. "What have you learned of this sudden buildup of the king's soldiers?"

Trey detailed what he had found out.

"You must get this information to your brothers immediately," Roan said.

"I plan to leave tomorrow at first light."

"*We* plan to leave tomorrow," Bliss corrected.

"If it were any other woman, I would advise against it," Roan said, "but with your powers, you would prove an asset to Trey."

"Dolca will be traveling with us," Bliss said, prepared for objections.

"Absolutely not," Trey said. "She still recovers from her illness and will slow us down."

"Trey is right," Roan agreed. "She can join you later."

"Unfortunately, she can't," Bliss said. "It is imperative that she go with us."

Both men stared at her, and she knew their thoughts. Did they question her or accept the wisdom of her ways?

"There is no other way?" Trey asked.

"I'm afraid not. It is best for her and the true king that she is kept safe on MacAlpin land."

"I will go with you," Roan said. "You may need help."

"You have just returned home," Bliss protested, though she knew he was right. It would be good for him to accompany them.

"You warned this day would come," Roan said.

"You told us that we would need to choose if we were to survive. The MacAlpins have proven themselves good friends, and so the Picts will join forces with them and help the true king take his throne."

"My brothers will be pleased to hear that," Trey said.

They spoke a while longer, then Roan left. He needed to make preparations for tomorrow and get some rest.

Bliss slipped into her husband's arms, laying her head on his chest. "I wish we could stay here and forget that anything exists except us."

His arms tightened around her, and she welcomed his firm embrace. If only life were simpler and they could remain as they were, without worry or fear. But it was not meant to be, and she wasn't sure if it ever would be.

"There will come a time for us," Trey said.

"Not before there is more bloodshed and suffering." That she knew for certain.

"Peace will eventually prevail."

Bliss didn't respond. That troubling feeling nagged at her again and caused her concern. Why couldn't she see what troubled her? Was it so disheartening that fate would not let her see it? Which meant . . . there was nothing she could do about it?

It was in fate's hands, and no amount of knowing would change it.

The realization worried her all the more, for she knew without a doubt that it concerned her and Trey. And she feared she might not like the outcome.

"You tremble," he said, stroking her back. "What disturbs you?"

At least she could be honest. "I do not know. I only know that it awaits us both."

"Good," he said. "Then we face it together."

"I never thought of it that way," she said, smiling up at him.

"We are husband and wife and will face everything together."

She had no response. The only thing she thought to do was . . . kiss him.

It was no quick, gentle kiss, but rather one filled with love and passion, and he responded in kind. They lingered in the kiss and in each other's arms. She ached for more and thought of tugging him toward the bed to let him know, but there was work to be done, and she couldn't be selfish.

Trey on the other hand . . .

"I know what's on your mind," he said, and returned to kissing her before she could respond.

When, finally, she got the chance, she said, "There is no time."

"There is always time," he said, and grinned, "for a quick one."

She grabbed his hand and pulled him to the bed, but once there, he scooped her up and plopped her down on her back, then dropped over her, his hands braced on either side of her.

Their hands fumbled as they both rushed out to touch the other, and they laughed at their eager, though bumbling, attempts.

"Leave this to me," he said, and took charge.

While it was a quick joining, it was no less satisfying. Actually, the haste heightened her excitement, and she burst with pleasure as soon as Trey entered her and happily exploded with passion again, along with him, a few minutes later.

They both sighed with contentment, and, as much as they would have loved to remain as they were, they knew that duty called, and no sooner than they stood and straightened their clothes, a knock sounded at the door.

They grinned, kissed, and went to the door.

The injured men were upset to learn that Bliss would be leaving, but not so Mary. She was pleased to know that Bliss would be meeting with Deryn and letting her know that the family was together and would reunite with her soon.

Bliss met with Dolca while Trey spoke once again with Roan. The older woman was thrilled to learn that they would be leaving in the morning.

"I am eager to meet with my granddaughter. There is so much to tell her."

Bliss grinned. "I just realized that Trey forgot to tell you something that I believe will thrill you even more."

Dolca's eyes turned wide.

"You will not only meet your granddaughter but your great-grandson and -granddaughter as well."

Tears pooled in her aged eyes, though they sparkled with delight. "Twins. I am so blessed."

"But there is one other you are eager to meet, is there not?"

Dolca nodded. "I have kept the secret for many

years, fearing I would never live to see it made known and now . . ." She wiped at the few tears that fell.

Bliss rested her hand on the woman's arm. "You must carry your secret a while longer before it can be revealed."

Dolca nodded. "In some ways it has been burdensome, and in others I have not felt its weight. But I am glad the end draws near, for it has cost so many so very dearly."

"Are you sure you feel well enough for the journey?" Bliss asked, sensing the woman's weariness.

"You feel the exhaustion of these many years on me, but my strength has never waned. I will see this done, as it should be."

"I admire your courage."

"Your courage far surpasses mine," Dolca said. "You suffer the burden of many while I only a few. And where mine has an end, yours goes on forever. You are indeed heroic."

Bliss never thought of herself as brave. It took no courage to be who she was, who she had always been. She was truly no different from any of her people though she doubted any of them could understand that.

Trey did.

She knew he made an effort not to treat her as others did, and it made her love him all the more. He tried not to seek endless answers from her, and he didn't pursue issues when she made it clear that was all she had to say on a matter. He respected her and did not fear her like most did, though they claimed otherwise.

"You love Trey," Dolca said.

Bliss smiled and nodded. "Very much."

"But something troubles you."

While her abilities allowed her to sense things, she realized that age brought with it certain intuitiveness.

"My ears listen well while my mouth remains firmly shut," Dolca said with a laugh.

"As your secret has proven," Bliss said, and gave a sigh. "Unfortunately, I'm not sure what burdens me, and I think that is what disturbs me the most."

"Give it to fate and let it be."

"You give much the same advice that I do."

"My wisdom comes with age; yours has always been."

Bliss smiled. "You are so like my grandmum, teaching and reminding when I need it."

"Hester taught you well, I but remind now and again." A tear caught in the corner of Dolca's eye. "I miss your grandmum. She was a good friend to me."

"I miss her terribly, and though no one can replace her, you have filled a great void in my life, and I am grateful."

They hugged and talked and hugged again, their bond forever strong. Bliss advised Dolca to get a good night's sleep, for her mettle would be tested once she reached the MacAlpin keep.

Dusk was fading fast as Bliss approached her cottage, and she stopped suddenly as she sensed something so strongly that it startled her. She and Trey would not continue on with Roan and Dolca to MacAlpin village. Their arrival would be delayed, but why?

No answer came, but at least she had been warned.

She entered her cottage, disappointed not to find Trey there, and she shook her head. She had never felt disappointment upon returning home to an empty cottage. Actually, she had enjoyed the solitude, the time simply to be herself, no demands being made of her.

Perhaps that was why, while she wanted to find a man to love and spend her life with, she had hesitated. Could she really share her cottage with someone? Always having someone underfoot?

She laughed. If she had ever known love, she would never have thought of someone's being underfoot. But still, there were times she needed her aloneness, needed to recuperate from difficult healings. That was when she most sought the solitude of her cottage.

The thought rushed at her, and she was surprised that she had not considered it before though perhaps she hadn't wanted to.

Trey would expect to live with his family on MacAlpin land, and she expected to remain with her people on Pict land. Neither of them had mentioned it, but a wife was expected to follow her husband. Though Bliss had made friends with Mercy and Tara and loved visiting with them, she still looked forward to going home.

The idea of leaving her home, her people, disturbed her, and she wasn't sure what to do about it. After giving it too much thought, she decided, as always, that fate would show her what was best.

A faint rap sounded at the door, and Bliss wasn't surprised to see one of her people there offering her fresh-baked bread. Another villager arrived a few minutes later with a cauldron of stew. It never failed that when she was gone for a day or more, her fellow Picts would arrive with food for her. It was their way of seeing to her care, so that she would be there for them when they needed her.

Again the question haunted her. How could she leave them? They were her people and depended on her. Fate had better hurry and show her an answer.

"What's wrong?"

Startled, Bliss turned from where she stood by the fireplace to find Trey standing not far from her. She had been so engrossed in her concerns that she hadn't heard him enter. His unexpected arrival reminded her of another reason she was so comfortable in her home. She never worried about anyone's entering without permission—everyone respected her privacy. Could she expect the same at the MacAlpin keep, where it seemed no one had time to themselves?

His arm went around her waist though he didn't tug her up against him as usual. "Something troubles you, tell me."

It wasn't a command, but more of an urging, as if he wished to share in her dilemma. Did she discuss this with him now or wait? There was the possibility that it wouldn't need discussing, that they were not meant to live their lives together.

The thought worried her more than the possibility of leaving her home. It made her realize that when the time came, the problem would be solved, and getting distressed over it now did no good.

"I have no doubt that you can settle my dilemma for me," she said.

"Tell me what it is, and it will worry you no more."

"I could not decide if we should enjoy the evening meal or feast on each other first."

Trey grinned, his actions answering for him. He gave her a kiss that was meant to stir both their passions, and stir them he did, Bliss tingling all over and growing wet with anticipation. Then he scooped her up into his arms and carried her to the bed.

Chapter 22

Morning came too fast for Trey and Bliss. While they had made love once before supper and another time after supper, it was the length of time they had talked while in bed that had prevented sleep. And he had been sorry when they had fallen asleep, for he couldn't recall a more enjoyable time. Bliss and he had talked about anything and everything. In that few short hours, they had learned much about each other, and he felt all the closer to her and fell all the more in love with her.

It was the moment that she had confided in him about a fear she had since she was young that he realized just how much she trusted him. And he swore to himself at that moment that he would never betray her trust.

She had claimed her fear nonsensical, foolish, but it was more foolish not to pay heed to the fear, for then it could easily conquer you. Bliss had not allowed her fear to stop her, though it reared its head now and again. She feared being in a dark place and never being able to escape. She had tried to make sense of it through the years, thinking perhaps it was something that was yet to happen to her though she hadn't sensed it as such, and so she had found no peace from it.

He had wrapped her in his arms and told her that he'd never let darkness get to her; he'd shield her from it forever.

Trey tucked her closer against him and kissed her awake. They needed to be up and ready to leave at first light. Trey could always sense when sunrise was close, and they didn't have much time.

She turned in his arms and cuddled against him. "You are so warm and comfortable. I could stay like this with you forever."

"You are staying with me forever," he said, as if issuing an edict. "Unfortunately, the sun will soon rise, and we need to be ready."

Reluctantly, she moved away from him and stretched herself awake. Trey knew that if they continued to remain in bed naked, they would not be leaving at sunrise, so he too reluctantly hastened out of bed and dressed.

Bliss chuckled. "Don't trust me?"

He grinned. "I don't trust *me*."

She followed suit, slipping hastily into her garments. And when she turned to him, her face no longer held a smile.

He waited, knowing from the concerned look in her eyes that she had something to tell him.

"I have sensed something about our journey that you should know."

He walked over to her. "Tell me."

"We don't continue on to MacAlpin keep with Roan and Dolca."

"Why and where do we go?"

She shook her head. "I wish I knew, but I have no answer to either question."

"I'm glad you told me of this. We'll see about taking extra provisions with us," he said. "Do Roan and Dolca make it safely to my home?"

Bliss nodded. "Without a problem."

"Then it doesn't appear that it is the soldiers that separate us."

"I thought the same myself," she confirmed.

"It is a puzzle," he admitted, and though he did not like being unable to solve it, at least he could be prepared. Then he realized something. "Could it be that you are summoned to heal someone?"

Her eyes turned wide. "That is a possibility."

"We will remain aware," he said, and she nodded in agreement.

He took her in his arms then and kissed her, a gentle kiss that stirred passion nonetheless. "Thank you for sharing this with me."

"Husbands and wives do that . . . share."

She more and more acknowledged him as her husband, and he had had no problem acknowledging her as his wife. They were one, joined forever, and nothing would separate them.

"Ready to go?" he asked.

She took hold of his hand. "Now I am."

He kissed her again and gave her hand a squeeze. "Together. Always together."

Their pace was slow in consideration of Dolca's age though she seemed to keep up with them well enough.

It would be another day's journey to MacAlpin keep, and while Trey was eager to get home, he knew a delay was inevitable. What Bliss had seen would surely come to pass, and so he would make certain that Roan took the information that he had learned to his brothers. And also let them know he would be home as soon as possible though he once again would advise Roan and also let Dolca know that his marriage to Bliss was not to be discussed. He wanted the privilege of announcing it to his family.

The air grew colder as they continued, and Trey had no doubt flurries would fall before long. Winter was making itself known.

Several hours later, with thick gray skies blocking any sign of the sun, they stopped for rest and sustenance. Trey and Roan took turns scouting the surrounding area, while Bliss and Dolca enjoyed the brief repose. With no signs of soldiers in the area, they felt it safe to continue and cover as much ground as possible before dusk.

By the time they made camp for the night, Trey could not help but wonder if perhaps this was one time Bliss could be wrong. Perhaps they would continue on with Roan and Dolca. He supposed he was hoping they would though in his heart he knew that when Bliss had a vision or sensed something, it would surely come to pass.

And it did, early the next morning, shortly after they had doused their campfire and begun the journey that would see him home soon. A young lad of about ten, skinny, with long brown hair, suddenly stumbled out of the surrounding woods and collapsed not far from them.

Trey was quick to go to him, cradling his limp body in his arms. Bliss was quick to work on healing him though it became apparent all too soon that it was food, drink, and rest he needed.

When they finally roused him, and he was able to speak, his first words were concern for his mother. "My mum needs help."

"Easy, lad," Trey urged, as the young boy struggled to stand.

"My mum is alone," he said, forcing himself to his feet. "The soldiers came and took my da and me, claiming we were to fight for King Kenneth. My mum is close to birthing a babe, and my da helped me to escape so I could get home to help her."

Bliss rested her hand on the lad's shoulder. "We will help you."

The lad collapsed to his knees in tears. "I fear for my mum and da."

"First, let us see to helping your mum; and then we'll see what we can do for your da," Trey said. He was growing angrier at the abuse the common people suffered. And he knew time was growing nearer for the true king to take a stand and claim the throne. He would be glad to see it done so that the people could return to their land and, hopefully, live a peaceful life.

He wished the same for himself. He would fight and do what he must to help the true king, but it was a life with Bliss he wanted the most.

"Your name, lad?" Trey asked.

"Ian."

With a few more questions asked, Trey had all

the information he needed. "Ian," he said, with a firm hand on the lad's shoulder, "you're going to be traveling on with Roan and Dolca to MacAlpin keep while Bliss and I go help your mum and bring her to you."

Ian got to his feet with a bit of help from Trey. "I'll be going with you and the lady," he said adamantly. "My da trusted me to help my mum, and I won't fail either of them. I go with you."

Trey couldn't imagine the exhausted lad's taking another step, but before he could say anything, Bliss spoke.

"Of course you'll come with us," she said. "Your mum will be glad to see that you escaped and returned for her."

Tears filled his brown eyes. "I need to get home to her and get her someplace safe."

"We'll see to that, Ian," Trey said, "but as for now, you must be hungry. You'll eat something before we leave."

Trey's firm tone left no room for argument, and so, when Dolca placed a comforting arm around Ian's thin shoulders, he went without protest.

"I'll check the area to make certain no one has followed him," Roan said, and was gone.

Trey turned to Bliss. "You've seen something regarding the lad?"

"Only that it is necessary for him to go with us."

Trey reached out and took her hand. "This could prove dangerous. We're bound to run into soldiers. It would be better if you and the lad continued on with Roan and Dolca and let me see to bringing his mum home."

"You have birthed a babe?" she asked with a smile.

"She will give birth?"

Bliss nodded and continued smiling. "A beautiful little girl, and her brother will be as protective of her as he is of his mum."

"As I am of you," he said, running his finger down along her cheek and lightly over her lips. "I will be glad when we finally have time for us."

"We need to leave," Roan said suddenly appearing. "I found fresh tracks to the south, a single one followed by many. They send a scout ahead."

They didn't waste any time; they gathered their things though Roan did ask Bliss, "You will be at MacAlpin keep soon?"

"We will be there, though when, I'm not sure."

"You will make it there, that's all I need to know," Roan said, and with that, he and Dolca were gone.

"I'm ready," Ian announced.

Trey admired the lad's courage. "Stay close and remain silent. We will need to go around the soldiers to avoid them. If nothing stops us from keeping a good pace, then we should reach your home by nightfall."

"I'll keep up," Ian said, nodding, though Trey wondered if he was trying to convince himself.

They traveled single file, not saying a word. They went off the well-worn path to avoid soldiers, the uneasy terrain making it difficult to keep a steady pace. If Trey traveled alone, he would have covered much more ground in a much shorter time, but, then, who would birth the babe?

Bliss was needed and, according to her, so was Ian, but why? How could a lad of ten help them? Ian's hand went up to alert the two that he was about to stop, and he did, abruptly. Had he heard footfalls? He couldn't be sure, and so he listened.

Trey startled with Bliss's sudden appearance at his side. He hadn't heard her steps, and why not? Had she trod so lightly, her steps were undetectable?

"Farmers escaped from the soldiers," she whispered.

He waited a moment, and, sure enough, two men stumbled out of the woods right in front of them. What surprised Trey was that Ian ran to one.

"Da," he cried, and fell down on his knees beside the man.

The man, a bit bloody and dirt-ridden, turned wide eyes on Ian before his thick arms reached out and wrapped around the lad.

Bliss had gone to the other man, dropping to her knees and shaking her head. She didn't hesitate to take hold of his hand, and the man held tightly to her as if he feared letting go.

He struggled to say, "I'm dying."

Trey went down on one knee next to Bliss and was surprised to see that she didn't deny the man's claim.

"Peter," the man said, and Ian's da made his way over to the man, with Ian clinging tightly to him, and reached out to take his hand.

"Corwin," Peter said, squeezing his hand to let him know he was there. "Please, help my wife Rona and my son Darren. See them safe."

"You have my word," Peter said with tears in his eyes.

"Tell them both that I—" He gasped for breath, and Bliss closed her eyes and laid a heavy hand on his chest.

Trey saw that it eased the man's pain though not enough for him to speak.

"I'll tell them you love them," Peter finished for him.

A telltale smile caught at Corwin's lips before he took his last breath.

Ian started crying, and Peter fought back his tears, trying to stay strong for his son, but Trey knew what the lad had to be thinking . . . that could have been his da.

Bliss remained as she was, her hand on Corwin's chest and her eyes closed. Trey wasn't sure what she was doing, but he felt that he shouldn't disturb her, and so he saw to moving Peter and Ian away.

"Tell me what happened," Trey said, though out of the corner of his eye he kept a watch on his wife in case she was in need of him.

"The group of farmers that the soldiers had taken prisoner decided they would rather die trying to escape than fight for King Kenneth. Many of us made it, spreading out so that the soldiers would have to divide to find us." He nodded toward Corwin. "He had suffered several beatings by the soldiers, being the most outspoken one, though his strength is what made us all act, especially after Ian's successful escape. If he could do it, why not the rest of us?"

"You made a brave escape," Trey said.

"A necessary one though I believe one or two may have been struck down, but most fled. Whether any were recaptured or not, I do not know. I only know that I wanted to find my son." He wrapped his arm around Ian. "And get home to my wife."

"We go to your home now to get your wife and bring her to safety," Trey said.

"We will also need to go get Rona and Darren, Corwin's family," Peter said. "I gave my word."

"And I shall help you keep it," Trey said.

Bliss joined them. "We must hurry and bury him; the soldiers hunt the woods."

Peter looked at her a moment, his eyes turning wide when he saw the markings at her wrists. "You're a—"

"Healer and my wife," Trey said.

Peter bobbed his head respectfully. "My wife will be grateful for any help you can give her."

"I'd be pleased to help her," Bliss said. "Now let me see to your wounds while Trey sees to Corwin."

Trey was again impressed with the lad when he left his da's side and went straight to work helping Trey with Corwin. He knew it couldn't be easy for him, but he found the strength anyway and helped Trey lay the man to rest.

Bliss let him know that Peter's injuries were minor and he was fit to travel. She was concerned with their swift pace, but Trey wasn't, and he was right. Peter wanted to get home to his wife, and, injured or not, nothing would stop him.

Ian remained close to his da's side as they continued, their pace a bit swifter than before. Dusk was fast settling, and they were still a distance away, but none suggested they stop and continue in the morning.

With darkness near, Trey made them all travel closer together, and they had no choice but to slow their pace. He had made certain to keep a firm hold of Bliss's hand. He would not see her separated from him, and so they traveled in pairs, father and son and husband and wife, until finally Peter hurried up ahead of Trey.

"My farm is just over the rise," he said with relief.

They all were pleased to see smoke pouring from the chimney, and father and son broke into a run.

Bliss squeezed Trey's hand. "We must hurry."

He didn't question why, he ran along with her.

As they all drew near the cottage, a shrieking scream pierced the night air.

Peter and his son stopped dead for a moment, then ran, Peter screaming, "Emma!"

Chapter 23

Bliss laid the freshly scrubbed little girl in her mother's arms.

Emma cradled her close and reached out and grabbed Bliss by the wrist. "I don't know how to thank you."

Bliss smiled. "You did all the work and suffered much of the labor while alone."

"But if you hadn't arrived when you did, I would not have had the strength to—" Tears choked off her words.

"Fate had other plans," Bliss said.

Emma smiled and wrapped her arms around her daughter.

"I'm sure that your husband and son are anxious to see you and the babe. I'll go fetch them and give you some time alone."

Emma nodded once again, choking back tears.

Bliss left the cottage to find Ian and Peter waiting right outside the door. She smiled and stepped aside, and the two rushed in.

Trey walked over to her. "Are you all right?"

His concern for her above anyone else amazed

her, not that he didn't care how mother and child fared. He simply wanted to know first how she was. It was so very nice to know how important she was to him.

She drifted closer to him, and his arms instinctively wound around her. "I am fine, and mother and daughter are doing well."

"Well enough to travel soon?" he asked, his hand gently massaging up and down her back.

She rested her head on his chest, welcoming his soothing touch. "Emma is stronger than she knows and will do anything to see her family kept safe. I would suggest that we leave in the morning, find a safe place to camp, and leave Emma and the babe there, and Ian to watch over them while Peter, you, and I go to fetch Corwin's wife and son."

"You have it all planned," he said on a laugh, "though tell me. Is there a reason that you need to go along?"

She glanced up at him. "I don't want to be away from you."

His smile faded as he leaned down to kiss her, a gentle touch of the lips before tasting more deeply. And when done, he said, "Nor I you, but I also want to see you kept safe. If it is not necessary for you to accompany us, then I prefer you remain with Emma and the children."

"I can't say it is necessary," she answered truthfully. "I only know that I have the overpowering need to remain with you."

He kissed her again though lightly this time. "And I am selfish and want you with me, but—"

She stilled his words with her fingers pressed

against his lips. "Let us stay together while we can."

He gently pushed her hand away and frowned. "What do you mean *while we can*?"

"I don't know," she said, feeling as troubled by her words as he did.

He tightened his grip on her. "I will let no one take you from me."

You can't stop fate. Her thought sent a chill through her.

"Not even fate," Trey said, as if he knew her thoughts.

"We stay together then," she said, trying to convince herself that there was nothing to worry about when she knew that there was.

"We stay together," Trey confirmed. "You, Peter, and I will settle Emma and the children safely, then go fetch Rona and her son."

Bliss smiled, pleased and relieved that he had agreed. She had no idea where this need to remain with him had come from. Could it be possible that they would not stay together, and she was beginning to sense their eventual separation?

She hoped not. It might have been only a short time since she had grown accustomed to him, but it seemed that they had become as familiar as longtime friends, talking, trusting, sharing, and . . . loving.

"How is it that I have fallen so deeply in love with you?" she asked, her eyes going to his.

"I have no answer, for I do not understand myself how easily, willingly, and so unconditionally I have fallen in love with you."

"I want it to be forever."

"You obviously worry that it won't be; therefore, I wonder if you know something and are not telling me."

"I don't know, that's just it," she said. "I do not know if we are meant to be together forever."

He grinned and stole a quick kiss before saying, "I *know* that we are meant to be together forever, so do not worry yourself over it. We have joined as one and will remain so."

Bliss had to smile; he spoke with such conviction that she could not help but believe his words. "You have a knowing of your own," she teased.

"Don't tell anyone," he whispered, "but I get it from my wife."

She laughed. "I am not some contagious illness."

He hugged her close and nuzzled his lips at her neck before whispering in her ear, "You are contagious to my heart, and I'll have it no other way."

They kissed then, a hungry, needy kiss that more than stirred their passion.

"When we reach your home, I wish to spend as much time alone in your bedchamber as possible," she said, her body already deeply aching for him.

"That is a wish I will happily and eagerly grant."

Peter gave a shout to them from the open door, waving to them to join him and his family.

They smiled in resignation and went to join the happy family.

Trey understood where Ian had gotten his stamina and determination. It was from his mother, Emma. The woman was up early the next morning, and, while her newborn daughter slept, she prepared a hot pottage. After they had all eaten their fill, Emma had to be made to sit and rest while Ian and Peter saw to gathering food, clothing, and blankets to take with them.

It was a few hours after sunrise that they were finally on their way. Corwin's farm was not far from Peter's, and so it had been decided that a spot would be found halfway between the farms for Emma and the children to wait.

It was midmorning when a spot Trey felt would be safe enough was found, and Emma settled. Ian took his responsibility seriously, asking Trey for a weapon so that he could protect his mum and sister if necessary.

Trey understood that because of the lad's recent bout with the soldiers, he felt vulnerable and needed something that would help give him a sense of security. He gave Ian a dagger though not without instructions and warnings. He could see the relief on the lad's face after the brief lesson finished. Ian now felt more capable of defending his family.

Peter thanked him for helping his son. "I'm a farmer, not a warrior like you. It is good he learns from a warrior."

Trey rested a firm hand on the man's shoulder. "You bravely escaped your captives; I'd say you're a mighty fine warrior."

With courage instilled in father and son, goodbyes were said, with tears, and the trio departed. If all went well, they would be back by nightfall, and so far Bliss had not mentioned any delays, so Trey was hopeful.

Silence once again was their traveling companion, Trey wanting nothing to interfere with keeping alert to surrounding sounds. A few times he stopped, having heard a sound and made sure he paid heed to his own instincts before proceeding.

He saw no point in troubling Bliss each time. If she sensed anything, she would be right there to tell him, and so he did not bother her with every little sound. What concerned him more was the weather. It felt like snow. He had expected at least a light coating yesterday, and, with the temperature dropping, he feared more than a dusting.

They were close to the farm when Bliss hurried to his side, grabbed hold of his arm, and whispered, "Soldiers."

"We go slow and quiet," he said, looking at Peter, who nodded.

Raised voices could be heard as they drew closer to the farm, though they remained hidden in the woods. When they were finally able to get a look, they saw two soldiers yelling at Rona, her son, barely five years, clinging to her leg, his eyes wide with fear and tears.

From what they could hear, the soldiers were accusing her of hiding her husband and threatening harm to her and her son if she didn't tell them where he was.

"Wait here," Trey ordered.

Peter stepped forward. "I'll help."

Trey shook his head. "They search for you as well; better they don't see you."

Peter looked upset but did as Trey said.

Trey walked out of the woods and headed straight for the soldiers.

"Now here's a big one that can fight for the king," one soldier said, as Trey approached.

"I have no use for King Kenneth," Trey said, and his fist flew out so fast the soldier had no time to respond. He went down hard and fast.

The other soldier was so shocked that he didn't react as fast as he should have, which gave Trey enough time to land a solid blow to his jaw, knocking him out.

Peter and Bliss came running as soon as the two went down.

"Peter," Rona cried out when she spotted him. "Is Corwin with you?"

Peter's saddened expression answered her, and she collapsed to the ground, crying, her young son crying along with her though he didn't know why.

Bliss knelt alongside her, slipping a comforting arm around her as Peter recounted the tale of her husband's bravery and that, because of him, so many men went free, and how in the end, Corwin had cared only for his wife's and son's safety. That was why they were here, to take her and Darren to safety.

"We need to hurry," Peter warned, and Bliss helped the woman to stand.

Though Rona continued to shed tears, she did what she had to do and got herself and her son ready to leave.

Trey and Peter saw to securing the soldiers so that they could not follow once they revived or alert any nearby troops. They were done in no time, as was Rona. Peter picked up the young lad and hoisted him onto his soldiers, Rona sending him a grateful smile.

They hurried off, Trey wanting to reach Emma and the children by nightfall. He felt uneasy though he couldn't say why.

A little after nightfall, they arrived, and Rona dropped down beside Emma, Darren clinging to her, and the two women cried in sadness and relief.

Trey pulled Bliss aside away from the others. "Something troubles me."

Bliss nodded. "I've felt it myself though I don't know what it is."

He pulled her into his arms. "I will be glad when we are home, where I know you will be safe." He could feel the sudden change in her, a quick almost undetectable bristle that vanished as soon as it had appeared. "What's wrong?"

She had no chance to respond, Peter calling out to them both. He was worried that soldiers would or had already gone to his farm in search of him. Would they be able to track them here?

They discussed all the possibilities, and though Trey knew what had to be done, he said nothing about it. He would wait for the right time though he knew there would be no keeping his plan from Bliss. No doubt she already knew.

Peter took the first watch, leaving Trey to curl around his wife beside the campfire and keep them both warm. The others had already fallen asleep from sheer exhaustion and relief from the day's sadness.

"Our return to your home will be delayed yet again," she whispered, "but it cannot be helped."

"It won't be a long delay, just a slight detour." He nuzzled at her warm neck, his hand beneath the blanket playfully creeping up to gently squeeze her breast. He truly should have thought better of his actions since the simple touch began to grow him hard.

"That is not fair, husband," she murmured, and he heard passion stir in her voice.

She stirred his even further simply by calling him husband. He liked when she did that, acknowledged the importance of who he was to her.

"To neither of us," he whispered against her ear, and felt her shudder. Damn but he wished they were alone.

"Please stop, Trey," she whispered so softly that he barely heard her. "It does not take much for me to want you and for that want to grow . . . and to pain me if left unsatisfied."

He moved his hand away from her breast reluctantly. "I didn't mean to—"

"Love me so much?"

Her teasing tone brought a smile to his face. "You know me too well, *wife,* and that pleases me."

"Since I have pleased you, it is only fair that you owe me one."

He laughed softly in her ear. "And I will see that you get a good, hard, and long pleasing."

She chuckled. "See that you do, husband."

"You have my word."

They woke the next morning to snow just beginning to fall. It could prove a blessing or a problem. If the snow continued, it would hide their tracks, but if it stopped, their tracks would be visible, and they could be found easily. If the snow worsened, that would present a bigger problem, especially with a new babe to worry about. They hurried and gathered their things and were on their way, hoping to cover as much ground as possible before the snow stopped or worsened.

It was only midmorning when the snow began to slow, and Trey brought them to a stop. He saw the worried look on Peter's face and knew what he was thinking.

"Snow or not, I knew this time would come though the snow has made it even more of a necessity," Trey said. "Peter, you need to travel on to MacAlpin keep with everyone while Bliss and I make tracks that the soldiers will follow."

"They will look for more than two sets of tracks," Peter protested nervously.

"Not so," Trey said. "The soldiers don't know if your son or you made it home, and since you were not seen at Rona's place, they do not know you travel with her. They will assume she left with me, who no doubt would carry her son, leaving two sets of tracks. The snow covered your farm, so the multiple tracks cannot be seen. With the place empty, the soldiers will assume that you or your son made it home and left, thus looking for two sets of tracks.

"The snow still falls, but not for long. Bliss and

I will wait here to see that the snow covers your tracks. And then we will go in a different direction. Once the soldiers find our tracks, they will assume it is either Rona and the warrior or your son, or you and your wife, and follow us."

Peter looked ready to protest.

Trey didn't allow it. "You take yours and Corwin's family and see that they get safely to my home. Leave the rest to me and Bliss."

"Bliss should come with us," Peter said.

"She will not leave her husband," Emma said, "just as I would not leave you."

"If you keep a good pace, you can make MacAlpin village by nightfall and have a warm bed for your newborn to sleep in tonight," Trey said.

Peter held out his hand, and Trey clasped it firmly. "I am indebted to you and will proudly serve the true king."

Ian stepped forward, his thin chest proudly extended. "As will I." He held the dagger out, returning it to Trey.

Trey shook his head. "You keep it, lad, and practice."

Ian grinned from ear to ear. "I will make the true king proud."

"No doubt you will," Trey said. "Now hurry and be off; though before you go, I have one favor to ask."

"Whatever you want," Peter said.

"My family does not yet know of my marriage to Bliss, and I wish to tell them myself, so please do not mention I have a wife. I want to surprise them."

"They will be surprised and pleased," Emma said with a nod and a smile.

Quick good-byes were said, and the group moved on, the light snow soon covering their tracks.

Trey took Bliss's hand, and a peaceful contentment washed over him. He had missed holding hands with her; though it truly hadn't been that long, it seemed that it had. And he missed having her by his side while they traveled. And though he worried over her safety, he was glad she had remained with him.

"Are you ready to lead the soldiers on a merry chase?" he asked.

"Romping through the snow has always been a favorite pastime of mine."

He kissed her quick. "I like romping."

"In the snow?"

"Almost anyplace."

"I'll have to see how true that is."

"By all means let me prove it to you."

"Now?" Bliss asked with a smile.

Trey grinned. "Before the day ends . . . we'll romp."

Chapter 24

Bliss was happy though their present situation called more for caution. It didn't matter to her. It only mattered that she was with Trey, and they had time together just the two of them. She knew it would not last long and that soon . . .

She did not want to think beyond this moment, for she knew that their time together would be limited, and there would come a time when they were . . . *separated*.

She did not wish to think about it and had wished she had not known, for she wondered what would cause it and how long they would be apart. Unfortunately, she sensed no answers, and that disturbed her all the more.

Their pace wasn't as rushed as usual, Trey wanting to make certain their tracks were easy to follow. They had waited until the snow had completely covered the ground and any remaining tracks that had been made before they left.

Bliss sensed Trey's intentions. He would make a wide loop before heading home, which meant another day or two of travel. She smiled, her happiness growing.

"Do I dare ask if that smile of joy has to do with me?" Trey asked teasingly.

"It has everything to do with you," she admitted with a light laugh.

"Tell me more," he urged with a nudge of his shoulder to hers.

"I was just thinking how happy I am being alone with you, just the two of us."

"The possibility of the soldiers' finding us doesn't worry you?"

"I don't sense our capture though I imagine it is because we remain cautious, and I am not foolish enough to think that things cannot change at the next turn. It is just that I believe this time is special for us since—"

Bliss almost bit her tongue. She had had no intention of letting Trey know that she had sensed a separation between them. It would only cause him worry when he needed to focus on the present.

"What was about to slip off your tongue that you hadn't planned on telling me?" he asked, not at all upset.

"You have enough on your mind." She hoped to keep it from him though she knew it would be a useless effort.

"You only burden me more by not telling me."

"We separate," she said, her heart feeling the harshness of her words.

Trey stopped abruptly, looked around, and hurried her to a grove of trees that provided a modicum of concealment.

"Tell me," he demanded.

"There truly isn't anything to tell, which is why I didn't want to mention it. I have sensed that somehow we are separated, but I don't know when or for how long."

"Can you sense that we do come together again?"

She shook her head. "I haven't seen beyond the separation."

He braced her back against one of the trees, his hand going to rest just above her head against the thick tree trunk. "It is probably no more than a mission or battle, for I will not be kept long from your side."

His kiss came quick, its potency stunning her senses, and her arms were just as quick to go around him and hold him close. Their tongues mated while their bodies pressed hard against each other. Their need to join was unbearable, and the deepening kiss only added to the passion that they both knew could not presently be satisfied.

Trey tore his mouth away from hers. "Duty will call, so there will be separations, but also reunitings"—he grinned—"that both of us will thoroughly enjoy."

He brushed his lips over hers and stepped away.

Bliss wasn't happy that he moved away from her though she could sense the reluctance in his steps. She knew that the distance was necessary or else they would soon be on the snow-covered ground . . . romping.

She could tell he wished to say more, or perhaps ask more, but he didn't, and that he had explained their separation so as not to make it sound worrisome. It troubled her that she caused him more worry and reminded herself to be more careful about holding her tongue in the future; though she had never had a problem doing so before, she did with Trey. It felt so natural to share with him that it was difficult to keep things to herself. It seemed so right to discuss everything with him.

He didn't judge her or scold her or belittle her; he was genuinely interested in all she had to say, and that had gladdened her heart. Finally, there was someone to share her life with, and it felt amazing.

"We stay as one," Trey said, and held his hand out to her.

"Always." She smiled and took hold.

They hadn't walked very far when they both suddenly stopped.

"Two or more approach," Bliss whispered.

Trey didn't hesitate; he hurried her behind a thicket of bushes. "Wait here. I'll be back."

She watched him break off a branch and wipe the ground clean of their foot tracks, then he purposely made new tracks and disappeared in the opposite direction from where she hid.

Why hadn't she sensed that someone approached sooner? She shook her head, annoyed with herself. She had been too busy with thoughts of Trey. Her knowing had always come easily, for there had been nothing else to fill or worry her thoughts. Now she was so concerned with Trey that it interfered with her knowing, and that was not good.

Even now, when she should be focused on what could happen, she was too busy thinking of Trey. Not good. She breathed a quiet sigh, kept her eyes on her surroundings and her ears attuned to all sounds.

As soon as quiet descended around her, she sensed the approach of two soldiers. She remained as still as could be and listened to the footfalls draw nearer.

"At least we found their trail," one said.

"We'll get that Highlander, and when the king's guards get done with him, he'll be begging to fight for the king," the other said.

"And no one need know that he bested us," the one sneered.

"As for the woman and child—"

"She'll pay for fleeing with the Highlander," the one said angrily.

"Look here, one set of footprints, and they're deep."

"He carries the fool woman and child. Let's go; we'll catch them fast enough now."

Bliss heard them hurry off, but she remained where she was; she would take no chance—she would wait for Trey.

It wasn't long before he was at her side, pulling her to her feet and cautioning with his finger to remain silent as he hurried them off in yet another direction. It wasn't for some time before he broke the silence.

"Those fools will track the trail I left long before they realize it takes them nowhere," he said.

"Then we can return to your home now," she said with a sense of disappointment.

He shook his head. "The two fools aren't the only soldiers in search of those farmers who escaped. I don't want to take the chance and lead any of them to Peter and the others. We'll leave foot tracks that will lead whoever finds them on a useless trail before circling and heading home."

"How long till then?"

"We'll reach home by nightfall tomorrow."

She smiled and squeezed his hand.

"I thought you would like that; it is the most we can delay. I need to get home to my brothers. The time draws near for the true king to step forward and claim the throne."

"I know, but at least we'll have this brief time, and for that I am grateful."

They continued walking, in circles at times, and as the day wore on, and dusk was about to claim the land, Trey turned to her.

"We need a warm, safe shelter tonight, for I intend to make love to you."

She smiled, though she asked, "Do you think it is safe?"

"The soldiers have searched all day on foot and no doubt are as exhausted as we are and have probably already camped for the night. I'm surprised we can't hear their complaints and loud snores. Besides, do you sense any soldiers near?"

She shook her head, knowing that he asked so as to put her mind at ease.

"Good, then tonight is ours," he said with a satisfied grin.

"Where will we find"—she smiled—"you knew I would sense a place."

"I *hoped* you would."

"It is a short distance from here, tucked in the woods, a bit worn but usable enough," she said. "A gift, I believe, from fate."

"A good gift; I gratefully accept."

As they drew closer to the abandoned cottage, her heart grew heavier, and, at first, she wasn't sure why; and then she realized that not soon after tonight, they could possibly separate. She didn't want to believe it, and she certainly didn't want to tell Trey. It would weigh too heavily upon them both and interfere with their night of love.

She would say nothing, though . . .

He was staring at her when she looked his way.

"Are you going to tell me, or do I have to ask again?"

She had to smile though the occasion certainly didn't call for it, but she couldn't help herself. It was wonderful to know how attuned he was to her and how he didn't get annoyed with her over it. He simply waited for her to accept how closely they were tied.

Duncan and Mercy may have had real, solid chains that bound them, but Trey and she were bound by a solid force that no one could destroy.

She was about to share what she had sensed when a vision hit her so hard that it drove her to her knees.

Wild and screaming, Leora rushed at her. "Bring him home. Bring him home now, I need him. Now! Now! Now!"

"Now! Now! Now!" Bliss yelled, as her eyes sprang open.

She was in Trey's arms, his expression one of sheer determination.

"I was about to shake you senseless to wake you."

"It was a brief vision."

"Leora?"

Bliss nodded. "She wants you to return home. She says she needs you."

"She is dead. What can she need from me?"

"I don't know, but I do know we will find out soon."

Trey scooped her up in his arms. "But not now, not here, not tonight."

She was glad when he carried her to the cottage and said no more.

Once inside, there was some preparing to be done. A fire needed starting, the small space needed sweeping, and the bed needed tending. They both went to work, wanting it all done as soon as possible.

"I'm thinking that I would prefer a cottage of our own rather than a bedchamber in the keep," Trey said, sending a grin her way as he stoked the fire. "More privacy."

The words spilled out of her mouth before she could call them back. "What of my cottage?"

Trey stood and slipped off his shirt. "A place to visit."

It wasn't that she had expected a different answer. After all, women followed where their husbands went, but then, to her, Trey wasn't like other husbands. He was different, and that was what she loved about him. She also had to consider that he served the true king. He had a duty . . . but, then, so did she.

He stepped toward her, and she took a step away. He was too appealing bare-chested, and this issue needed to be discussed before she surrendered to him, and perhaps that was her worry. That she would surrender everything to him, and what would be left of her, her people, her ways?

The thought suddenly frightened her. Was love demanding too much? Or was she surrendering too much?

"We need to talk," she said, her hand going up to stop his approach.

He laughed. "Now is not the time for talk."

She kept her eyes on his face, the sight of him half-naked making her hands itch to touch him. "Appease me."

He grinned wickedly. "I'd rather pleasure you."

"Consider it a prelude to our lovemaking."

His grin vanished in a flash. "A necessary one?"

She nodded.

"This night was meant for us. Can this not wait?"

She supposed she could let it go for now and discuss it another time with him, but that would be one more step to complete surrender. Would she lose another part of herself? Her abilities were part of who she was, and, while at times, she found them a burden, she could not live without them. They defined her.

"Your hesitation tells me you are thinking it over and therefore perhaps it is not as important as you think."

That was enough for her to hear. "It's more important than you'll ever know."

He quirked a brow. "Then let us talk and be done with it."

"It cannot be discussed and dismissed easily."

"If it is nonsense, it can be discarded easily enough."

She told herself to be patient. He was eager to make love to her and annoyed that a discussion should delay their pleasure. She had to make him understand the importance of this matter to her.

"It's about my home," she said.

"You'll love your new home," he assured her with a smile, as if the matter were settled easily.

She shook her head. "Not *your* home; *my* home."

His smile disappeared. "*My* home is *your* home."

"No, it isn't. I have a home with my people—"

"You belong with my clan now."

"I cannot simply desert my people," she said.

"You are not deserting them. We'll visit with them."

"And what if I wish to remain there a while?" she asked.

"If such a time comes, I'll see what can be arranged."

A shiver ran through her, as if part of her was slipping away. She had come and gone as she pleased for so long that it was strange to think she would need to seek anyone's permission to do as she pleased.

"Do not fret over it. We will see that you can visit often with your people and they can come to the keep when in need of healing."

She shook her head. "That will not do. My door is always open to my people, and there are times I sense when I am needed."

"They must understand that your marriage will take you away from them, to a new home. It is part of marriage. A wife makes a home with her husband. We will make a good home together."

"I have no doubt of that. It is where that home will be that troubles me."

"You know I serve the true king," Trey said, as if no more discussion was necessary.

"So what you are saying is that there is no room for discussion."

"What is it that truly bothers you? It can't be this senseless chatter about where we will live. You know a wife goes with her husband. So what is it that has you stopping us from making love?"

"I am to abide by a rule that has me surrender my home without thought to what I lose?" she said, more adamantly than she had intended.

"You think you lose, not gain?" he said with a raised voice. "That is what you think of our marriage."

Her voice rose as well. "Our marriage is not in question here."

"Then tell me what is."

His demanding tone irritated her. "You should know."

He threw his hands up. "I do not have your abilities, and why don't you just use them to answer whatever it is that frustrates you and be done with it."

Her eyes narrowed, and her lips clamped shut.

"Don't even think about remaining silent. We'll have this out and be done with it."

"You tell me to find the answer myself, then order me not to remain silent. Make up your mind."

He shook his finger at her. "This was a discussion best left for another time."

"You are the one who encouraged me to share all my thoughts with you."

"Not when I hunger to make love to you," he snapped.

She felt a pang to her heart, but her chin went up. "I didn't know there would be specific times to discuss things with you."

"That's not what I meant, and you know it." He rushed his fingers through his hair again. "Damn, but you're frustrating me, but then you know that too. You know everything."

"And that bothers you?" she more accused than asked.

He stomped over to her and placed his face so close to hers that their noses almost touched. "You know the answer to that too. Now tell me what truly troubles you, and let's be done with it, though I doubt by now either of us are in the mood for making love."

His words hurt, and she stepped back. Had she approached this matter at the wrong time? Was this rift between them entirely her fault? Would she lose a night of making love with a husband she dearly loved because she had thought only of herself?

Or was she once again surrendering another piece of herself for love?

"Now you say nothing," he snapped, "which is what you should have done in the first place." He turned his back to her, walked to the fireplace, and braced his hand on the mantel.

She stood where she was: shocked, disappointed, feeling guilty, all feelings foreign to her. Her world had always made sense, but then she had been in control of it. Love had taken that control from her and had taught her what . . . to share?

But hadn't that been what she was doing when she had attempted to speak with him?

Not truly, and he knew it; he knew her. He knew there was more to the matter than the issue of her new home. So why hadn't she been honest with him? Thus far he had not grown angry with anything she had discussed with him . . . until now.

He certainly had grown angry, and she understood why. He wanted to make love, not talk, and yet she needed to talk before . . .

She shook her head. She had wanted him to ease her doubts, her misgivings and her fears that this sudden marriage had been forced on her.

She glanced over at him and winced, the scars on his back looking as angry as he had. He had suffered so much, and she had felt most of it when she had helped heal him. He was a good, caring man, and, suddenly, the need to end this senseless rift between them overwhelmed her, and she walked over to him.

With a bit of reluctance but an overpowering need to touch him, she rested her hand on his back.

As soon as her hand connected with his warm flesh, he turned in a flash and grabbed her wrist.

Anger mixed with passion in his eyes and in the next second he scooped her up into his arms.

"I'm sorry for my harsh words. I wanted nothing more than to make love with you. I could think of nothing all day but making love to you. Even when I led those two fools on a merry chase, I was thinking of what I would do to you tonight. Let me love you. And then we will talk until sunrise if you wish."

She smiled and nodded, and hurried them to the bed.

Chapter 25

Trey kissed her like a starving man, then quickly shed his plaid and boots and helped her out of her clothes. When he had shed the last of her garments, and she lay naked on the bed, waiting for him to cover her, he took a calming breath, his body so hard for her that it hurt, and slowly moved over her to cradle her hips between his knees.

He brought his mouth to hers and kissed her lips gently though he wanted nothing more than to ravish them. "I'm sorry for disappointing you."

She shook her head in protest.

He nodded. "Yes, I did disappoint you. I promised I would always be there for you, and I wasn't this time, and I regret it."

"I should have waited," she said.

"No, you needed to talk with me, and I could think only of making love with you."

"Not a bad thought," she said with a smile.

"A selfish one."

"Not so," she said, "for I get great pleasure from making love with you."

"I won't let it happen again. I prom—"

She pressed her finger to his lips. "Do not promise, for it is one you will not be able to keep."

He nipped playfully at her finger, then kissed her lips gently. "I'm going to kiss every part of you."

"Do I get to do the same to you?"

"Only if you want this night to end fast."

She laughed and shook her head. "I'd rather what you promised—a night of making love, though"—she grinned and slipped her hand down between his legs to stroke him—"I wish a night to do the same to you."

His hand grabbed hold of hers and moved it off him. "I will make certain of it, but tonight . . ." He smiled slowly, the smile turning wickedly sinful as it spread; and then he kissed her.

Bliss had shared many a kiss with Trey, but this one was as if he kissed her for the first time. She couldn't say what it was about it that made it feel that way, she just sensed it. It was as if this moment they were starting their life together as husband and wife.

The thought tugged at her heart and made her senses explode, her body responding like it had never done before. It was as if his kiss had brought every fiber to life. Her skin prickled with passion, her nipples turned hard, aching to be suckled, her stomach fluttered with anticipation, and a tingling desire raged between her legs.

He had only begun, his lips now at her neck, and already she was mad with the want of him. She would never survive this. She would be crazy with—she nearly bolted off the bed when his lips claimed one nipple, and his tongue played unmercifully with it.

She moaned and squirmed beneath him. "Trey."

His tongue moved to her other nipple, and his hand gripped her breast as his tongue and teeth alternately forced the bud to turn even harder.

"Trey, I can't wait."

"Not yet," he said, continuing to torment her.

"Please, I can't wait," she pleaded. "I want you so badly."

He glanced up at her and, with a smile, released her breast. "I'm going to make you come over and over and over tonight."

His hand had traveled down over her stomach while he spoke and was now slipping between her legs as his mouth returned to torment her nipple.

She jumped when his thumb grazed her pulsating nub; and then his fingers slipped inside her. His thumb and fingers worked in a rhythm that had her body arching, aching for him to slip inside her, but he didn't.

He teased and tormented her until she thought she'd go mad. While she knew he could pleasure her easily his way, she preferred sharing this moment of madness with him. She wanted him inside her, deep inside her. And so she slyly maneuvered her hand down until she was close enough to grab hold of him.

His body tensed, and she groaned with pleasure at the way the thick size of him fit so snugly in her hand. She then did what he was doing to her—she played with him.

"Bliss," he said in a whispered warning.

"You're hard for me," she murmured in his ear. "Bury yourself inside me and pleasure us both."

He groaned. "Damn, Bliss—"

She intensified her playful tugs. "It's been too long since you've been inside me. I need you to fill me."

Her words did the trick. He moved so fast that it stunned her. He drew her legs up over his shoulders and grabbed her bottom as he plunged into her in one swift motion.

She gasped with pleasure as he drove repeatedly into her, inflaming her passion to unimaginable heights. Her moans grew with each thrust, and she slipped her legs off his shoulder to wrap them around his waist and draw him closer.

His rhythm intensified, and she could feel his own passion building as wildly as hers. It wouldn't be long now for either of them. They would climax together, she could feel it, she wanted it, and she wanted them to be one.

It hit them so hard and quick that they both cried out at the same time, exploding together in a climax that seemed to go on forever, rippling through them again and again and making them shiver down to their souls.

Trey collapsed on top of her, and she welcomed him. Tingles continued to run through her, and she didn't want the deliciously delightful feeling to leave her just yet.

He went to move off her, and she grabbed hold of him to stop him, but she couldn't, and when he took her with him, rolling her over to rest on top of him, she smiled and settled her head to rest on his chest.

"I love the feel of you inside me," she said.

"Then I will reside there often."

She glanced up at him and grinned. "As often as you'd like."

He stroked her face. "I am a lucky man to have you as a wife."

"Oh!" Bliss cried out and slipped off him, her hand rushing to her stomach as she jumped out of bed.

Trey was beside her in an instant, his hand resting over hers. "What is it? Did I hurt? Are you in pain?"

Her eyes turned wide, and she smiled. "We made a child."

It was his turn for his eyes to grow wide, and he stared at her, speechless.

She moved her hand from beneath his and pressed his hand against her stomach. "I felt it the instant he took hold and nested."

"He?"

She nodded and grinned. "A son. I carry a son."

She felt his hand press more firmly against her, and a smile spread across his face. "You will know each time we make a child?"

"It would seem so. Oh, Trey, it is so amazing to feel life take hold." She shivered, the chill of the room wrapping around her.

Trey scooped her up and settled her on the bed, tucking a blanket around her. She grabbed his hand as he turned to walk away.

"I go to add more wood to the fire."

Reluctantly, she let him go. She wanted him beside her, holding her, sharing this special moment with her, and he did. He returned, climbed in beside her, and took her in his arms to cradle her close.

"I cannot believe I am to be a father," he said.

"You will be a good one," she assured. "I have seen how patient and caring you are with children. You will be an excellent da." She grew quiet for a moment. "You do want to be a da, don't you?"

He lifted her chin so that she looked up at him. "Nothing could please me more than to know that our love made a child this night."

She kissed him quick. "Your words warm my heart and grow my love for you even more."

He grinned. "Do you know what truly pleases me?"

"What?"

"That you cannot keep anything from me, and it seems that the closer we grow, the more difficult it is for you even to try."

Her brow scrunched for a few moments, then she nodded. "You know, you're right. I seem to just blurt things out."

"Or they disturb you so that you must talk about it."

He hadn't forgotten that she had wished to talk and was offering her this time to do so, to listen and discuss with her.

"There is nothing I want to discuss right now," she said.

"When you're ready, I am here to listen."

She smiled and kissed him again. "You have made me so happy."

"We make each other happy and nothing—absolutely nothing—will separate us."

She wanted to believe him, but her knowing told her otherwise although it was not always easy to understand her knowing. Perhaps there was more to it than what she had sensed.

She sighed, contented, and snuggled against him. "Remember that you promised me a whole night of lovemaking."

"And so we shall, after a brief rest."

"Just a brief one," she said on a yawn.

His yawn matched hers. "Brief," he repeated, and, within minutes, they were both asleep.

They woke sometime in the night and made love again, slower this time, though their climax was just, if not more, intense than the previous one.

They drifted off to sleep once again and woke just before daylight and joined quickly, as if starved for each other. They slept again, though briefly, then hurried to get dressed and be on their way though not before Trey took her in his arms.

"You feel all right?" he asked.

"I should not even know that I carry a child." Her words made her realize their importance. "It would be better for none to know that I am with child."

He looked ready to protest but hesitated a moment before speaking. "I see the wisdom in that since many would not understand, but I want you to know that I would shout it out for all to hear that you carry my son."

She smiled though she cringed. "Another fact that would be best kept between us, at least for a while."

He nodded and slipped his arms around her

waist and drew her against him. "The birth will be an easy one?"

"I do not know."

"I do not wish you to suffer."

She chuckled. "That is something I agree with though pain is inevitable with birthing."

He cringed. "The thought that you will suffer to—"

"Giving our son life will cause me no suffering," she assured him. "I have attended many births, and while there is pain, there is joy. Every mother has smiled when the babe is placed in her arms." She chuckled. "Perhaps it is because there is no more pain though I think it is more because of the small babe that grabs at the heart as soon as a mother holds her child in her arms. And I look forward to that moment when I hold your son in my arms."

He looked about to ask a question, then thought better of it and stopped.

"Ask me," she urged.

He tightened his arms around her. "Will I be there with you when you birth my son?"

"I do not know," she said with a sad shake of her head.

"I tell you right now, wife," he said adamantly. "I will be right there for you. Nothing will keep me away—not even the true king."

She wrapped her arms around his neck. "That tells me much about you, husband, and pleases my heart."

"Good; then know you and I shall have a good life together, and I will allow nothing or no one to interfere with it."

She didn't want to sense or know anything at that moment. She simply wanted to believe him, and so she kissed him, gently at first, but it turned heated all too soon and he rushed her to the bed, and there, with clothes hastily shoved out of the way, they made love.

It was a fast, intense joining, and though neither made mention of it, they both worried that it could possibly be their last, at least for a while.

It was well after sunrise when they took their leave, and it was a long tedious day of making tracks, backtracking, and making tracks again to confuse and frustrate the soldiers.

By early afternoon, they spotted a stream and stopped to rest by it and share a bite to eat.

"I've sensed no soldiers all day," Bliss said, cuddled beside her husband and wishing they could share another night alone.

"It concerns me that we've come across none."

"Why?"

"I wonder if they abandoned their search for a greater cause."

"You think they are close to waging war?" she asked, and tried to sense if that was happening.

"It would seem the logical conclusion," Trey admitted.

"True and yet—" She shook her head. "I can't say I sense it though something doesn't seem right. It is as if the king waits for something—a message, I think."

"From whom?"

"I don't know."

"It is good that we will reach home by nightfall," Trey said. "It is time I speak with my brothers."

Bliss knew he was right. It was time for him to return home, and yet, as they continued walking, drawing ever nearer to his home, the feeling of them separating grew stronger. Something awaited them at Trey's home that would somehow cause a separation between them, Bliss was sure of it, and with each step, she was beginning to realize what it might be.

Hard as it was to believe, the thought grew stronger and stronger within her.

Clouds followed them overhead and seemed to grow heavier with each step. The crisp air grew chillier, and it felt like snow.

Bliss was relieved when Trey stopped just before dusk claimed the land and took her in his arms.

"We'll be home soon. Is there anything you need to tell me?"

There was so much she had to say though words slipped from her mouth before she could stop them. "I love you and I always will."

"That sounds like you bid me farewell."

She shook her head. "It is a reminder."

His smile revealed relief. "A reminder I wouldn't mind hearing often."

"Then you shall."

He kissed her, a long and lingering kiss, and afterwards, he whispered, "I will make love to you tonight."

Bliss smiled though she knew it was not meant to be.

Chapter 26

Snow was falling lightly and dusk settling over the land when Trey and Bliss entered the MacAlpin village. Trey wasn't met with the usual cries of welcome home. Instead, villagers nodded and smiled, then turned and whispered to each other.

"Something is wrong," he said with a glance to Bliss.

"I feel it as well," she confirmed.

They clung more tightly, as if their hands were bound by metal.

Inseparable.

Trey intended it to stay that way.

They hurried up the keep's steps and entered the great hall. Trey smiled, seeing his family gathered around the trestle table in front of the fireplace, their usual gathering spot. He was relieved to see that they were all there, along with a few faces he didn't recognize. His da and mum, Duncan and Mercy, Reeve and Tara, Bryce, and there was a petite woman sitting next to him, and a thin old man and Dolca sat across from them.

He was about to call out to them when Mara

spotted him and yelled out, "My son is home." She hurried over to him, throwing her plump arms around him. "Thank the Lord you've returned safe and sound."

His mum's green eyes had betrayed her worry when she had bid him good-bye several weeks ago. She hadn't said it, but Trey knew she hadn't wanted him to go. She had thought he required more rest and healing, but the simple fact was that she feared for him. And he could understand why. He had been near to death when the Picts had found him, and if it hadn't been for Tara's fine stitches and Bliss's healing hands, death would have claimed him.

Mara turned to Bliss. "You were with him, this is good. You were there in case he needed healing."

"He is well healed, Mara, there is no need for worry," Bliss assured her.

"Bless your heart," Mara said with a grin, and hugged her.

Trey noticed that the others remained at the table—quiet. His brothers were never quiet, especially when one of them returned home. There was always good-natured ribbing and endless questions.

"Come sit," Mara instructed, urging them with gentle shoves to the table.

"I have something to tell you all," Trey said gently, squeezing Bliss's hand.

His da stood, "We have something—"

A piercing scream ripped through the hall, and Trey could have sworn the scream held his name. When he turned to see the source of the crazed shriek, his eyes rounded, and his heart began to pound in his chest.

"Leora?" he said, barely above a whisper.

The woman he loved and believed dead was running toward him, and he didn't think twice, he let go of Bliss's hand and ran to her. She threw her arms around him and clung so tightly that he thought she'd squeeze the life from him. But then he also held her tight, perhaps wanting to make certain she was real, alive, and not a ghost.

"I thought you dead," he finally said, releasing her and holding her at arm's length to look at her. She was much as he remembered her, though thinner, but nonetheless beautiful. Her long blond hair fell in waves down over her shoulders, and her skin was flawless. Her full lips were as ripe for kissing as they had always been.

"A ruse by the king's soldiers," she said, wiggling out of his grip to snuggle up against him. "The king held me prisoner all this time until he finally realized that I held no knowledge of the true king, then he sent me to"—she shivered—"I cannot speak of the hell he sent me to."

He eased her away from him. "How did you get here?"

"A tale left for another time, though it was through the good graces of Bryce and his woman Charlotte that I was able to return here."

He shook his head. Had he returned home to the same family he left? Could he possibly be still recovering from his wounds and trapped in a dream? Nothing seemed to make sense except . . .

He turned and saw Bliss. She stood where he

had left her, her face pale as freshly fallen snow. He immediately left Leora and went to his wife's side.

His arm went around her and tucked her close, and asked, "Are you all right?"

She stared at him, her eyes shimmering with unshed tears. "The visions all make sense now. She was calling you home to her."

He went to speak, but her words stopped him. "You should speak with her first before you tell everyone about us."

Trey was ready to protest, but the wisdom of her words sunk in. It would not be right to blurt out in front of everyone that he had wed. He owed Leora the truth first, and privately, before he made the announcement.

"Is something wrong with Bliss?" Mara asked, walking over to them.

"A long journey, I but need to rest," Bliss said.

"She can rest in my bedchamber," Trey said.

"Leora resides in your bedchamber," Mara whispered. "She can use Reeve's, since he and Tara make their home in her cottage."

"It isn't necessary that I remain in the keep," Bliss said.

"Yes it is," Trey and his mum said in unison.

"Trey?"

He turned to find Leora only a few feet from him.

"Who is this woman you worry over?"

Mara answered. "This is Bliss, a healer of extraordinary power. She saved Trey from death."

Leora gasped again and hurried over to Bliss, grabbing her hands. "I don't know how to thank you for saving Trey. His love is what kept me going all through my horrible ordeal. Without it, I would have withered and died. Bless you."

Trey watched Bliss's eyes begin to flutter and her face turn paler, and he knew that, in a moment, she would be in the throes of a vision. His arms reached out and caught her just as her body was about to crumble to the ground.

"Oh my Lord, is she all right?" Mara asked.

Trey didn't answer his mum. He knelt, cradling her body in his arms and watched her. If she didn't come out of it soon, he'd shake her out of it. And he couldn't help but wonder if Leora's taking hold of Bliss's hands had thrown Bliss into a vision.

"Trey, perhaps—"

"Not now, Mum. I'm doing what's best for Bliss."

Her eyes began to open, and relief swept over Trey, along with curiosity. What had she seen?

He didn't care for the dazed look in her eyes as she struggled to sit up.

"Easy," he urged as he helped her to sit and lean against him.

She laid her head on his chest. "I need to rest."

"I'll take you—"

"No," she said, as he helped her to stand. "You have important things to discuss with your family."

Mara stepped forward. "I will help—"

"No," Bliss said gently and reached past them both, taking the hand extended to her. "Dolca will help me. We are old friends."

The older woman slipped her arm around Bliss. "I will see her settled safely for the evening." She looked to Mara. "Could you have food sent to her room?"

Mara nodded. "Of course."

Trey stared after his wife as she was led from the room, with Dolca's arm firmly around her. He wanted to be the one going with her. It was where he belonged, by his wife's side. He suddenly grew annoyed with himself. He should have made their marriage known immediately. He had no intention of being kept from his wife's side, and definitely not her bed.

She might be too worn-out to make love, but he'd sleep by her side tonight—that he promised himself though a little niggling of doubt tormented him. And damn if he could chase it away.

Leora wrapped her arm around his. "We have much to discuss."

He rested his hand over hers. "That we do, but first I must speak with my brothers."

"Can it not wait?" she asked, her bottom lip protruding in a pout.

"No, it can't," he said, and directed her to the table where his family sat.

His brothers rang out a greeting as did their wives, their voices no longer silent. Each let him know how glad they were that he was home.

"You've missed much in your absence," Reeve said. "Bryce has found himself a woman, and a good one at that."

"Yes," his wife Tara agreed with a nod and a smile. "She was able to knock Reeve right off his feet."

"Is this true?" Trey asked with a laughing grin.

"He made a foolish move that left him vulnerable."

Trey looked at the slim, petite woman with hair the color of golden honey and shook his head. "You're just a bit of a thing. How could you possibly—"

"Charlotte also rescued Leora from a well-hidden prison," Bryce said with pride.

"I am indebted to you," Trey said.

"No need," Charlotte said. "I was there to rescue my da"—she pointed to the thin man with gray unruly hair sitting opposite her—"and, in the process, freed others. Leora was among them."

"It is so good to be home, to be with you," Leora said, keeping a tight hold on Trey.

"Dolca told us how busy you have been helping others," Mercy said. "It is good that Bliss was there with you to help."

Trey simply nodded. As much as he wanted to announce that Bliss was his wife, he knew it would not be fair to Leora after all she had been through, and so he held his tongue, even though it was difficult.

"I want to hear more about what I have missed, but we need to talk," Trey said, looking from one brother to the other and settling last on his da.

"I'll have hot food waiting for you," Mara said.

Leora clung tighter to Trey's arm. "It has been so long. I do not wish to separate from you."

Separate.

The word hit him like an arrow to the heart. Could this be what Bliss had seen, this minor separation? He also realized just how accurate her vi-

sions of Leora had been. And he couldn't help but
wonder again about her latest vision. What had it
shown her?

"Besides," Leora said, "there are things I learned
about the king while held captive that might be of
help."

"We would be most interested in hearing them,"
Carmag said, "but another time."

Mara slipped her arm around Leora and, with a
firm yet gentle urging, eased her away from Trey to
the table. "Join us women in a chat."

"Yes, you've hardly said a word since your arrival," Mercy said. "Do share with us."

"I'd love to hear what happened to you," Tara
said.

"And how you came to be in such a horrid
prison," Charlotte said.

Leora looked from one to the other, put a hand
to her head, and returned to Trey's side. "I'm sorry,
but my head pounds," she said, her fingers rubbing
her forehead. "I will wait for you in our bedchamber. Please do not be long." She kissed his cheek
and walked away, without a word to anyone else.

Trey wondered if it was difficult for her with
the other women here. She had been the only other
woman besides his mother in the keep. Now his
brothers all had women, two of them already wed.
And Bryce had a woman, something he had never
expected.

The men retired to the solar to talk. The door
was no sooner closed than Trey spoke.

"The king is heavily building his army to the
north."

"I hadn't expected that," Carmag said. "He takes a risk, gathering his men there with winter upon us."

Trey continued to detail what he had seen, including how the farmers were being ripped from their lands and the women left to care for themselves.

"It sounds like the king is desperate for more soldiers," Duncan said.

Bryce shook his head. "No, he attempts to rob the true king of men who would fight for him."

"A foolish plan," Trey said, "for it makes the people hate him even more."

"King Kenneth doesn't care about the people," Reeve said. "He thinks only of himself."

"We need to send some men north to keep watch on the king's soldiers' encampment," Carmag said, and the brothers agreed.

Trey gave Bryce a hearty slap on the back. "I can't believe I return home to find that you have a woman."

Bryce grinned though it faded slowly. "And I can't believe you don't seem thrilled to see that the woman you love is alive and well and here waiting for you."

"He's right," Reeve chimed in. "You looked more as if you wished to escape her than hold her."

"I have to agree with my brothers," Duncan said. "And your concern for Bliss was blatantly obvious. Want to tell us something?"

Trey looked to his da, who simply nodded. There wasn't much he kept or could keep from his brothers, and that they could be trusted went without saying. He rubbed at his chin, shook his head, and, with a smile, said, "Bliss and I are wed."

Trey hadn't expected complete silence to meet his announcement and was relieved when Bryce spoke.

"Are you sure about this? Bliss is not like other women."

"Something I am grateful for," Trey said, his smile spreading.

"Don't you worry that there is nothing you will be able to keep from her?" Reeve asked.

Trey threw the question back at him. "Do you think there is anything you can keep from your wife?"

Reeve laughed. "True enough."

Carmag rested a hand on his son's shoulder. "I remember how much you loved Leora and how inconsolable you were when you thought her dead. Are you sure that your love for Leora is gone?"

"What difference does it make?" Duncan asked. "He is wed to Bliss. There can be no changing that."

Carmag squeezed his son's shoulder. "I am familiar with the Picts' ways. Marriages can be ended at their choosing and with only a few words spoken."

"Damn, I should have married a Pict," Reeve said with a laugh.

"You would end your marriage to Tara that easily," Trey snapped.

Reeve's laughter died quickly. "I but joke. I love my wife and would never think of ending my marriage . . . but, then, I haven't loved another woman as strongly as I love Tara."

"Why did you wed so fast?" Carmag asked. "Why did you not wait until you returned home and share the happy occasion with your family?"

Trey hadn't been prepared for questions. He had believed, or had he hoped, that his family would simply accept the marriage and not pry. But he should have known better.

"Once your mum finds out, and I would not wait long to tell her, she will want answers," Carmag said.

His da didn't have to remind him. He knew his mum would question and probe until . . .

He shook his head.

"True love doesn't die easily, my son," Carmag said. "Make certain this is what you want."

Chapter 27

Bliss appreciated Dolca's help and had been glad for her company, but what she now sensed would soon bring her to tears, and she simply wished to be alone.

"Dolca, I need to—"

"Think," the older woman finished.

"I forget how wise you are."

Dolca walked over to where Bliss sat on the bed and offered her a comforting hand. "I am here whenever you need me."

Bliss gave her hand a squeeze and smiled. "It will go better than you think. Do not worry."

"I did not give you my hand with expectation of—"

"I know you didn't," Bliss assured her, "but I cannot control what I sense or see."

"I've often wondered if what you and your grandmum shared is a gift or a curse."

Bliss didn't respond; she just smiled, and was glad when Dolca closed the door behind her, for at the moment she felt cursed. With a heavy heart, she sensed that Trey was being warned of his marriage to her. She wasn't surprised that he had confided in his father and brothers. She had seen for herself how close the family was and could not blame them for warning him.

Trey had returned home with a bride after being gone for only a few weeks. His family would be foolish not to question the circumstances. And to add to the problem, the woman he loved was not dead, but alive and well and loved him as strongly as—

Bliss threw the soft wool blanket off her and got out of bed. She walked over to the hearth and held her cold hands out to the flames' heat, rubbing warmth into them.

When Leora had taken hold of her hands, Bliss had sensed that she wasn't telling the truth, but about what she wasn't sure. She also sensed that she was worried about something, but what would concern her when she was finally home with the man she claimed to love?

Bliss walked over to sit on the edge of the bed. Many secrets were about to be revealed. How they would affect Trey and her, she didn't know, and she wondered if she was better off not knowing.

She was about to climb back in bed when she sensed that someone needed healing. It would happen like that with the Picts. She would sense when someone would arrive at her cottage or that someone needed her, and she would go to the person's home before she was summoned.

This, however, was a bit different. It was an odd sensation, almost as if someone called to her. The more she paid heed to it, the stronger the summons grew, and she hastily slipped into a dark blue wool gown that Mara had brought for her. It was a bit large and revealed a bit more of her breasts than she would have liked, but it was warm and clean. Her stockings were being laundered, so she slipped her bare feet into her leather boots and, tossing her cloak over her arm, quickly crept out of the room and down the stairs.

The voice directed her to a narrow passage that sat away from prying eyes, and, before she knew it, she was out of the keep and walking through the village. Her footprints quickly disappeared behind her, the snow having turned heavier.

It wasn't until she came to the far end of the village that she stopped and tapped at a cottage door. It swung open.

"Good, you heard me," Stone said. "Hurry in out of the snow."

Bliss shook the snow from her cape and entered. "Someone is ill?"

"I am fine, Stone worries too much," Willow said from where she sat in the bed in the corner of the room.

Bliss walked over to her after Stone took her cape to hang on a peg. He quickly followed behind her.

"Her stomach has not been well," he said, sitting on the bed beside her.

"Can't keep much in it?" Bliss asked though she knew the answer and already knew her problem though it wasn't a problem.

Stone jumped up off the bed, realizing the cause, "Good, lord, Willow, why didn't you tell me?"

"Why didn't you know she carried your child?" Bliss asked with a smile. "And when did this happen?"

"You want details?" Stone grinned.

"Stop teasing her, Stone," Willow chastised and held her hand out to him. He took it and joined her on the bed. "It just happened. One day I looked at him and knew that I loved him."

"It was the same for me," Stone admitted.

"He didn't bother to wait to see if I felt the same," she chuckled. "He blurted it out before he ever kissed me. And I did the same. We've been joined as one since that day."

"I am happy for you," Bliss said, "and there is no need to worry that you will lose the babe. She will be a healthy one and much like her da."

Stone sat speechless for a moment, then shook his head. "I am going to have a daughter?" He took Willow's hand in his. "I've been feeling your fear, but I thought it was because you were ill. You frightened me. I thought you seriously ill, your fear was so great."

"It was foolish of me, but having lost one babe—"

Bliss put her mind at ease. "You will lose no more, and it is a large brood you'll have."

Willow reached out to her. "I am so glad you were here and that Stone sent for you."

Bliss squeezed her hand. "His love is so great for you that it doesn't always allow him to see clearly of things to come for you both. So I will tell you both now. You will have a good, long, and happy life together." She yawned. "Forgive me, I am tired from my long journey here."

ugh be careful. Your mum can sniff out
a secret like a prized hound."

The brothers laughed; Trey didn't.

Bryce clamped a hand on Trey's shoulder. "We
will wish you well whatever your choice."

"I would pay heed to da's words though," Reeve said. "Mum is as good at uncovering secrets as she is in keeping them."

"You should go and talk with Leora," his da said. "Since her arrival, she has talked with no one. All she would say is that she wanted you."

Carmag spent a few more minutes outlining who would be sent to scout the soldiers' encampment and the area around it. They also discussed briefly the failed attempt of having a spy infiltrate the king's castle. Though none would say it, they all knew that time was drawing near, and what they had worked so hard for would soon be upon them.

They would fight to the death if necessary to see the true king claim the throne.

The meeting dispersed, the men going to find their women and Trey reluctantly heading for his bedchamber and Leora. His father's words haunted him.

Love doesn't die easily.

He had been devastated when he had believed Leora dead. He would have given anything to get her back, and now that he had her back?

His father's words rang strong in his head again.

Love doesn't die easily.

He agreed. Love didn't die easily, and, therefore, he had to ask himself if he ever truly loved Leora, for right now he wanted nothing more than to hurry to his wife, climb in bed with her, hold her close, and never let her go.

Instead, he did the honorable thing and he rapped lightly on the door to his bedchamber before opening it and entering. The room was quiet, the hearth's glow the only light.

He walked toward the bed though he slowed his steps as her familiar scent drifted around him. After he had lost her, he had spent many a night with his arms wrapped around her pillow, breathing in her sweet scent. She had always smelled like a field of freshly bloomed wildflowers.

It had upset him when her scent began to fade. It had been like losing her all over again.

He approached his bed to find her sprawled across it, the wool blanket tangled around her. He had to smile, recalling how many times he had woken to find himself clinging to the edge and chilled from having no covers.

The thought hit him suddenly like one of Bliss's visions. He slept wrapped around Bliss. They fell asleep cuddled together, and they woke that way. And whenever in bed, they were always wrapped in each other's arms.

He stepped closer and saw that one leg lay exposed, pale and slender and silky soft. Leora was always soft to the touch and had responded to his touches most willingly—a good portion of the time.

Bliss had simply surrendered to his touch all of the time. Her passion constantly simmered at the surface, and all he needed to do was place a hand on her, and desire would stir in her eyes.

There was no choice here for him to make. Bliss was his wife and carried his child and, most importantly, he loved her like he had never loved before. Standing by the side of the bed staring at Leora made him realize that and made him question the love he had believed he had for her all the more.

She stirred and turned restless, as if in the throes of a bad dream. He thought of Bliss and how frightened he would get when she became lost in a vision. It angered him that all he could do was sit by helpless, unable to do anything but hold her. And it worried him that she would get stuck in a vision when he wasn't with her, and what then?

Leora's fitfulness worsened, and he couldn't stand there and watch her suffer. He sat on the edge of the bed and gently stroked her arm.

"Easy, Leora," he whispered, "you're safe now."

She sprang up, startling him and stunned him even more when she threw her arms around him and pressed her body against his. The soft wool nightdress provided only a thin barrier between her abundant breasts and his chest. And guilt washed over him like a tumbling wave. This was not right; he belonged with his wife.

"I'm so frightened, Trey, please hurry into bed and hold me."

That was not going to happen. He *would not* betray his wife; he *did not want* to betray his wife. And as much as he wanted to tell Leora that he was wed and intended to remain so, now was not the time.

Just as he was about to ease her away from him, she tilted her head and planted her lips on his.

Bliss gasped, her hand rushing to press against her stomach.

"Are you all right?" Roan asked.

Bliss forced a small smile to her face. "Yes, a sudden vision that startled." It was the truth, and how could a vision of Leora kissing Trey not startle her?

"Langward will heal?" Roan asked.

"This wound should have been seen to immediately," Bliss said, wishing her focus could have remained on the vision so that she could have made some sense of it. But the young Pict needed her attention more at the moment, and so she let it go.

Besides, if she believed and trusted their love, she knew that there was nothing for her to worry about. Though what of that separation she had seen? She shook her head; she had no time for this now.

"The others did what they could for him, and once they arrived here, one of the local women cleansed it and did what she could."

"There is a small piece of the arrow that pierced his arm embedded in his wound. It must be removed for me to heal him properly. You will need to help me, and you will confirm what I already know, that it is a soldier's arrow that struck him."

Roan nodded.

"The soldiers attacked the Picts," she said, already knowing that it was true.

"Aye, they did just as you once predicted."

Bliss felt the knot in her stomach worsen and worried over the future, for she could not see it clearly. Had fate yet to decide it?

The cottage was small where Roan and she worked on Langward, but at least they had shelter,

Roan explaining that Carmag had offered it to the Picts anytime they passed through MacAlpin land. It sat a distance from the village, alone, with no neighbors in sight. A place no doubt frequented by travelers needing shelter for a night.

It didn't take long to tend Langward's wound though it did take longer to heal him. She had sensed that the wound had turned poisonous and had seen indications of it while working on him. That meant she would need to spend more time healing him with her hands.

Battling fatigue, she knew her strength was dwindling, so she placed a shield around herself so that no one could disturb her and she could concentrate on healing Langward. She rubbed her hands together and went to work.

Trey had feared that the kiss would flood him with a wave of memories that would cut deep, but it didn't. Where had the passion gone? It had been there once; he wouldn't deny that. But not now, and not for either of them—that he strongly sensed, and he didn't need Bliss's ability to confirm it.

He eased Leora gently away from him. "You are overwrought from all you have suffered, and, no doubt, your head still pains you."

"It does," she said with a sigh that sounded more like relief.

"And there is much for us to discuss."

"Like when do we wed?"

"That and much more," he said, not wanting to

start any discussion that could lead to tears and disappointment.

She moved away from him to snuggle beneath the blanket. "Remove your garments and join me as you always did."

That was definitely not going to happen. The only one he'd shed his clothes for and climb into bed with was Bliss.

"I can't bear being alone," she said with tears in her eyes. "The nightmares are"—she shuddered— "Please, I don't want to be alone."

Guilt twisted at his stomach. How could he not empathize with all that she had suffered and help ease a burden he would only add to.

He sat on the side of the bed, and she reached out to him. He took hold of her hand, her slim fingers wrapping around his.

"Thank you for being so understanding," she said. "But then you have always been an honorable man and a considerate lover"—she yawned and closed her eyes—"a man worthy of being king."

He sat staring at her as she drifted off to sleep. He laid her limp hand at her side and couldn't help but recall how often she had made mention of his being king. She had been well aware that of the four brothers, one of them was the true king. She had seemed convinced that it was he.

His da's words certainly had stirred a hornet's nest. Suddenly, Leora had seemed different than he had remembered her. He left the room with haste, not wanting to chance her waking again.

Reeve's bedchamber wasn't far from his, and he was eager to see his wife and talk with her. He stopped abruptly, two things suddenly heavy on his mind. One, he carried Leora's scent on him, and, two, he had no doubt his wife already was aware that Leora had kissed him.

Had she seen the whole of it, or had she wondered over it?

He didn't want to wait to find out, and since she knew of the kiss, the scent would not matter. Or would it? He hurried to Reeve's bedchamber and eased the door open, not wanting to disturb her if she had fallen asleep.

Trey hurried over to the large bed and stared at it. It was empty.

Chapter 28

Trey raced through the keep, searching for his wife. No matter where he went or whom he spoke with, no one had seen her. He couldn't understand how she could just vanish without a trace. Someone had to have seen her somewhere.

The one person he hadn't truly wanted to see, though she knew everything that went on in the keep, was his mum. She had an instinct about her and could always tell when he and his brothers were lying. He didn't want to lie to her, but he wasn't ready to discuss his problem.

"Have you seen Bliss, Mum?" he asked, entering the great hall as she was leaving it.

"She's where Dolca settled her in Reeve's bedchamber."

Trey shook his head. "I stopped by to see how she was doing, but she wasn't there."

Mara wrinkled her brow. "That's odd. She was so tired that I assumed she'd be fast asleep by now."

"I thought the same myself," Trey said, his worry growing.

"Shouldn't you be with Leora instead of concerning yourself with Bliss?"

When she hooked her arm with his and walked them to the table in front of the hearth, not even waiting for an answer, he knew he was in trouble.

"Is there something you want to tell me?" she asked, pointing to the bench for him to sit.

His mum's intense stare had him keeping his mouth shut. How he'd get out of this unscathed he didn't know.

"You may have been shocked to see that Leora was still alive, but you didn't seem as happy to see her as I expected you to be."

"It's the shock of it all," he said, feeling safe to blame his reaction on it. "I had thought her dead, and here she is, alive. Weren't you just as shocked?"

"It near knocked me off my feet to see her alive though it was with tears and a hug that I greeted her." Her brow wrinkled. "It was strange though that she chose to keep to herself while waiting for your return. Leora was like a daughter to me, but now . . ." She shook her head. "She has changed though no doubt not through any fault of her own."

He seized on her words. "You're right, Mum, Leora is different, and I think she and I need time to get to know one another again."

Mara's hand went to rest on her hip, and she grinned. "Don't be thinking you can lie to me and get away with it. What's going on? You were more concerned with Bliss's well-being than Leora's return."

Part of the truth might be enough to appease her. "I'm in love with Bliss."

Mara's hand flew to her chest, and her eyes spread wide. "Are you sure?"

Trey smiled. "More sure about it than anything I've ever been in my life."

"What of your love for Leora? You were devastated when you thought her dead. I didn't think you would ever recover. Now you tell me that, within a few weeks, you have fallen in love with someone else."

"I cannot explain to you or to myself," he said. "I hadn't expected it or planned on it. It just happened."

"Well, at least you haven't wed Bliss. It will give you time to see if perhaps you made a mistake and still love Leora."

He wasn't about to tell her that Bliss was his wife and would remain his wife. But he did intend to let her know what Bliss meant to him.

"My love for Bliss is not going to change. I am happiest when I am with her and miss her when she isn't near"—he stood—"which is why I intend to find out where she has gone off to."

Mara rested her hand to her son's chest. "Be sure about this, Trey. True love is rare to find, and you don't want to lose it."

He took hold of his mum's hand. "I know, and that's why I go to look for Bliss."

She sighed as if in resignation. "You were always a stubborn one."

"I thought I was the stubborn one," Reeve said, entering the hall.

Mara laughed. "You do have your moments though your fists usually settle things for you, and since you're here, help your brother find Bliss."

"I thought she was in my bedchamber, sleeping."

"She's not there," Trey said.

"Perhaps someone needed healing," Reeve suggested.

"Then I would have been summoned," Mara said.

"Well, she couldn't have just disappeared," Reeve said.

"Who disappeared?" Bryce asked, Charlotte at his side, as they entered from outside, Odin trotting happily alongside her.

"You're covered with snow," Reeve said.

"That's because it's snowing out," Bryce informed him with a grin.

Mara shook her head. "You two wander off at the oddest times."

"What is that thing?" Trey asked, shaking his head though he didn't wait for an answer. "By chance, did you happen to see Bliss?"

Charlotte patted the big dog on the head. "This is Odin, my trusty and loving companion. As for Bliss, I saw her walking toward the far end of the village."

It came to him in an instant, and without a word to his family, he turned and hurried toward the door.

"Where are you going?" Bryce called out.

"Willow's place," he answered without looking back.

"I'll join you," Reeve offered, coming up behind him.

"The hour grows late." Trey stopped at the door. "Go see to your wife. I can do this on my own."

Reeve yanked two fur-lined cloaks off the pegs by the door and tossed one at his brother. "I'm going with you . . . just in case. As for *my wife,* I know exactly where she is. She's sound asleep after being well satisfied."

"Bryce and Duncan are right, you do need a beating," Trey said, shoving a laughing Reeve out the door.

The village was quiet, the snow falling steadily. There was sure to be a good accumulation by morning. Trey hoped he'd find Bliss at Willow's place. He didn't want to think of her having gone off somewhere in the snow, in the dark of night and alone. Or was she alone?

What troubled him the most was that he couldn't sense anything about her. While they traveled together, he could sense things about her so easily. But at this moment he could sense or feel nothing, and he grew fearful. Had something happened to her?

Trey's fist came up as he approached the door, anxious to pound on it, gain entrance, and see his wife sitting there safely.

The door sprang open before he even reached it. Stone stepped out. "Bliss was here, but she left sometime ago."

"Where is she?" Trey demanded.

Stone shook his head. "I don't know."

"Look and find her, do what she does," Trey snapped.

Stone kept his voice calm. "I do not have the power your wife has."

Trey kept his voice to a harsh whisper. "You know that we are wed."

"It was easy to sense, and I will guard your secret well. But Bliss's power comes naturally, passed down from one to another, growing ever stronger in each person. While I inherited some ability, more of it was learned and grew stronger with practice."

Trey's fear mounted. Where could she be?

"Call out to her, and she should hear you . . . unless?"

"Unless what?" Trey demanded.

"Unless she shields herself from letting anyone in or . . ."

Trey shook his head. "No, even if she were dead, she would come to me like her grandmother comes to her."

"So she can sense and see beyond this world." His smile was one of envy.

"How can I penetrate any shield she erects?"

"You cannot," Stone said. "But if you both truly love each other, and you continually reach out to her, she will eventually hear you, if only as a whisper. Fate allows nothing to stand in the way of true love." Stone rested his hand on Trey's shoulder. "Reach out to her. It is the only way you will find her."

Reeve followed beside Trey when he turned and headed back to the keep.

"We could organize a search party," Reeve offered.

"No, I will do as Stone says and reach out to her."

"I must ask you. Doesn't her power frighten you? A wife who knows your every thought?"

Reeve pretended to shudder. "I love Tara beyond reason, but I would not want her in my head."

"It's not like that, and, besides, it eases my worry over keeping her safe to know that she can sense me and I her, though I worry that perhaps her sensing that Leora kissed me is what made her erect the shield."

"Cheating on your wife so soon?" Reeve chuckled.

"You really do need a beating. I said Leora kissed me; I did not return the kiss."

"But you did not stop her, did you?"

Trey shook his head. Reeve was right—he hadn't stopped Leora from kissing him.

"Had to know if you still enjoyed it, didn't you?"

Trey didn't answer.

Reeve grabbed hold of his brother's arm, forcing him to stop. "I had asked Tara if she loved the first man she was to wed. And she did. She had told me that she had loved him and knew she wanted to wed him when they first met. Naturally, I felt jealous, but she told me that with me she felt not only loved but safe, and she hadn't felt that way in a very long time.

"You loved Bliss enough to wed her—" Reeve stared at his brother. "Why did your eyes shift so suddenly? What didn't you tell us?"

Trey started walking.

Reeve grabbed his arm again. "Tell me, or you'll be having this talk in the solar with the others."

"Don't threaten me," Trey warned.

"Then tell me what you're keeping from us."

"Nothing of importance."

"Let me be the judge of that."

"No," Trey snapped sharply, and walked on without him. He had no intentions of telling anyone how he and Bliss came to be husband and wife. It would create more strife than it was worth, and, besides, it meant nothing now. He loved Bliss, and that was all that mattered.

He rushed into the great hall, dropped his cloak on the peg, and was relieved to see that no one was about. He didn't want to delay reaching out to Bliss or delay receiving a response. Their love was true, so she would certainly hear him. Or did he need this to prove the strength and depth of their love?

He entered Reeve's bedchamber and began pacing in front of the hearth, his thoughts on nothing but Bliss.

Bliss. Bliss. Answer me. I love you.

He repeated it over and over and over.

Bliss woke with a start. "Trey?"

She looked around the room, expecting to see her husband; his voice had been so clear in her head. Roan slept soundly on the ground in front of the hearth, while Langward slept peacefully in the narrow bed. She stretched the aches from her body as she sat up, the wood chair not very comfortable for sleep.

Bliss.

She stilled. That was her husband's voice, but how. She hadn't removed the protective shield when she finished working on Langward. She had been so exhausted, and if she hadn't been able to get some sleep, she would have been useless when needed.

How had Trey penetrated the shield?

Bliss, answer me. I love you.

She gasped lightly, and tears came to her eyes. He loved her, truly loved her.

Had she doubted his love? Did she need this to prove it to her?

She grinned like a fool. If that was so, she didn't care. His love had the power to penetrate her shield, and that was all that mattered.

She reached out to him. *I'm all right, Trey.*

Good Lord, Bliss, where are you?

Langward required healing. I'll be back in the morning.

I'll come to you now.

It is late.

I don't care. I want to be with you. Tell me where you are, or I will not leave your thoughts.

She laughed softly and explained where she was, wanting him there.

I will be there soon. I love you.

Happiness rushed over Bliss, and she shuddered. She couldn't wait for Trey to get there. She missed him and would be relieved to have him beside her. They truly were one, and nothing, absolutely nothing could tear them apart.

Trey hurried down the stairs relieved and with a smile on his face . . . until he saw what awaited him in the great hall.

He approached his da and brothers with a confident stride. He had no intention of being waylaid. "Whatever you have to say to me, it will wait until morning."

"No, it won't," his da said.

Trey shook his head at Reeve. "You had to say something. You couldn't wait."

"Do not blame your brother," his da said. "Anything that could possibly put the true king in peril cannot wait."

"How could my situation be perilous to the true king?" Trey asked annoyed.

"We don't know, but we don't want to take a chance," Bryce said. "Tell us what brought you to wed Bliss."

"Why did you wish to wed me?" Charlotte asked, entering the hall.

"I thought you were sleeping," Bryce said.

"I woke, and you were gone, so I came looking for you," she said, "and I'm waiting for an answer."

"I love you and cannot see life without you," Bryce answered and held his hand out to her.

Charlotte smiled and took hold of his hand. He quickly wrapped his arms around her and tucked her against him. "Then don't you think your brother feels the same about Bliss?"

"Why then did he rush into marriage?" Duncan asked. "We all brought the women we love home to wed. Why didn't he? And by the way, Charlotte, no one is to know of his marriage."

"What marriage?" Mercy asked on a yawn as she entered the hall.

"Who got married?" Tara asked, following behind Mercy.

"If we're not all quiet, Mum will be joining us soon," Reeve said, drawing his wife into his arms as Mercy drifted into Brycc's outstretched arms.

"Mum's already here and has been for some time." Mara stepped out of the shadows. "Did you all think that when I came upon each of you slinking around the keep, I didn't know something was afoot?"

No one said a word, and Mara marched over to Trey.

"Can this not wait until morning?" Trey asked, but he already knew the answer.

"No," Mara said sharply. "I think Bliss is a good woman, and I am forever grateful that she saved your life, but to wed her so fast?"

"You are married to Bliss?" Leora screeched, rushing off the stairs and into the room to fall to her knees a few feet from them all. "No! No! You can't be."

Trey went over to her and reached down to help her up.

She slapped his hands away. "You don't know what you've done. Now King Kenneth will kill my da."

Chapter 29

Bliss woke Roan. "I must go back to the keep."

Roan sat up. "I cannot let you go on your own, and I cannot leave Langward."

"I will be fine," she assured him. "The woods will guide me, and my husband needs me. Langward is well on his way to healing. Feed him the brew I have prepared and bring him to the keep when he feels up to traveling. You will need to speak with the MacAlpins about this attack."

"I do not like your traveling on your own," Roan said.

"I have done it many times, and at the moment, there is nothing for me to fear. I will be fine."

Bliss left the safety of the cottage and followed her instincts, the snow tapering off as she traveled. She had decided against telling Trey she was on her way home. He would worry, and he presently had enough to deal with.

She couldn't help but wonder if fate had a hand in what was happening tonight. Had she grown tired of waiting? Was she forcing secrets to be revealed?

Whatever the answers, Bliss was glad of one thing . . . Trey's love.

She tucked her cape tightly around her and hurried her steps. It wouldn't take her long to reach the keep though by then more trouble would be brewing.

Trey was still trying to comprehend what Leora had said as Mara and Mercy helped the weeping woman to the table in front of the hearth and wrapped a soft wool blanket around her shivering body.

He noticed that she had gotten much thinner than he had first realized, her gown hanging on her where once it had clung to her every curve. He felt bad for what she must have suffered, but it also made him wonder who this woman was. Had he ever known her? Had she ever loved him?

He shut his eyes for a moment against the unthinkable. Had she been a spy for King Kenneth all this time? He opened his eyes and saw on all their faces that their thoughts were similar to his.

Trey walked over to Leora and gently moved his mum aside. She looked ready to protest, but the resolve on his face warned her otherwise, and she stepped aside.

"It's time to tell me the truth, Leora," Trey said, sitting on the bench beside her.

The others gathered behind them, all eager to hear.

Her thin hand slipped out of the blanket and took hold of his. "I never meant to hurt you. You are a good man."

"What have you done?" Trey asked, not knowing if he'd be relieved or hurt by her answer.

"You must understand that I had no other choice. King Kenneth took my da and held him prisoner. The only way he would even consider freeing him was if I"—she choked back tears—"if I infiltrated the MacAlpin clan and pretended to fall in love with one of the four warriors, one of whom would be king. I was to feed all information I learned to him and try to find out who was the true king. When I did, he promised he'd release my da."

Trey sat silent. Their love had never been real, and yet he had believed it was. How could he have been so blind? He had brought peril on the true king. Did he continue to do so all in the name of love?

"You never found out the true king's identity, so why was your death staged? Why did you leave?" Trey asked.

"The king was in a fury. He had discovered that a spy had infiltrated his court at the deepest level and was going mad with the need to find him. So he insisted I return and tell him everything I knew and help him find the spy."

"We pulled our spy out before he could be discovered, and he didn't go that deep in the king's court," Trey said.

"It wasn't your spy," she said, shaking her head. "I helped the king discover that his mistress was a Pict, and her intention all along was to waylay his plans to destroy the true king."

Mercy gasped and rushed forward, Duncan fast to follow her. "My mum was no Pict."

"You must be Mercy, the king's daughter,"

Leora said, "and from what I have learned, it is the truth. Your mum was a Pict."

"But she had no markings," Mercy said.

Leora shook her head. "I do not know anything about that. I only know that she was a Pict."

Mercy turned to her husband, and he wrapped her in his large arms.

"Why did you return here?" Duncan demanded.

"You all seemed to thwart the king's plans at every turn, from taking his stepdaughter to robbing him of a significant bride price. He believed he had another spy in his court, and the only way for him to find out was to send me back here. He insisted I wed Trey and gain his full confidence as only a wife could."

"He used the threat of harming your da to force you to do this?" Trey asked.

"He had my da moved to one of his hidden prisons, where they do unspeakable—" She shook her head as tears trailed down her cheeks. "I couldn't let my da suffer when I had the chance to save him. And now it is all for naught; my da will die a horrible death."

"What were you doing in one of those prisons?" Charlotte asked.

"I had been there only a day and was about to escape, allowed to escape, and make my way back here when you suddenly showed up. I couldn't believe my good fortune."

Charlotte nudged Bryce in the side. "Remember Donald's story?"

Leora's eyes turned wide. "Donald is my grand-da's name. You've met him?"

"He's here," Bryce said. "Charlotte and I met him while on a mission. He had lost all desire to live until he discovered we had met his son."

Leora jumped up. "My da escaped?"

"He did," Charlotte said, "and he helped me find my way to that prison so that I could free my da. The king had put you in the same prison he had banished your da to."

Tears streamed down Leora's face. "Can you tell me where you last saw my da?"

"He's here with your grandda," Bryce said.

"Take me to them please," she pleaded. "I will tell you everything in detail from start to finish, but first, please let me see my da and grandda."

"It's not possible to see them tonight," Bryce said. "Your da prefers to live a distance from others, so his place is a bit of a walk from here."

Leora's shoulders slumped, as if in defeat. "There is something else you should know though I cannot confirm it, for I heard it in whispers and only recently. There is talk that the king plans something against the Picts."

"The Picts will not take kindly to any intrusion from the king," Trey said.

"The king does what suits him," Leora said. "And when things do not go his way, those around him suffer." She shivered, as if recalling such a time.

Mara stepped forward. "I think Leora should get some rest. We all should. It's late, and we can talk in the morning, after a good night's rest."

The women drifted off, knowing that the men needed to talk alone, and Mara, with Mercy's assistance, helped Leora to her room.

"It makes no sense that the king would attack the Picts," Bryce said. "It would be a foolish battle move on his part, and I do not believe he's that foolish though I do believe he plans something."

"Perhaps Leora lies to us," Reeve said.

"For what reason?" Duncan asked. "Her da is safe."

"Perhaps the Picts know something," Carmag suggested.

There was a moment of silence before Bryce turned to Trey. "Whether you want to or not, there is something you need to consider. One woman used you to suit her own needs; does another one do the same?"

Trey took a quick step forward but stopped, keeping his clenched fist at his side when he wanted nothing more than to plant it in Bryce's face.

"It's a question that needs answering, son," Carmag said.

"We protect the king above all else," Duncan reminded.

"Just tell us how your marriage came to be, and this can all be settled," Reeve said.

Would it or would it create a larger problem? Bryce's comment had wounded him. Leora had made a fool of him. She had led him to believe that she loved him. He had been sure that she loved him, and he had suffered greatly when he thought her dead. And now to find out it had all been a ruse . . . just like his marriage to Bliss?

Was he seeing only what he wanted to see as he had done with Leora, or was Bliss different? Leora had reason to trick him. She wanted to save her da. What of Bliss? What could she want from him?

He needed answers as much as his brothers did. And they were right, the true king came above all else.

Trey told them everything, from the time he came upon Bliss, to the many detours they had encountered, and he also informed them of how easily the marriage could be dissolved.

"Then you truly aren't wed," Duncan said, as if he sounded relieved.

"You can spend more time with Bliss and make certain it is love that brought you together and not some plan of the Picts to help protect their people that brought this marriage about," Reeve said.

"That would be wise of you to do, Trey," his da advised.

Trey looked to Bryce. "And your thoughts, since I'm sure you have them?"

"The Picts have been our friends, and I do not believe there is any deception on their part, but one can never be sure, especially during these troubling times. I would suggest that you take your time and think this through, not for the sake of the true king or your family, but for you."

"What do you mean?" Reeve demanded. "He's been made a fool of once—"

"The precise reason he needs time to think this through," Bryce said. "Don't you think he's asking himself that very question? Don't you think he now wonders if Bliss truly loves him? Don't you think he wonders if love is even worth the trouble it has caused him?"

Reeve nodded and looked to Trey. "I may have faced possible death in wedding a death bride, but I had no doubt that Tara loved me, and that made all the difference. Bryce is right—you need to make sure for yourself."

"I agree," Duncan said. "I never once doubted Mercy's love for me, but I wonder if I would have been so easily accepting of it if I had been deceived by a woman. Though I must say Bliss has been a good friend to our family. She healed Mercy and she healed you and she keeps the secret of the true king's identity."

"But does she truly love me?" Trey asked, voicing his concern aloud.

"If you feel you must ask that, then you are not the man I thought you were."

The men turned to see Bliss standing a few feet away, her cloak sprinkled with snow and her cheeks flushed red from the cold.

At that moment, seeing the hurt in her eyes, Trey knew that he was a fool ever to allow himself to think that she might not love him. He felt as if he had betrayed their love, a love he had come to know, to accept, to revel in as honest, solid, and everlasting.

He stepped forward, and her hand went up in a flash as she took a step back.

"Do not come near me. You are not the man I wed. Until *he* returns to me, bother me not." And with that, she hurried from the keep.

Chapter 30

Trey didn't hesitate; he ran after her. The snow was falling heavily again, and he could barely see her, but it didn't matter. He had to make this right. He had to make amends for being an idiot.

He thought he saw her duck around a cottage, no doubt in an attempt to lose him, and so he was fast to follow, but she wasn't there. She seemed to elude him at every turn, and it upset him. He drove her away when only a short time before he had let her know how eager he was to be with her. How had he ever allowed himself to doubt even for a moment that her love was real and no ruse?

He had come to know his beautiful, unselfish wife in the short time they had been together. She hadn't hid herself from him, she had been open and honest and loving. And it hadn't been possible for her to hide her desire for him. She had responded like only a woman in love could, but, then, hadn't Leora done the same.

He stopped, paying no heed to the snow that accumulated more heavily on his hair and shoulders, having failed to grab a cloak before chasing after his wife. Taking a closer look, he'd have to admit that it was different with Bliss than it had been with Leora.

Bliss responded to his every touch, whether innocent or intimate, it didn't matter. It was obvious she desired him. It was as if her passion for him simmered on the surface and waited eagerly for his touch.

He turned hard with the thought.

Damn, now all he could think about was making love to her, burying himself deep inside her and hearing her moan with desire for him. It was like an addictive melody to his senses, one he longed to hear and would never grow tired of.

Instinct finally kicked in, and he turned and caught sight of her; he followed. She was headed to the woods, her haven. It would shelter her and keep her safe, so attuned was she to its magic.

He hurried after her. He had no intentions of letting her spend the night alone in the woods. She belonged with him, in his bed, and that was where he intended to take her.

He hastened his pace, catching up quickly, and soon he'd be able to reach out and . . .

Bliss stopped abruptly and spun around, holding her hand up to warn him not to come any closer. "I want to be alone."

"That's not going to happen," Trey said with a shake of his head. "You're coming home with me."

"We need time apart. It is what I saw and what must be."

He shook his head again. "Not this time."

"You can't deny fate."

"I'm not," he said, and took a step toward her. He was glad she didn't retreat. "It was never distance that you saw that would separate us; it was doubt and fear."

"I have no doubt that I love you, and as far as fear?" Her smile was sad. "My only fear is losing you."

"I feel the same."

She shook her head. "I don't believe you."

"You can't be serious. You're letting your fear interfere with your instincts. You can feel what I feel for you. I can't hide it from you." He spread his arms wide. "Look, I have nothing to hide—my love is there for you to see."

"You doubted."

"I won't deny that," he conceded. "Leora's return confused me, though thinking on it more, it actually frightened me. It made me question. What if, like her, you didn't truly love me? What would I do then? How would I live without you?"

"I should have realized that she never loved you," Bliss said, as if it were her fault. "In my visions, she kept claiming that she needed you; but never once did she say that she loved you."

"It isn't your fault. It's mine for even doubting briefly that you loved me."

Bliss pressed her hand to her chest. "It hurts to hear you say that. My love for you is eternal. It always has been and always will be. I have dreamt of the man I would call husband all my life, and that man is you; I have not a sliver of doubt."

He stepped forward again, eager to scoop her up and carry her back to the keep and make love to her.

She jumped back. "While I have not had a shred of doubt, you did, and you must settle that in your heart and mind before we can be together again."

Trey nodded slowly, his brow scrunched in thought.

"When your heart is certain, return to me," she said sadly, as if it pained her deeply to say it.

Trey nodded and went to turn, but instead swung around to reach out and scoop her up in his arms and yank her tightly against his chest. "You're mine and always will be. There is nothing to think about." He walked at a fast pace. "I love you, wife, and that love will only continue to grow with time, which means I will love you more and more each day."

"I—"

He silenced her protest with a kiss, before saying, "I will hear no more foolish objections from you. I intend to take you to our bedchamber and make love to you. All night, if we're both not too exhausted."

Her soft laughter sounded like a gentle melody floating on the night air.

"We belong together, Bliss. Fate decreed it, and what fate decrees, nothing can separate."

He kicked the door to the keep open and walked in, then kicked it closed.

His da and brothers still lingered in the great hall, and they stared at him, though Reeve grinned.

"Don't disturb us," Trey commanded, and disappeared up the steps.

Once in the bedchamber, Trey didn't waste a minute. He stripped himself fast as Bliss took a couple of steps back, then he stripped her, not giving her a chance to protest since he kept kissing her as he shed her garments.

When he was done, he hoisted her up so that she had no choice but to wrap her legs around his waist. Then he carried her to the bed and lowered her, burying himself slowly inside her as he did.

He loved the initial moment of entering her. She was always ready for him, always slick with moisture, as if just the thought of making love with him made her wet and that excited him and grew his erection harder and made sliding into her easy.

She gasped, though in moments she was moaning with delight as his rhythm quickened. It would be a fast joining—they both knew that and they both needed it to be. Though it hadn't been long since they had last made love, it had been much too long for them. It was as if their bodies, their minds, and their hearts could not live without it. Making love nourished them in ways neither understood but would not deny.

He grabbed her hips, forcing her to meet his potent thrusts more vigorously.

His name spilled from her lips in a whisper, and he knew it would grow stronger and louder as she begged him to bring her to climax. She wanted him; only he could drive her wild with passion, only he could satisfy her burning need, only he could deliver the climax that would leave her shuddering with satisfaction.

She belonged to him, body, heart, and soul.

The thought had him driving into her with such passion that she shouted out his name, and he knew, he could feel, her climax near. He moved with power that brought him pleasure and her satisfaction as he sent her flying over the edge.

He felt her explosive climax, heard her cry out his name, forcing him to join her. He burst in climax with her. So strong was it that it felt as if it went on forever. Not surprisingly, he sensed and felt another climax hit Bliss, and he kept his thrusts strong so her pleasure would be great.

When passion finally faded, leaving tingles to run through them, Trey stretched out beside her. He tucked her close to his side, smiled, and, with a slightly labored breath, said, "I love the way you're always wet and ready for me and how you moan and tighten around me just before you explode with passion."

"And I love that you sometimes enter me slow and easy and other times"—she didn't need to pretend to shudder, she did—"it's fast and hard."

"That's because I cannot wait; my need for you is too great."

"I feel the same," she admitted, snuggling closer against him.

He ran his hand over her breast, teasing the nipple. "I can't stop touching you. I can't stop thinking about you. I can't stop wanting you, and I will never stop loving you."

Contentment filled Bliss like never before. She eased herself over him, covering his warm, damp body with her sleek, moist one and rested her head on his chest. His arms went around her, his hands stroking down her back and along her backside.

She sighed with pleasure, cherishing the intimate moment with him. "I knew I would find love, but never did I think it would be as strong as the love I have for you. There is, however, one thing that I don't understand."

"And I know exactly what it is."

She raised her head, her eyes wide. "You do?"

He nodded. "You sensed it would be a while before we made love again and yet here we are and you wonder how you could have been wrong."

She smiled. "You know me well."

He laughed. "Every inch of you."

"Then if you know me so well, you must know the answer."

"I do," he said proudly. "It is a simple one. Time is different for us. A full day is even too long for us to go without making love. The intimate act connects us in a way it does no other. It is as if making love nourishes us, gives us strength, and so we hunger for it like others hunger for food."

"You know, I think you may be right," she said with surprise. "There are times I feel empty, as if somehow I need filling, then you . . . touch me. And I know it is you who will fill me to overflowing."

He kissed her, lingering on her lips before slipping his tongue inside to tease, taunt, and tempt. He hadn't expected to grow hard so soon after such a powerful climax, but to his surprise, he did. And the stronger the kiss grew, the harder he grew until . . .

He quickly rolled her on her back and slipped over her.

"I want to make love to you again," he said, his hand cupping her breast and his tongue darting across her nipple until it turned hard. "Slow and easy this time."

She smiled and reached down to stroke him. "And this time, I get to touch and taste as well."

Much later, their bodies exhausted and sleep ready to claim them, Bliss realized that she had forgotten to tell him about the attack on the Picts. She thought to wait until morning since nothing could be done about it tonight, and they both needed sleep.

"Something troubles you?" Trey asked.

"We grow ever more attuned to each other."

"And that troubles you?"

"No, not at all," she assured him. "It pleases me. It's just that I recalled something I meant to tell you and wondered if I should wait until morning, but it appears that, having sensed it, you should hear it now."

"Tell me."

"Roan and his group were attacked by the king's soldiers."

Trey tightened his arms around her.

"Now something troubles you," she said, sensing his concern.

"Leora told us that she heard talk that the king was possibly going to attack the Picts."

Bliss was silent for a moment. "That makes no sense. It would only cause us to side with you, and the king cannot be so foolish as to believe that with the Picts being neighbors of the MacAlpins these many years, the two would not have formed some mutual allegiance so that peace could prevail."

"Bryce voiced similar concerns."

She sat up shaking her head. "The king must have another reason for planning to attack the Picts, but what could it be? The attack would generate severe retaliation and guarantee the Picts' joining forces with the MacAlpins."

She wished she could sense something, have a vision, anything that would help solve the pending problem. But what she got would offer little help.

"You don't sense anything, do you?"

Bliss yawned and eased down alongside him. "I only know that the answer will soon present itself."

In no time, they both drifted off to sleep in each other's arms.

Trey woke just before dawn, and while he wanted to stay beside Bliss, be there when she woke and make love to her, duty to the true king came first, especially now, when battle lay much too close on the horizon.

He eased out of bed, tucking the covers around her. He took a moment and looked at her, as if just realizing she was his, they were wed, and she carried his child. It amazed and pleased him that they belonged to each other. It all had happened so fast. One day he was mourning the death of the woman he had loved, or thought he had loved, and the next he was falling in love.

Fate.

He smiled. Perhaps fate *was* much wiser than he had believed. Though the lesson had been a difficult one, fate had given him the opportunity to distinguish lasting love from passing love. He couldn't be more grateful or more grateful that fate had given him Bliss. If not for her, he would no doubt have been thrilled with Leora's return, only to later discover her betrayal and once again mourn, only this time he would have mourned a love that was never true.

He kissed his wife softly on the cheek, and whispered, "I love you."

She smiled, as if hearing him, and cuddled beneath the blankets. He wished he was there beside her, touching her, kissing her and . . .

He got up and dressed lest he surrender to his passion and climb into bed with her. He could delay no longer; his brothers and da needed to know what he and Bliss had discussed last night.

Reluctantly, he left his sleeping wife.

Chapter 31

Trey entered the great hall, knowing that his da or one of his brothers would be there. He wasn't the only one to rise before dawn. His da, mum, and Bryce were there, talking, and though he wanted to join them, he slowed his steps. As soon as he reached the table, before he even sat or said a word, his mum would assault him with questions.

He hastened his step, figuring it was better to get it over with and smiled when he saw his mum's mouth open before he reached the table.

"Don't you go grinning at me," she warned, shaking her finger at him. "I want to know why you haven't taken your time in deciding if this marriage is right for you. You just learned that the woman you thought loved you never did and that she betrayed you." She shook her head. "Why are you grinning like a fool?"

"Why wouldn't I grin? I don't feel an ounce of guilt over falling in love and loving another woman more than I ever loved the woman who betrayed me. If it wasn't for falling in love with Bliss, I'd be, at this very moment, not only mourning a love that never existed but angry as hell for ever having loved Leora in the first place."

"And you're not the least bit angry?" his mum asked.

"More upset that I've been duped—"

"We all were," Bryce said. "We all accepted and trusted her as a member of our family. Never once would any of us have believed that she was a spy. It still seems more tale than truth, but then, desperation causes people to do desperate things."

"My concern is that you don't get hurt again," Mara said.

"Bliss would never hurt me," Trey said, and was quick to raise his hand to silence his mum before she could argue. "My love for Bliss is far different than what I felt for Leora, and I have only realized that since falling in love with Bliss."

"I think Bliss will make a good sister," Duncan said, entering the room.

"I don't know," Reeve said, following behind Duncan. "She knows too much. There'll be no keeping anything from her."

"That's a good thing," his mum pointed out. "Then your wives will be able to keep a closer watch over all of you. Besides, you shouldn't be keeping anything from your wives."

"See what I mean," Reeve said, grinning and shaking his head as he took a seat at the table.

"You don't need a seer to have your wives know what you're up to," Carmag said. "Wives have the uncanny ability to know everything."

Mara gave her husband's shoulder a playful slap. "Even before you know it yourself."

They laughed.

Trey didn't want to interrupt the playful banter, but there were things that needed discussing. "We need to talk."

Laughter died off, and expressions turned serious and attentive. Mara didn't excuse herself; she knew it wasn't necessary. She was as trustworthy if not more so than anyone there.

"Bliss informed me that Roan's men were attacked by the king's soldiers."

There was stunned silence for several moments before his da spoke. "How badly?"

"One Pict was injured, no more. They are fierce fighters."

"That they are," Bryce said. "And for whatever reason, it would seem the king is anxious to make enemies of the Picts. It still makes no sense. King Kenneth is a good strategist when it comes to battle, and this is not a wise move on his part."

"Bliss believes the same," Trey said.

"Has she offered any insight as to why the king might be doing this?" Bryce asked.

Trey shook his head. "Not yet, but she believes the answer will soon present itself."

Conversation turned silent when servants began to enter the great hall to prepare the tables for the morning meal. Warriors would soon arrive and share the meal and receive instructions for their daily duties.

The keep was coming to life, and any further private discussion would have to wait.

Tara entered the room with Leora, who looked as if she hadn't slept a wink. That she was nervous and troubled was obvious, and Tara kept a supportive arm around her, as if the woman required help walking.

"Have something to eat," Mara said, waving Leora over to the table.

Leora shook her head. "No thank you. I would like very much to be taken to my da and grandda now if you don't mind."

Trey stood, a sudden thought striking him. Would a daughter of his have the courage to do what Leora had done? Not that he would want her to put herself in danger, to sacrifice so much to save him. The question probably would have never come to mind if he hadn't known he was to be a da, but knowing that made the difference. He could understand why Leora had sacrificed everything to see her da safe.

Leora moved away from Tara and hurried to Trey. "I am so sorry. I never meant to hurt you."

For a moment, he saw the woman he had loved standing before him, and he felt a catch to his heart. He felt sorry for her yet relieved for himself, and he had wished it could have been different. It could have been different if only . . .

"You never trusted me or my family enough to help you. You chose deceit instead. If you had only confided in me or in any of us, we would have helped you. And it would have saved us both much suffering."

She hung her head. "I made a poor choice."

Trey lifted her chin. "You let fear rule, and when you did, sound reason slipped away."

"I'll leave, go away. You'll never see me again. Just, please, let me see my family."

Trey shook his head. "You still don't understand. You never did. I would never keep you from your family." He stepped aside and called out to one of the warriors. "Malcom, take Leora to Old John's place and make certain that he knows that he and his family are welcome to remain part of the MacAlpin clan."

Tears ran down Leora's face, and she reached out, placing a hand on Trey's arm. "I am truly sorry I hurt you. And I am glad you found love. You deserve it."

She walked over to Malcom, and he escorted her out the door.

The great hall filled with talk and laughter as more warriors entered, and the women joined their husbands, and the twins were passed around to uncles and aunts as the parents took turns eating. Bliss was the last to make an appearance, and Trey stood so that his wife could sit beside him on the bench.

"I've no want for food," she said, her hand going to her stomach. "I'm going to see Dolca."

Trey went to her, his hand covering hers and lowered his voice. "You are not feeling well?"

"Just a bit," she said softly.

He didn't voice his concern, not wanting his family to know about the babe just yet. Instead, he said, "I'll take you to Dolca."

She shook her head, then stepped around him. "Mercy, do you mind showing me where Dolca is staying?"

Trey realized that Bliss had a far different reason for asking the favor of Mercy. Obviously, she believed it time for grandmother and granddaughter to meet.

"I'll take you," Duncan said, pushing away from the table to stand.

Mercy stopped him with a gentle touch to his arm. "I will take Bliss."

Tara smiled down at Conall, sound asleep in her arms. "I'll look after this little fellow for you."

"And I'll watch after Kate," Charlotte offered, hugging the smiling babe against her.

Mercy thanked them, gave her husband a quick kiss, and joined Bliss.

Trey hugged his wife close, and whispered, "Are you sure you feel well enough?"

She smiled and kissed his cheek, then whispered, "Your son makes his presence known."

A stab to his heart and gut turned him silent as she walked away with Mercy. It amazed him to think that his son grew inside her, and all he could think about was how very much he loved them both, and his son had yet to be born. He would keep them safe; no matter what it took, he would keep them safe.

His thoughts turned to Leora, and, once again, he realized how difficult it must have been for her when the soldiers took her da away. She must have felt so helpless and fearful. If only she had trusted him.

Slipping on fur-lined cloaks that were kept on pegs by the door, the two women left, hurrying out into the cold and snow.

Trey turned to rejoin his family, and they all sat staring wide-eyed at him.

Naturally, it was his mum who spoke. "Anything you want to tell us?"

"There is something you wish to tell me, isn't there?" Mercy said, as the snow fell lightly but steadily on them.

When Bliss woke this morning, she strongly sensed it was time that Mercy met her grandmother. More and more she sensed the urgency that longtime secrets be revealed. It was time the truth became known . . . it was time for the true king to step forward.

"There is something you need to know, but it is for Dolca to tell you."

Mercy nodded, and they walked in companionable silence until Mercy stopped in front of a small cottage.

"Will this upset me?" Mercy asked, before approaching the door.

Bliss smiled. "It may upset and surprise, but I believe it will also bring joy."

Mercy released a worried sigh, nodded, walked to the door, and gave it a rap.

Dolca welcomed them in though Bliss stopped in the doorway and suggested she leave them alone. Neither woman would have it, Mercy tugging her in, insisting she stay, and Dolca agreed with her.

They gathered around the small table, a hot brew in front of each though none touched it.

Unease filled the small space, and so Bliss got right to the crux of the matter. "Dolca is your grandmother, Mercy."

Mercy remained silent for a moment, as if trying to make sense of what she had just heard. "You're not the king's mother, and my mum's mother has long been dead."

"A tale your mum told you to protect you," Dolca said.

Mercy shook her head. "First, I'm told that my mum is a Pict, and now you tell me all I thought about my mum's past is not true?"

"Your mum wanted to keep you safe. You would not have been safe if you knew the truth," Dolca said. "Let me tell you about your mum, who she truly was and why she did what she did. And then you will learn for yourself what a truly loving mother she was."

Bliss could sense Mercy's anguish and pain as the story unfolded. All she had been told, all she believed her mum to be, was nothing but lies, and, in the end, all her lies were to protect her children.

Tears streamed down Mercy's cheeks, and she reached for Bliss's hand and held on tight until, finally, Dolca finished.

All Mercy could do was stare at the woman. It took her a few moments to gather her thoughts and find her voice.

"All these years I thought—" Mercy could not finish. "Mum sacrificed everything for me and"— she shook her head—"I can't believe I have a brother."

Dolca rested a gentle hand on Mercy's shoulder. "It is time for all of this to be known."

Mercy nodded. "Yes, secrets have been kept long enough. I wish I had known this sooner."

"Things are revealed in their own time," Dolca said.

"Very soon, all will be revealed," Bliss said. "At least now you know just how much your mum loved you."

"And why my father hates me," Mercy said.

"Your mum made a fool of the king," Dolca said. "Can you imagine what he felt when he discovered who she was?"

Mercy wiped at her tears. "And what that made me. No wonder he wanted me dead."

"Your mum would have been proud of you," Dolca said with tears in her eyes. "And she would have been happy that we have finally been reunited."

Mercy smiled though it was with a touch of sadness. "It is wonderful to learn you are my grandmum. Another time you will tell me more about my mum?"

"I will tell you everything so that you come to know your mum and what a brave and amazing woman she was. And I am eager to meet my great-grandchildren."

The sadness faded as Mercy's smile grew. "It will be so wonderful for my children, Conall and Kate, to know their great-grandmum."

Dolca pressed a hand to her chest. "Did you say your daughter's name was Kate?"

Mercy nodded. "I have always loved the name ever since my mum told me stories of a brave little lassie called Kate."

Dolca couldn't stop tears from falling. "Kate was your mum's true name."

Tears fell again, though this time Mercy smiled. "I am happy that my daughter bears the name of such a courageous woman."

Dolca nodded. "Yes, your mum would have been exceptionally proud of you."

Bliss sensed relief wash over the two women and happiness prevail. She only wished her stomach would settle. It had grown steadily worse since being there; she wasn't feeling well at all. She had laid her hand on her stomach while the women talked, hoping she could settle the unease, but it hadn't worked. Trey's son growing inside her was already a stubborn one, and she couldn't help but smile at the thought.

"You must come to the keep now and meet your great-grandchildren," Mercy said.

"I would like that," Dolca said.

Mercy looked to Bliss. "I can share with the others what grandmum has told me?"

Bliss nodded. "Aye, you can, and more secrets will be revealed because of it."

The three women slipped on their cloaks and left the cottage. The closer they got to the keep, the worse Bliss felt, and she had no desire to enter the hall and take a chance of someone's realizing that she was ill. No doubt questions would be asked, and she worried that she would not be able to hide the obvious . . . she carried Trey's babe.

"I must see to something," Bliss said to the two women, who walked a few steps ahead.

They stopped and turned, and Mercy asked, "Are you all right? You look pale."

"I am fine," Bliss said, pleased that it truly wasn't

a lie. She was well. It was only the babe making himself known. "I will join you soon though please wait until I do before you tell anyone the news."

Dolca slipped her arm around Mercy and gently urged her forward. "Bliss is a fine healer. If she were ill, she would heal herself."

It seemed to satisfy Mercy, and the two women continued walking though Dolca glanced back at Bliss once, and Bliss nodded and smiled her appreciation. She recalled Dolca and her grandmum often communicating without words, and Dolca did it with her as well.

Dolca had graciously offered her cottage to her while she was gone, and, with her hand to her protesting stomach, she turned, hoping her stomach wouldn't empty itself before she got there.

Bliss was only a few steps from the cottage when her stomach protested most vehemently. She hurried a short distance to the edge of the woods, not wanting to be sick in front of the cottage. She was about to lean over, ready to heave, when an arm wrapped around her waist.

Chapter 32

Trey pressed his hand gently against Bliss's stomach, and she leaned back against him, taking a deep breath. He had been worried about her after she left the keep. She had turned much too pale while talking with him, and she had refused any sustenance. It hadn't surprised him when his mum had questioned him, not once but several times. It seemed she wanted confirmation from what she had already surmised, that Bliss carried his child . . . but Trey would not acknowledge it.

It would give his mum another reason to question his marriage to Bliss in ways that would only anger him, and so he kept their secret. Besides, he wasn't ready to share it. He liked that only Bliss and he and no other knew, and when the time proved right, and they agreed, they would share the news, but not until then.

"I don't know what power you hold, but you instantly calmed your son, and I am grateful," Bliss said, relieved to have her husband's back for support.

"He is a good son; he listens to his da."

"It would seem he is strongly connected to his da to feel him when he is nothing more than a sprouting seed."

Trey laughed softly. "A seed I enjoyed planting."

He barely heard her light laughter though he felt it. It raced through him, sparking his senses and tightening his groin. Now was not the time to grow hard for her.

Her hand slipped over his, resting her fingers between his splayed ones. "I am ripe for planting anytime, my soil always moist and ready for you."

The growling moan rumbled deep in his chest. "If you were feeling well, I would plant here, right now, in the falling snow, but since you're not . . .

He scooped her up in his arms knowing, that if he didn't retreat soon, they would be making love on the snow-covered ground. "You need to rest." He kissed her quick. "We'll plant later."

Bliss wrapped her arms around her husband's neck and laid her cheek against his and shivered.

"You are cold," he said, annoyed with himself for letting his groin rule. "I will take you back to the keep to rest."

"No, Dolca offered me her cottage for a while, and I would like to take advantage of its solitude."

His chest tightened at the thought that she wanted to be alone. He had intended staying with her and making certain she was well. Did he respect her desire to be alone or did he insist he stay and see to her care?

He wanted to spend all the time he could with her, for he knew that battle drew ever nearer.

Warriors were sent out today to MacAlpin land's farthest borders to camp, keep watch, and relay messages about the soldiers' movements. It was only a matter of time before the first skirmish erupted into full-fledged war, and the time would come for the true king to lead his people.

Trey entered the small cottage and walked over to the bed, much too narrow for two people though not if one lay on top of the other. He shook his head as he lowered her feet to the ground.

She giggled and looked up at him. "As much as I'd like to stretch out on the bed, it is much too small to hold us both, and, at the moment, I'd much prefer to snuggle against you and . . ." She took hold of his hand and rested it against her stomach. "Calm your son again."

Trey placed his cloak on the ground before the hearth, and, after she settled in his lap, he used her cloak as a blanket for added warmth. Once comfortable, he slowly stroked her stomach.

"When I said I wished solitude, I never meant that I wanted to be alone," she said.

He knew it shouldn't have surprised him that she had known his thoughts. She always knew his thoughts where she was concerned, and perhaps that explained why she was always moist with desire for him.

"I did not invade the privacy of your thoughts; I felt your disappointment and saw it in your eyes, just like now I see a flicker of desire."

"It burns constantly for you."

"As does mine for you," she said, and brushed her lips over his.

"I am having a difficult time keeping my hands off you."

"Perhaps you can convince your son to remain calm so that his parents can . . ." She touched her lips to his and kissed him gently.

He responded, telling himself that they could share a kiss, a tender one that led nowhere, but when had kissing Bliss ever led nowhere. Whenever their lips met, passion flamed, whether the kiss was simple or hungry didn't matter.

He felt it then, the unease in her stomach, and it forced him to end the kiss.

"Kissing will wait until you feel better," he insisted, and tucked her cloak around her.

"I could erect a shield so that you don't sense anything," she offered.

"No," he snapped though not meaning to. He softened his tone. "I will not have you shielding me from anything. I will share it all with you."

She grinned and laughed briefly. "Even when it is time to birth the babe?"

He cringed. "I hadn't thought of that."

"It is for me alone to do," she said.

He shook his head. "I never want you to think that you do anything alone. We have each other; we're never alone . . . unless you prefer to be."

"I have always embraced solitude, perhaps because I had no choice. But now, since falling in love with you, when I think in terms of solitude, you are always included. There may be times I need quiet, time to think and focus, but that doesn't mean I don't want you near." She smiled. "I have come to enjoy having you around."

"That is good," he said with a playful tap to her nose, "for you are stuck with me."

She shook her head slowly. "Never. Never will I feel stuck with you."

He tucked her closer to him, too afraid to kiss her again since his groin was tightening by the minute, and he knew that if he kissed her again, he'd spring as hard as a rock.

They sat silent, enjoying the heat of the fire, his hand having gone still, afraid it would inch down and find her moist and ready for him. And then . . . there would be no stopping.

She dozed off, and he watched her sleep, this woman whom he had magically fallen in love with or whom fate had delivered to him, or who had always been meant for him. It didn't matter; he didn't care how they came to be, he was simply glad they had. He couldn't imagine life without her. He couldn't imagine not being connected with her. He couldn't imagine loving an ordinary woman instead of an extraordinary one.

She belonged to him, and he belonged to her, and nothing, nothing would ever change that.

She stirred after only a few minutes, her eyes going wide. "I'm famished."

He laughed. "Hunger woke you from your brief respite?"

"Hours haven't passed?"

"No," he confirmed. "You closed your eyes only a few moments ago."

"I feel refreshed, as if I have slept for hours, and more hungry than I ever recall being."

Bliss scrambled to her feet before he could help

her up, and he laughed. "You truly are hungry."

She hurried them on with their cloaks and pushed a laughing Trey out the door. It didn't take them long to get to the keep, Bliss's rushed steps setting a fast pace.

The keep had quieted, all the warriors having gone off to their prospective duties. The MacAlpin family were the only ones left, along with Dolca, who looked to be having a grand time with her great-grandbabies.

It was obvious to him that Mercy knew that Dolca was her grandmother, but why hadn't others been made aware of it?

"I asked them to wait until I was here," Bliss answered, as if he had spoken the question aloud.

He eased their gait, not wanting to get too close to his family before he had a chance to say, "It seems that since learning that you carry my son, your ability to know and hear my thoughts has multiplied substantially."

Bliss stopped with a gasp and turned stunned eyes on him. "You're right. Your thoughts have gotten clearer in my head. It's as though I feel and know your every thought."

He shook his head. "That's not good. There are things you do not need to know, things that do not concern you, and things I do not want you worrying over."

She smiled. "How about things you want to keep private?"

He laughed. "Is that even possible? Keeping something private from you?"

Her smile vanished, and he knew he had made a mistake.

"I'll just erect that shield, then you'll have all the privacy you want."

He chuckled. He couldn't help it. "I have never known you to get angry with me. You're delightful when you're angry."

Her eyes narrowed, and she looked ready to give him a tongue-lashing when suddenly she stopped. "Where is this anger coming from? This is not me. I do not like it."

He almost chuckled though he thought better of it and instead went to speak, but she stopped him with a warning.

"Don't dare tell me again that I'm delightful when I'm angry."

Being wise, he said nothing.

She leaned against him for support, and he quickly slipped a firm arm around her. "I should eat," she said.

"Yes, you should," he agreed with a smile, and they went to join his family.

His chest swelled with such happiness that he thought he would burst. It had been so long since he had felt so elated, and he had thought he'd never know such a thrill again. But now, with Bliss as his wife, the strength of her love, and a son on the way, he finally knew contentment. Even with war looming on the horizon, he had confidence that the true king would prevent as much bloodshed as possible.

They had not been sitting long, Bliss enjoying the

fresh food brought to her, when Roan arrived, with Langward leaning heavily on his shoulder. Bliss took one look at him and stood. Trey was about to stop her but thought better of it. This was who she was and what she did. He admired and respected her for it, and he would not stand in her way.

She turned to him. "Can I put him in your bedchamber?"

"Put him in Reeve's. I have my bedchamber back, and I intend to make use of it."

"Are you sure of that?" she asked quite seriously.

He nodded. "I am."

She shook her head, and he wondered if he had just made a mistake though he couldn't figure out what it could be.

Roan looked to Trey as he approached. "We need to talk after I am done settling Langward."

Trey nodded and helped with the injured Pict. He didn't like leaving Bliss on her own after she hadn't been feeling well. He walked over to her where she hovered over the ailing Langward.

"Are you sure you are well enough to handle this?" he asked.

She smiled and pressed her cheek to his. "It is so good to know and feel how much you worry over me, but know that I am fine, feeling much better and looking forward to the noon meal."

He laughed, and he knew her words were not only truthful but meant to lighten his spirit. "If you need anything . . ."

"I will reach out to you."

"I will be listening for you," he said, and gave her a quick kiss before reluctantly leaving her.

He and Roan joined his brothers and his da in the solar. They were all waiting impatiently for news.

Roan didn't waste time. "The attack came quick and ended just as quickly. The strange thing about it was that the soldiers ended it after one shouted to the others that there was no woman there."

"They search for a woman?" Reeve said, sounding as puzzled as the others looked.

"It would seem so," Roan confirmed. "We assume they search for Bliss, the king having learned of her powers and wanting to use them to his advantage"—he shook his head—"though no mention was made of a seer or healer, so I cannot be sure."

"Who would they search for if not for Bliss?" Duncan asked.

No one had an answer, and, for some reason, Trey had the distinct feeling that it wasn't his wife whom the soldiers were after. The problem was he had no idea who else it could be if not for Bliss.

The men talked further, then Trey realized how exhausted Roan was and offered him food and rest. The Pict gladly accepted and went off with a servant. The others briefly discussed the situation but could find no answers, and so they all went their separate ways to see to the day's duties, with plans to discuss the matter later.

Since Trey had only just returned home, he had no pressing duties. And so he went to join his wife, only to find a servant girl watching over Langward. She explained that Bliss had finished tending the young Pict warrior and left.

Trey checked his bedchamber but found it empty, then it hit him; Bliss was hungry. There would be only one place she'd be.

Sure enough, he found her in the kitchen, talking with Etty and munching on cheese and freshly baked bread. He realized that she had barely had a chance to eat when Roan had arrived. She had left her food to attend to Langward.

As soon as she saw him, she hurried to his side and gave him a quick kiss, then offered him a piece of cheese. He accepted it with a smile, pleased that she was finally able to eat.

He spoke too soon.

Reeve entered the kitchen. "We need you in the great hall; one of our warriors has returned with urgent news."

Bliss looked from Trey to Reeve. "The king's soldiers have crossed the Pict border."

Chapter 33

The MacAlpin family was gathered in the great hall. Reeve joined his wife near the hearth, slipping his arm around her waist, Mercy and Duncan sat snug against each other at the table, Charlotte stood in front of Bryce, his arm draped protectively across her chest and his hand snug at her waist. Carmag, Mara, and Idris stood off to the side, speaking in whispers, and Roan and five of his men stood in a circle talking. When they caught sight of Bliss, they rushed to her.

"What do we do?" Roan asked.

"At the moment, nothing," she said to the surprise of all.

"Do you know whom the soldiers search for?" Roan asked.

"Aye, I do, and I believe others here know as well," Bliss said, turning and looking from one to the other until finally . . .

"Oh hell," Mara said, stepping forward. "I suppose it's time for the truth to be made known."

Dolca stepped forward as well. "Aye, it's been a long time coming."

Mercy smiled at her and hugged her husband's arm, which tightened protectively around her.

"You know who the king searches for among the Picts?" Roan asked.

Mara nodded. "King Kenneth searches for the woman who will be queen."

Silence hung heavy in the air, no one uttering a word.

Mara continued. "You are all aware that to be a true king of Scotland, you must be born of a Pict mother. The king then must marry a Pict if he wishes his heir to have a claim to the throne. It is the reason King Kenneth has no true claim on the title. He was not born of a Pict mother. His wife conveniently died shortly after he took the throne; he intended to wed Tara for her substantial dowry, then kill her, and, finally, after having learned that the future queen was with the Picts, I'm sure the king's plan is to find her and wed her himself."

Tara spoke up. "That means that Reeve is not the future king since I am no Pict."

"Is that relief I hear?" Reeve asked as he hugged her.

"Yes," she said, cuddling closer to him. "You're a handful now. I could not imagine how you would be if you were king."

Everyone laughed, the brothers' teasing remarks agreeing with her.

Charlotte was quick to point out. "That would omit Bryce and me since I am no Pict, and Mara is no Pict so that eliminates Trey, leaving Duncan to be the true king."

Dolca stepped forward. "I am the king's grandmother, and Mercy is his half sister."

There were several audible gasps from the women.

Charlotte took several steps away from Bryce. "It's you. You're the true king?" She shook her head. "I'm not a Pict. You knew this all along. You knew you could never wed me."

Bryce squared his shoulders and stepped forward, his head high, his muscles taut. "I am the rightful king, and you will be my queen."

Charlotte shook her head. "No, I will not. My da told me how important the true king was to Scotland. The good he would do, and how his queen would help him and bear him many children, one of whom would be king." She shook her head again. "I will not see you sacrifice that for me. It is not right."

"You will be my queen," he repeated, and stepped toward her, but she scooted back away from him. Odin made his way to her side, taking a protective stance next to her.

"Your queen waits for you amongst the Picts," Charlotte said. "And why don't you seem surprised to know you have a sister?"

Mara answered. "Bryce has known for some time that Mercy is his sister, and so have his brothers."

Bryce looked to Mercy. "I'm sorry I couldn't tell you and sorry that Duncan was forced to keep it from you, but it was a matter of protection for us both."

Mercy nodded. "I understand. It's just that all

that time I thought my mum was trying to find you to make me your mistress when she was—"

"Seeing to your protection," Bryce said, "seeing you safely reunited with your brother, the king. She gave her life for both of us."

Charlotte shook her head. "I don't understand any of it."

"Let me explain," Dolca offered, looking to Bryce for permission.

He nodded, and she continued.

"After Bryce's da was killed in battle, my daughter, Kate, knew that she had to do everything possible to protect the future king, and so a plan was set in motion. She had yet to receive her Pict markings, and so she decided that the best way to protect her son was to get close to his enemy. She had told Bryce time and again that if anything were to happen to her or his da, he was to go to Mara, her best friend, and she would take care of him. Once Kate was certain that Bryce had arrived at Mara's safely, she left, and it took her a little time, but she made herself known to King Kenneth. Since she was a beautiful woman, he could not resist her; and so she became his mistress."

Dolca looked to Mercy. "She had no plans to give birth to the king's child, but the herbs she took to prevent it from happening failed once, and so she gave birth to Mercy. She loved her dearly and knew that if the king ever found out that his daughter was half sister to the true king, he would surely kill her.

"Kate spied on the king for years, supplying the MacAlpins with information they could never have learned any other way. She would pass the information to me, and I would pass it to Mara. Not many men pay attention to gossiping women. When she learned that the king knew of her deception she—" Dolca choked back tears.

Mara continued. "She contacted her son and asked to meet with him so that she could be the one to tell him the truth. She also requested that he bring the piece of hide with him. It needed to be destroyed. No one could get it and learn the truth."

"What truth?" Charlotte asked.

"That his queen was not living among the Picts," Mara answered. "Bliss's grandmum predicted the birth of the queen and how important it was to keep her safe, and so when she was born, her mum and da, Picts, left Pict territory and set out on a journey to do just that and to teach her all she would need to know to be a great queen."

Idris stepped forward. "Forgive me, dear daughter, for not telling you the truth, but it was imperative that you be kept safe for the king."

Charlotte shook her head, as if trying to comprehend it all. "I'm a Pict," she said, as if saying it helped it to make sense. "What if I hadn't fallen in love with the king?"

Trey laughed. "Fate had decreed it. You and Bryce were always meant to be."

"You knew?" Charlotte asked.

Trey shook his head. "None of us knew about you. That was for the king alone to know, and we all believed that was why mum was not too happy when you showed up with Bryce. You were no Pict as far as we knew."

"I wasn't sure either since I was kept from knowing the queen's identity," Mara said. "It was only until later, when I spoke with Dolca, then with Idris, that I was told the truth."

"Again, I am sorry, Charlotte," her da said. "I did what had to be done. What I knew would make you happy, and I was so very happy when you introduced me to Bryce. I knew when I saw how much you loved him that your mum and I had made the right choice those many years ago."

Charlotte turned sharply to glare at Bryce. "When did you know I was to be your queen?"

"I knew nothing until after I fell in love with you and decided I would wed you whether you were a Pict or not," he said.

"That was a foolish and selfish thing to do," she scolded walking over to him, then smiled. "But I am glad to hear it."

He took her in his arms. "It is also why I have waited to wed you. We will have a wedding ceremony and huge celebration once I am crowned king. And then I will crown you my queen."

There were many misty-eyed women and grinning men as the king kissed his future queen.

Bliss leaned back against her husband, and it was a good thing she did. The vision hit fast, and she felt her body go limp and Trey's arms close around her.

Charlotte and she ran from the keep into the woods, snow covered the ground, and the skies were gray. She couldn't sense if anyone followed, and yet she knew danger was near. She urged Charlotte to go faster, then, suddenly, they both stood on the edge of an open field, and she felt it heavy around her . . . death.

She woke with a gasp and was grateful to find herself cradled in Trey's arms, where he knelt on the floor. He held her close and looked relieved to see that the vision had ended.

Everyone else stood in a circle around them, each looking more concerned than the other and for different reasons.

Bryce asked the obvious question. "What did you see?"

"Charlotte and I running from the keep and into the woods, snow on the ground, a cloudy sky, then an open meadow—" She grabbed her throat and coughed, unable to bring herself to finish.

Trey stared at her, letting her know that he knew she had not told them everything. She turned, pressing her face against his chest, silently imploring him to leave it be for now. Thankfully, he did, though she knew it was only a temporary reprieve. He would want answers, and she would have to tell him.

"It is time for this to end. I will not see any more of my people suffer," Bryce said. "The seer predicted that when I meet death on my own, that is when I claim the throne. It is time for me to face King Kenneth. It is for him and me alone to join into battle and settle this once and for all."

Bliss sensed that his words rang true. The true king would bring an end to this, and peace would reign, but who would live to see it?

It was a long evening, with so much to discuss. Dolca went into detail about Mercy and Bryce's mum, and caused many a tear to fall. There were so many questions that could finally be answered and so many secrets allowed to be revealed.

It seemed like yesterday that he and his brothers had been young and been told about the true king. They had all known it had been Bryce but since his mum never treated any of them differently, and Bryce had never tried to rule over them, they had grown up equals. That didn't mean they would not give the king his due and show him respect, but Trey knew that to them and to Bryce, he would always be their brother first and king second.

As the evening wore on, Bliss wore out quickly. With all that had happened since their return to the MacAlpin home, she hadn't gotten much sleep. And as anxious as he was to ask her about her vision, he was more eager for her to rest. When they reached his bedchamber, she immediately climbed into bed and fell asleep in seconds. He thought to undress her, but he didn't wish to disturb her, and so he lay down beside her and slept.

He woke just as dawn was breaking, as he always did, and was surprised to find the spot beside him empty. He sat up and didn't need to look far to find her.

She was pacing the floor in front of the glowing hearth, her expression troubled.

He got out of bed and approached her though he kept a distance from her. He wanted to reach out and take hold of her but wasn't sure if he should, at least not just yet. "You are upset. Has it anything to do with your vision?"

She shook her head, stopped pacing, then nodded and started walking again, only to shake her head once more.

Trey thought he'd see if he could sense what agitated her, but after several minutes of feeling nothing, he had had enough. He stepped in front of her and grabbed her by the shoulders. "Tell me what's wrong. We will handle this together."

"Fate—"

"Has sent me to help you," he finished. "Now tell me so that I may do what fate intended."

She spoke fast, as if she feared she wouldn't have the courage to finish. "Death hangs heavy in the air, and I know not whom it will strike."

Trey went cold inside, and every muscle in his body tightened in fear. "I will not let it take you."

"It is not your choice."

He knew he could not stop death, and yet he would battle death itself to keep her safe. A shiver raked her body, whether out of fear or chill, he did not know. "You are cold, come and let us talk in bed—"

"No," she snapped, and wrenched out of his arms. "I will not lie in that bed."

It took Trey a moment to make sense of her hostility, and when he realized the cause, he went to her side, slipped his arm around her, and hurried her out of the room.

"I'm sorry," he said once in the hall. "I should have never brought you here. Leora's feelings linger, don't they? How long have you been awake?"

"Hours."

"Why didn't you wake me? I would have moved us out of here."

"I was going to at first, then her feelings took hold, and I had to explore them." Bliss shook her head. "She is not a happy woman."

"She has been through much."

"Perhaps, but she is free now to be with her family, and yet I sensed that she is more unhappy than ever."

Her words got Trey thinking as he directed her down the hall. What if Leora still lied to them? What if she still spied on them?

Bryce and Mercy were in the great hall at the table when they entered.

Trey and Bliss were reluctant to approach, knowing the two had much to discuss. Bryce waved them forward, and they joined the half siblings.

"We've been talking for hours," Mercy said. "Neither of us could sleep and found the other one down here, so it gave us time alone to talk."

"She's told me so much about my mother that I never got a chance to know," Bryce said.

"And it has made me see her differently," Mercy said, "and love and admire her more than I thought I ever could." She grinned. "And to think it is my brother who will be king. I am so proud."

Bliss tensed suddenly, grabbing Trey's arm. "Soldiers approach."

Bryce bolted off the bench just as the bell tolled, signaling the same.

Bryce turned to Bliss. "Keep Charlotte safe."

"And yourself," Trey added, before he and his brother ran out the door.

Reeve and Duncan flew off the stairs and raced past them.

"You women stay together," Duncan ordered, before they disappeared out the door.

Carmag and Mara followed, scurrying into the hall, Carmag taking after his sons and Mara turning to the women.

"Get Tara, Charlotte, and the babies and bring them here," Mara ordered.

Mercy flew up the stairs, Bliss not far behind. "Duncan left the babes alone."

But once they reached the bedchamber, they found that Tara was already there with them. She scooped one up, and Mercy grabbed the other.

"Go to Mara," Bliss ordered. "I'll get Charlotte.

The women didn't argue; they fled down the stairs while Bliss went up.

Charlotte was hurrying out of the room as Bliss approached.

"What's happening?"

Bliss was about to explain when she suddenly grabbed Charlotte by the arm and propelled her forward. "We have to get out of here."

Fear ran through Bliss, for she knew that her vision was soon to come true.

Chapter 34

Bryce and Trey sat atop their horses, watching as a troop of soldiers approached the edge of the village. Duncan and Reeve were quick to catch up with them, while a line of mighty warriors stood at the ready behind them.

"The women are safe?" Trey asked.

"They gather in the hall with Mum," Reeve said.

Trey felt relief wash over him and was ready to battle alongside his brothers though for some reason he did not think the soldiers were here to fight. Something was wrong, and he didn't like it.

One soldier approached. "It is time for the MacAlpin clan to pay allegiance to King Kenneth, the true king of Scotland."

Trey felt uneasy, and it rippled through his mare. She became skittish, hard to control, and he fought to keep a rein on her.

Reeve moved his horse forward. "This is MacAlpin land, and the false king is not welcome here."

"This is the king's land, and you will obey—"

"We obey the true king," Reeve shouted with fury. "Now get off our land."

The soldier laughed. "It is not your land, and you will learn that soon enough."

It worried all the brothers that the soldiers left without argument. Something wasn't right, and as they rode back to the keep, their warriors remaining on the outskirts of the village in case the soldiers returned, the four felt on edge.

It was as they got closer to the keep that Trey sensed it, and he looked to Bryce. "Bliss and Charlotte are in trouble."

The brothers rode hard, leaping off their horses as they reached the keep and rushing inside.

Carmag was with his wife having remained behind to see to the protection of the keep and to protect the women. Mercy and Tara sat with Dolca, keeping the twins occupied. There was no sight of Bliss and Charlotte.

"Where is Charlotte?" Bryce demanded, Odin's head shooting up from where he lay sleeping by the hearth.

"And Bliss," Trey said, reaching out to her in his thoughts. *Where are you, Bliss? Where are you?*

Bliss heard her husband and let him know that she and Charlotte were hiding just inside the woods, watching six soldiers, led by Leora, entering the secret passageway into the keep. As soon as she was certain no other soldiers followed, Charlotte and she would return to the keep.

She was anxious to get to her husband and tell him what else she had sensed, that more soldiers than they thought surrounded the place and the sentinels who had guarded the borders had been killed, while the attention of the other sentinels had been diverted by soldiers' troop movements as the Picts made ready for an attack.

The king's various ploys had worked well. He had made everyone look elsewhere while his spy had snuck his men into the keep.

Bliss waited impatiently with Charlotte though she wanted to run, ached to run as far as she could, but she knew it was impossible to outrun . . . death.

Trey drew his sword and ran to the bottom of the stairs. His brothers were quick to follow.

"Soldiers enter through the secret passageway of the keep, Leora guides them," Trey said, once they were all gathered there. It angered him that he had once again allowed himself to believe Leora's lies.

"Charlotte?" Bryce asked, moving behind Trey.

"Bliss and Charlotte are making their way back to the keep and should be in the hall once we finish with this lot."

Bryce smiled with relief. "Then let's finish with these intruders."

The four brothers crept along the narrow staircase, stopping abruptly when they heard footfalls from above. Trey signaled to his brothers that they would need to strike fast and hard, taking the soldiers and Leora by surprise. It didn't matter how many there were, the MacAlpin brothers were known for their fierce fighting abilities. Few stood a chance against them when they fought side by side.

Trey nodded, making certain his brothers were ready, eager grins and nods letting him know they were not only ready but looking forward to the battle.

The brothers struck so rapidly that the six soldiers were caught off guard, and the altercation took no time at all. Within minutes, the only one left alive was Leora.

"Why?" Trey asked, his brothers nodding indicating that they wanted to know themselves.

Leora lifted her chin with pride. "King Kenneth is the rightful king and is more man than you or anyone of your brothers could ever be."

Trey shook his head. He could not believe that he had ever loved this woman. But, then, the woman he had loved had never truly existed. "The king and his selfish ways have corrupted you."

She laughed. "You are a fool. Old John's daughter died while trying to free her father. It gave me good reason to return to you and have you sympathize with my plight."

Trey fought the urge to hit her. "What have you done to Old John and Donald? You haven't harmed them, have you?"

"I never went to them. When I spied the cottage, I convinced your inept warrior that I wished to go the rest of the way alone, and he obliged me. I took off as soon as he was out of sight and went to find the soldiers I knew would be near." She raised her chin. "I am a favorite of the king. You would do well to return me to him."

Bryce stepped forward. "Then let us send you back to him and see if he'll have you now that you have failed him, and he no longer has any use for you."

"He will welcome me back," Leora said, smiling.

"Where does the king wait?" Bryce asked.

"Two meadows over, with more troops than you have warriors."

Bryce laughed. "Trey was right. You still don't understand us."

"Is it safe to leave yet?" Charlotte asked in a whisper, her eyes alert to her surroundings.

"I'm not sure, perhaps a moment more," Bliss said.

"This all was a ruse, wasn't it?" Charlotte continued in a hushed tone. "King Kenneth wished to draw out the true king. No doubt he waits nearby with troops to attack."

"He diverted attention from his true objective," Bliss said, "but Bryce and his brothers are no fools."

"True enough. Bryce and his brothers did not sit idly by when they received news of the troops' converging on the area. I was not made aware of what they did, but it was known that something was being done."

"I think they planned for every possibility and that a surprise awaits King Kenneth." Bliss turned suddenly grabbing Charlotte's arm and forcing her to crouch down. "Someone comes."

Leora was forced to sit at one of the tables in the great hall, two warriors standing on either side of her to make certain she didn't go anywhere until the true king was ready to release her.

"Shouldn't the women have returned by now?" Bryce asked, though he turned to Carmag before getting an answer. "Da, has all been seen to?"

"All is ready," his da assured him.

Trey took a moment to listen for his wife, and his hand snapped out to grab his brother's arm. "Soldiers have them."

The two men ran, their brothers right behind them. It didn't take them long to find the spot where the women must have scuffled with the soldiers.

"That's my Charlotte," Bryce said with pride. "She'd never let herself be captured without a fight."

Trey couldn't say the same of Bliss. Her mind was her weapon, and he wondered how she had used it. He wished she wasn't silent in his thoughts, for he could only assume that she had her hands full dealing with her situation.

'Tis the way it was meant to be.

Trey almost smiled. He had never thought that fate could have a voice, but he sensed that was who had spoken to him . . . Fate. And he decided to trust her.

"It is time for the true king to meet King Kenneth on the battlefield," Bryce said.

The brothers said nothing. They all knew that this day would come, when they would have to stand by and let the true king fight. It had been predicted: *when he meets death on his own, that is when he claims the throne.*

Was King Kenneth's death what Bliss had felt or would there be more blood shed than the false king's?

"We could exchange Leora for your women," Reeve said, "though I doubt the king cares enough about her for such an exchange."

"Then Leora will learn the folly of her ways," Duncan said.

Bryce looked to each of his brothers. "Come and let us make ready. The day we have planned and worked so hard for is here . . . the true king steps forward and demands his rightful throne."

Chapter 35

Bliss and Charlotte stood beside King Kenneth's horse and watched as the four MacAlpin brothers rode together toward the middle of the meadow, while behind them stood five rows of mighty Highlander warriors. To the sides of the meadows, three rows of Highlander warriors congregated. They all raised their shields and weapons cheering on the four brothers.

Charlotte grinned, then winced, the bruise at the corner of her mouth paining her.

"Bryce is not going to be happy when he sees that you have been injured," Bliss said softly.

"He knows I've taken worse and survived." Her grin grew. "Besides, we are the MacAlpin women, and we cannot cower in fear; we must be strong and able to stand at our husbands' sides, ready to fight if necessary or ready to cheer them on in battle. That is who we are; who we are meant to be." Charlotte chuckled. "And wait until Trey gets at look at your eye. I bet it looks worse than my bruised mouth."

Bliss had to laugh herself. She had never physically fought with anyone in her life. She had always used her wit to escape any kind of threat or injury, and it had always worked well for her.

That hadn't happened this time. She had realized too late that soldiers were nearly upon them, and there was no time to run. Charlotte didn't waste a minute, attacking the two soldiers, and, without thought, Bliss had jumped in to help her. The pint-sized woman was a fierce fighter, and they would have known victory thanks to her if two more soldiers hadn't joined in the melee.

At that moment it hit Bliss—she might be a Pict, but she was also a MacAlpin woman, strong, proud, and fierce, defending her husband and his people in their way. Fate had wisely sent her a love that allowed her to step out of who she was and become so much more.

Her heart swelled with joy, and she knew that this day would end well for the MacAlpin clan.

Bliss jumped as, despite the pain it caused her, Charlotte joined the warriors' cheering and hooting loudly for the four brothers.

Bliss was about to do the same when the king's hand swung down at Charlotte. Bliss didn't hesitate. She pushed Charlotte out of the way and focused all her strength to her hand as she grabbed the king's wrist and squeezed.

Her vision blurred for a second; and then she smiled. "Death stalks you this day; choose your actions wisely."

He yanked his wrist out of her hand, and that

was when they both realized that silence surrounded them.

Bliss looked to see that all eyes were on them, but the one that caught her attention the most was her husband's. He did not look on her with worry or fear, or even anger . . . but with pride.

She not only carried the pride of being a Pict, but the pride of being a MacAlpin woman.

At that moment, Trey, Reeve, and Duncan bowed their heads to Bryce and backed their horses to stand a few feet behind the true king.

Bryce raised his hand, and a warrior brought Leora forward. She kept her chin high and her stature regal.

"I have someone who belongs to you and you have two who belong to me," Bryce called out.

King Kenneth laughed, and shouted, "Do with her as you wish. She means nothing to me."

All color faded from Leora's cheeks.

Bryce looked down at her. "This is the man whom you want as king? Go to him."

Leora raced over to the king, but before she could reach him, one of his soldiers grabbed her and hurried her off, kicking and screaming for the king.

"I am not as charitable as you," King Kenneth yelled. "I will keep your women. When you are dead, I will wed your intended. After all, she is meant to be queen . . . my queen. As for the other, she will serve me well as a seer."

"And do you pay heed to her warning? That today you die."

The king's cheeks burst bright red, and his lips moved though no words came out of his mouth. His fury mounted, and he raised his fisted hand. "You will rue this day."

Bryce shouted out for all to hear. "This day I claim my rightful heritage . . . I am the true king of Scotland."

A deafening cacophony of shouts, cheers, and hoots filled the air.

King Kenneth grew angrier, and Bliss could feel the soldiers around her grow alarmed. They doubted their ability to win this battle.

"Do you have the courage to meet me alone in battle?" Bryce shouted above the din of the warriors. "Or are you the coward so many believe you are?"

Silence fell like a thud of a stone being dropped to the ground.

Bliss knew at that moment that King Kenneth would pay no heed to her warning about choosing to act wisely. Without thought or common sense, King Kenneth rode forward to meet his death.

It wasn't a quick fight, both men being equal in strength and skill. But there was something about Bryce that was different. And as Bliss watched, along with everyone else, as the two men battled each other, she realized what that difference was . . . Bryce fought without fear.

They swung their swords with the potency of two powerful men, rolled and jumped and maneuvered their way out of endless jabs. They took severe blows to their faces and bodies until, finally, the true king delivered the final blow straight through King Kenneth's heart.

It was done. In that one instant, life changed for all, and everyone knew it. Cheers filled the air, and, with a bloodcurdling scream, all the true king's warriors rushed forward to finish the battle and protect their king.

Epilogue

The sacred grove shimmered with sunlight though snow fell lightly. It seemed that the heavens smiled down on this joyous day. The true king was wedding his queen in Pict fashion. Only the MacAlpin family was in attendance to hear Bryce and Charlotte exchange words of love and commit to each other.

Trey stood with his arm around Bliss, his mum sending him a look that asked if the woman carrying her future grandchild was feeling well. It had been his fault that his mum had found out about the babe. He had been beside himself with worry when he had seen Bliss's bruised eye and had anxiously asked how she and his son faired . . . in front of his whole family.

Mara had gone wild, then became even more ecstatic when Reeve proudly announced with a firm arm around his wife that he also was to be a father.

Mara had cried tears of joy and repeated throughout the day that her fondest dreams had come true. She would have tons of grandbabies to fuss over.

Trey smiled at his mum to let her know that all was well. Bliss was fine although he sensed she wasn't, and it had nothing to do with the babe.

He knew what troubled his wife, and he waited until the ceremony was done and his family drifted off, and, with a nod to Bryce that he would follow them soon, he turned his wife around in his arms.

"It was a beautiful exchange of vows," she said teary-eyed.

Since having realized she was with child, her feelings were more open to him. It proved difficult at times since he thought it was his duty to ease her every worry until she finally explained that she preferred he simply listen to her whimpering complaints and ignore them.

She had not expected him to solve her every annoyance, complaint, and problem, though there was one dilemma he knew he could solve and easily.

"Yes, it was a lovely ceremony for a planned one, but I thought ours was much better."

She scrunched her brow as if trying to recall. "I don't remember us having a ceremony here."

He eased her over to the spot where Bryce and Charlotte had exchanged vows. The sunlight filtered down on them like golden dewdrops. He took her hand.

"Don't you remember what you said to me here that night?"

She nodded. "The words were meant for the husband I would love."

"That's me, the husband you would love, and I recall your words well—'I take Trey MacAlpin as my husband. I give my heart to him and only him. And I will love him for all the days of my life and beyond.'"

"You remember," she said, surprised.

"Why wouldn't I? They were spoken with such feeling that they touched my heart and had me eagerly responding."

"What do you mean?"

"I mumbled something after you, though I didn't admit to it. Now I will. I spoke words that were meant to seal our fate."

A tear tickled at the corner of her eye. "Tell me."

"I, Trey MacAlpin, take Bliss as my wife to love and honor all the days of our lives together, for without her, there is no life . . . Bliss is my life."

Tears streamed down her face. "I love you, Trey MacAlpin."

"And I you, wife," he said, and kissed her, sealing the gift of love that fate had given them.

Kiss of Surrender by Sandra Hill

Trond is a thousand-year-old Viking vampire angel who's undercover as a Navy SEAL. But it's not all bad. Working out with SEALs like Nicole Tasso is a perk. Nicole knows Trond is hiding something strange, but it's not easy figuring out a man she finds as attractive as she does annoying. Will Trond and Nicole get their stories straight . . . before it's too late?

King of the Damned by Juliana Stone

Given a chance to atone for his past, Azaiel, the Fallen, must find out if the League has been breached. What he doesn't foresee is the lovely Rowan James, a powerful witch out for vengeance and in need of an ally. Wanting Rowan means risking salvation, but will these desperate souls find love...or be forever damned?

The Importance of Being Wicked by Miranda Neville

Thomas, Duke of Castleton, has every intention of wedding a prim and proper heiress. That is, until he sets eyes on the heiress's troublesome cousin. Caroline Townsend has no patience for the oh-so-suitable men of the *ton*. Suddenly Caro finds herself falling for a stuffy duke . . . while Thomas discovers there's a great deal of fun in a little wickedness.

How to Deceive a Duke by Lecia Cornwall

When her sister runs off the night before her arranged marriage, Meg Lynton saves her family by marrying the devilish Nicholas Hartley herself. Nicholas never wanted to change his wicked ways for a wife—until he discovers Meg's deception. Now, the Duke will have to teach the scheming beauty how to be a duchess, kiss by devastating kiss . . .

THE BLACK COBRA QUARTET from #1 *New York Times* bestselling author
STEPHANIE LAURENS

The Untamed Bride

978-0-06-179514-5

He is a man who has faced peril without flinching, determined to fight for king and country. She is a bold, beautiful woman with a scandalous past, destined to become an untamed bride.

The Elusive Bride

978-0-06-179515-2

He's focused on his mission, then sees a lady he never dreamed he'd see again—with an assassin on her heels.
She secretly followed him, unaware her path is deadly— or that she'll join him to battle a treacherous foe.

The Brazen Bride

978-0-06-179517-6

Shipwrecked, wounded, he risks all to pursue his mission— only to discover a partner as daring and brazen as he.
Fiery, tempestuous, a queen in her own realm, she rescues a warrior—only to find her heart under siege.

The Reckless Bride

978-0-06-179519-0

He races to complete their mission against escalating odds— his task made more perilous when he loses his heart.
She's determined to defy convention and live a solitary life— until she tastes the reckless pleasure found only in his arms.

At Avon Books, we know your passion for romance—once you finish one of our novels, you find yourself wanting more.

May we tempt you with . . .

- **Excerpts** from our upcoming releases.

- Entertaining **extras**, including authors' personal photo albums and book lists.

- Behind-the-scenes **scoop** on your favorite characters and series.

- **Sweepstakes** for the chance to win free books, romantic getaways, and other fun prizes.

- Writing **tips** from our authors and editors.

- **Blog** with our authors and find out why they love to write romance.

- **Exclusive content** that's not contained within the pages of our novels.

Join us at
www.avonbooks.com

AVON

An Imprint of HarperCollins*Publishers*
www.avonromance.com

*G*ive in to your Impulses!

These unforgettable stories only take a second to buy and give you hours of reading pleasure!

Go to *www.AvonImpulse.com* and see what we have to offer.

Available wherever e-books are sold.

AVONIMPULSE

IMP 0811